Praise for the Gou [illegible]

SIMMER DOWN

"The writing is breezy yet polished, the plotting adept, the overall tone funny without trying too hard . . . The Josh-Chloe pairing is perfect—he loves to cook and she loves to eat."
—*Cozy Library*

"A delicious new series with engaging characters, a unique pet, a fascinating milieu, the right touch of romance, and lots of fantastic food and recipes—what more could any mystery reader want?!" —*The Romance Readers Connection*

"The talented authors Jessica Conant-Park and Susan Conant have created a pleasant blend of romance, food, and mystery. Any fan of romance or mystery will find it an enjoyable read with lots of recipes included. Enjoy."
—*New Mystery Reader*

"This is a fun Gourmet Girl Mystery . . . Readers will enjoy the heroine's escapades as she risks her life to uncover the identity of a killer. The mother-daughter team provides the audience with a delicious chick-lit cozy filled with lists, recipes, and asides as Chloe takes on Beantown."
—*The Best Reviews*

"Packed with delicious recipes . . . the Gourmet Girl Mysteries have quickly become one of my favorite culinary mystery series." —*Roundtable Reviews*

STEAMED

"This delectable collaboration between Jessica Conant-Park and her mother, Susan Conant, author of the Cat Lover's and the Dog Lover's mystery series, introduces an appealing heroine . . . This scrumptious cozy, the first of a new series, has it all—charming characters, snappy dialogue, and mouthwatering recipes." —*Publishers Weekly*

continued . . .

"All the right ingredients—fresh characters, a dash of humor, and a sizzling romance. *Steamed* is hot." —Elaine Viets

"Famous writer of mysteries involving cats and dogs Susan Conant teams up with her daughter to write a refreshingly charming chick-lit mystery." —*Midwest Book Review*

"*Steamed* is a gem. It grabs you from the start, as the heroine is witty, down-to-earth, and rolls with the punches. Great competition to anything Diane Mott Davidson has ever offered. I am thoroughly hooked. Top this already winning combination off with some decadent-sounding recipes, and I can guarantee *Steamed* will be topping the bestseller list in no time." —*Roundtable Reviews*

And praise for the novels of Susan Conant

Award-winning author of the Dog Lover's Mysteries and the Cat Lover's Mysteries

"[An] absolutely first-rate mystery. I loved it!"
—Diane Mott Davidson

"Mystery lovers know a champion when they see one."
—Carolyn G. Hart

"A fascinating mystery and a very, very funny book . . . Written with a fairness that even Dorothy Sayers and Agatha Christie would admire." —*Mobile Register*

"Hilarious." —*Los Angeles Times*

"Fun, fast-paced . . . with the most eccentric and quirky of characters." —*Publishers Weekly*

Gourmet Girls Mysteries
by Jessica Conant-Park and Susan Conant

STEAMED
SIMMER DOWN
TURN UP THE HEAT

Dog Lover's Mysteries by Susan Conant

A NEW LEASH ON DEATH
DEAD AND DOGGONE
A BITE OF DEATH
PAWS BEFORE DYING
GONE TO THE DOGS
BLOODLINES
RUFFLY SPEAKING
BLACK RIBBON
STUD RITES
ANIMAL APPETITE
THE BARKER STREET REGULARS
EVIL BREEDING
CREATURE DISCOMFORTS
THE WICKED FLEA
THE DOGFATHER
BRIDE AND GROOM
GAITS OF HEAVEN
ALL SHOTS

Cat Lover's Mysteries by Susan Conant

SCRATCH THE SURFACE

SIMMER DOWN

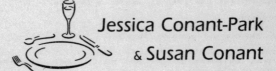

Jessica Conant-Park
& Susan Conant

Jessica Conant-Park

BERKLEY PRIME CRIME, NEW YORK

THE BERKLEY PUBLISHING GROUP
Published by the Penguin Group
Penguin Group (USA) Inc.
375 Hudson Street, New York, New York 10014, USA
Penguin Group (Canada), 90 Eglinton Avenue East, Suite 700, Toronto, Ontario M4P 2Y3, Canada
(a division of Pearson Penguin Canada Inc.)
Penguin Books Ltd., 80 Strand, London WC2R 0RL, England
Penguin Group Ireland, 25 St. Stephen's Green, Dublin 2, Ireland (a division of Penguin Books Ltd.)
Penguin Group (Australia), 250 Camberwell Road, Camberwell, Victoria 3124, Australia
(a division of Pearson Australia Group Pty. Ltd.)
Penguin Books India Pvt. Ltd., 11 Community Centre, Panchsheel Park, New Delhi—110 017, India
Penguin Group (NZ), 67 Apollo Drive, North Shore 0632, New Zealand
(a division of Pearson New Zealand Ltd.)
Penguin Books (South Africa) (Pty.) Ltd., 24 Sturdee Avenue, Rosebank, Johannesburg 2196, South Africa

Penguin Books Ltd., Registered Offices: 80 Strand, London WC2R 0RL, England

SIMMER DOWN

A Berkley Prime Crime Book / published by arrangement with the author

PRINTING HISTORY
Berkley Prime Crime hardcover edition / March 2007
Berkley Prime Crime mass-market edition / March 2008

Cover art by Alana Machnicki.
Cover design by Rita Frangie.
Cover logo by axb group.
Interior text design by Kristin del Rosario.

For information, address: The Berkley Publishing Group,
a division of Penguin Group (USA) Inc.
375 Hudson Street, New York, New York 10014.

ISBN: 978-0-425-22089-4

BERKLEY® PRIME CRIME
Berkley Prime Crime Books are published by The Berkley Publishing Group,
a division of Penguin Group (USA) Inc.
375 Hudson Street, New York, New York 10014.

PRINTED IN THE UNITED STATES OF AMERICA

10 9 8 7 6 5 4 3 2 1

Acknowledgments

Endless thanks to Alexa Lewis and David Grumblatt for their tremendous help with proofreading and to Bill Park for his wonderful recipes. We are also grateful to our wonderful editor, Natalee Rosenstein, and to Michelle Vega.

ONE

I hate the week after Christmas.

Or I used to, anyway. When I was growing up, I kept trying to convince my Protestant family that we were Jewish and consequently had to celebrate Hanukkah for a full week instead of Christmas for one short evening and a single all-too-brief day. But this year, I, Chloe Carter, have an actual boyfriend, and everything has changed for the better—even my post-Christmas blues. Now, on December 27, I was not, for once, bemoaning the end of carol singing, and it didn't bother me at all that I'd have to wait almost twelve months to tear through my presents like a six-year-old and then finish off every Christmas cookie in sight. On the contrary, I was brimming with excitement at the prospect of spending New Year's Eve with my boyfriend.

So, in the midafternoon, I was seated at my kitchen table pretending to concentrate on work for my social work school internship while actually being distracted by my gorgeous Josh, who was busy cooking. How I got lucky enough to find a chef as the love of my life, I don't know. What could be better than good food and good sex all rolled into one? Well, not "rolled into one" in the sense that we were smearing food all over each other as foreplay. I mean, ewww! How gross. If I have to watch one more B movie with couples seducing each other with strawberries and whipped cream, or licking champagne off each other, or wagging their tongues in the air to catch dangled tidbits of food, I think I might gag. Still, there's no denying the food-love link.

I could seriously stare at Josh for hours while he cooked; he was so focused and serious and skilled and . . . well, so cute, besides. I couldn't get enough of his dirty-blond hair, piercing blue eyes, and slim build. And he was loving and funny and loyal. We'd been together only since September, but we were already spending most nights with each other, usually at my place. The apartment he shared with his roommate, Stein, was, like most apartments inhabited by heterosexual males, messy and filthy. Discarded chefs' clothes were everywhere, and unidentifiable odors emanated from dark corners. With some justification, Josh and

Stein blamed the state of their living quarters on chefs' hours; in fact, neither of them was ever home for long. Whatever the reason, I seldom went there.

Josh had lost his last chef job right after we'd met and had been struggling to find a new home in which to park his culinary talents. He'd spent the past few months picking up hours by helping out chef friends of his who'd needed him to fill in now and then at restaurant after restaurant. His only steady employment had been at Eagles' Deli, around the corner from my apartment in Brighton, where he'd been putting in a few days a week. Stein owned the booming deli and always needed the help, so the time Josh put in at Eagles' gave the best friends and roommates a chance to catch up with each other.

After chasing after every job lead possible, Josh finally hooked up with a man named Gavin Seymour, who was opening his first restaurant, Simmer, on posh Newbury Street, right in the heart of Boston. Gavin knew that if he was going to open a restaurant, he'd need the hottest location possible—and restaurant locations in Boston don't get much hotter than Newbury Street. So, when the property became available, Gavin jumped right on it and paid what must have been a fortune for the lease. Nestled in the bottom of a brownstone and located among top restaurants and high-end shops, Simmer was strategically set up for success. And with Josh at the helm, there was no way it could fail.

In the three weeks since Josh had accepted the position of executive chef, he had been working more or less normal hours, days only, instead of working until late at night as chefs almost invariably did. Opening a new restaurant was a tremendous amount of work, and Josh had been swamped with hiring a kitchen staff, contacting food purveyors, assisting Gavin and the contractor in remodeling the kitchen, and, most importantly, at least in my book, writing a menu.

I'd been loving his schedule, which meant more time together, but all that was about to change when Simmer opened on New Year's Eve. For now, though, I'd savor every minute I had with Josh. Technically, I was on winter break from my first year at Boston City Graduate School of Social Work, so I was free to follow Josh around like a lovesick puppy. In fact, although classes had ended, my field placement, as it was called, took no notice of the holidays. Since September I'd been interning at the Boston Organization Against Sexual and Other Harassment in the Workplace, which I'd taken to calling the Organization, as if we were some sort of Mafia cell. The Organization was headed by my supervisor, Naomi Campbell, who was not, of course, the internationally famous supermodel and, in fact, had only a vague notion of who the other Naomi Campbell was. Naomi failed to find anything amusing about her name or, frankly, about much else. Totally driven to rid the world of harassment, she felt that since harassment didn't break for the holidays, neither should we. The Organization consisted of Naomi and me plus a bunch of invisible board members who made themselves known only by signing hundreds of petitions and notices that Naomi was forever having me type up. We worked out of a minuscule downtown office, and my primary social work contribution so far had been to address the daily feelings of claustrophobia that came from finding myself trapped in the gloomiest, messiest one-window office in Boston. My other major responsibility was to handle hotline calls from women dealing with office jackasses who thought that attempting to fondle a coworker was acceptable behavior.

Although I completely believed in the work I was doing, Naomi's extreme dedication and overzealous work ethic grated on me—that and her New Age, hippie, hold-hands-and-tell-me-your-feelings style. One of my New Year's resolutions was to avoid our morning "staff meetings," a term that I found ridiculous not only because *staff* meant Naomi and me, but because *meeting* meant my being pressured to verbalize some sort of spiritual feeling about what the day would bring. Last week, for example, while gripping my hands in hers, Naomi had closed her eyes and whispered, "Today I will look inside myself to find strength, sensitivity, and courage. I will reach out to my sisters in need and take on their challenges as my own." Then she'd waited for me to take my turn. I usually snuck in a good eye roll before she opened hers and before I compliantly faked my way through some copycat bullshit.

I liked some of my classes and parts of my internship, but for the most part I was finding that I didn't fit in with my earnest, do-gooder classmates. I definitely considered myself a liberal, politically correct twenty-something, but I wasn't all about marching the streets for causes, petitioning against this and that, or engaging in long discussions about oppression and injustice in the world. So far, I'd managed to keep my true character hidden from my peers. In brief, I wasn't the most devout social work student there was. I blamed my uncle Alan for my being one at all.

When my mother's brother died a few years ago, his will revealed what I considered to be blackmail; I would receive an inheritance only if I completed a graduate program of my choosing. Uncle Alan's estate would pay for school and give me a monthly stipend distributed by his lawyer, and if and when I earned my degree, I could collect the rest of the money. In other words, Uncle Alan had no confidence in my ability to further my education on my own. Not that I'd actually *had* any plans of my own ever to poke my head into a classroom again after college, but I wasn't about to turn down a lucrative opportunity just because of a few insults about my ability to get my act together and find a career. After rifling through piles of graduate school catalogs, I'd narrowed my choices to two different easy-sounding programs: one in social work, the other in performing arts. Since my most recent acting experience had been in elementary school when I'd played Nana the dog in *Peter Pan*, I'd figured that a career on the stage was out. Plus that snot-nosed Eric Finley had called me Nana until we'd graduated from high school. Who knows? Maybe I would've been a brilliant thespian if it hadn't been for Eric's tormenting me.

So, social work it was. I was getting through mostly unscathed and enjoying the advantages of a school schedule versus some dreary nine-to-five job. And having a winter break meant that I could sit at home today and admire Josh as he worked on his food. The new restaurant, Simmer, wasn't quite finished. As of today, there was still no electricity in the kitchen, so Josh had been working out of my condo to test dishes and feed recipes into his laptop. Although I didn't exactly have a gourmet kitchen, even my small space was better than the eat-in kitchen Josh had at his apartment. By some act of God, I'd been able to convince my landlord, Chuck, that I'd move in only if he installed a garbage disposal and a small dishwasher. Not realizing that he could've rented this condo unit to about a million other people for more money, even without the new appliances, he'd agreed. And with Josh cooking out of here, I was even happier than ever to have those two kitchen accessories. He'd been testing a lot of recipes this month. Three or four times a week, he'd come over with bags loaded with beautiful fresh produce, meat and fish wrapped in white butcher's paper, wine for reducing in sauces (and drinking), fresh pasta sheets, and packages of aromatic herbs. I'd learned that a chef's grocery shopping looked distinctively different from mine. When Josh shopped for the restaurant, there was nothing frozen or precooked; everything was fresh and raw and gorgeous. Since Gavin was picking up all the shopping costs, Josh spared no expense in buying the highest-quality ingredients he could from specialty shops around the city. And I was a delighted taste tester.

Today, he was not, however, testing recipes but preparing food to serve at the Food for Thought event going on tomorrow night. The annual charity fund-raiser, which was held at Newbury Street art galleries, paired social service agencies with local restaurants. Inside each of the posh galleries, one agency and the restaurant paired with it got to set up a booth to showcase services and food. When Naomi had first brought this event to my attention, my inclination had been to run screaming from something that was going to interfere with my vacation. I quickly realized, though, that Food for Thought was not some bothersome and negligible event; it was a high-class, high-publicity Boston affair and was the perfect opportunity to promote my boyfriend's talents. *Boston* magazine always did a piece on it, and local restaurant reviewers would definitely be there. Gavin and Josh were thrilled to be involved, and the timing coincided perfectly with Simmer's grand opening. It took only a little conniving to have the Organization and Simmer assigned to each other. Our tables were to be featured at the trendy Eliot Davis Gallery, which was just a few doors down from Simmer. Oh, and, yeah, I could help promote the harassment hotline I was in charge of. I keep forgetting that.

I was much more excited about Josh's end than mine. Naomi was forcing me to learn about "marketing the agency," as she called it. So far, the activity mostly consisted of her calling me six hundred times a day to see whether I'd finished making idiotic posters and flyers about the Boston Organization Against Sexual and Other Harassment in the Workplace.

Speaking of which, the phone rang. One peek at caller ID made me sigh.

"Damn Braids, again," I grumbled, referring to Naomi. She had the misfortune to think that plaiting her four feet of brown hair into zillions of fat braids that poked out of her head was attractive.

"Hi, Naomi," I said with resignation.

"Hey, there, partner," she chirped. "How are the materials coming? Are you just about finished?"

I glanced down at the drawing I'd done of a male stick figure trying to fondle a female stick figure. I drew a big X across the image and scrawled ILLEGAL across the top of the page. "Doing great," I lied while crumpling the paper up and tossing it into the trash. "I'll e-mail you something at the office later to print out."

"Wonderful. You know, this is a significant opportunity for us to really get the word out."

Getting the word out, I'd learned, was hard-core social work jargon. If I wanted to appear studious, I'd need to start tossing it around. *I need to get the word out about the sale at Banana Republic!* Or maybe, *It's vital to get the word out about salon-quality hair care products!*

"Oh, listen," continued Naomi, oblivious to my daydreaming, "I have one other assignment for you. I want you to work on a list of things in life that cause you to feel anger. This is an exercise that will really help you get in touch with who you are, where your fears and strengths come from, and how you can best work with your clients. When I was in school, my supervisor had me do it, and I found it incredibly enlightening." I could practically see Naomi's face suffused with exhilaration at the prospect of *my* enlightenment.

"I'll start on that right away," I said, turning to my laptop and writing:

Anger-Inducing Experiences
by Chloe Carter
1. Being forced to write stupid lists by psychotic supervisor.

"You know, Chloe, the holidays are a great time of year to do some introspective thinking and get a good look at yourself. Reassess where you are at professionally and personally, and set goals for next term. In fact, I think I'll do the same assignment I've given you to work on. We can compare them in a few days!"

Oh, Naomi, I'm giddy with excitement!

"Before I forget, I got a message on my voice mail at the office that was for you. The woman didn't leave a name, but I think it was a follow-up call about a sexual harassment issue at her job. You can call into my messages and listen if you want. I think it's that same woman I'd spoken to a few times before passing her on to you. Remember?"

I had mastered the basics on handling sexual harassment hotline calls, but some of the callers were in really dicey situations, and my limited experience sometimes left me at a dead end when I tried to help. Also, unbeknownst to Naomi, I frequently jumped outside the hotline instruction manual to suggest slightly radical alternatives. In this woman's case, I think I may have advised her to chomp on garlic-stuffed olives so she could fend off the man harassing her with her stinky breath. That suggestion, as I recalled, hadn't gone over too well, and I'd transferred the anonymous caller to the thoroughly professional Naomi.

"I think I know who it is." Naomi sighed. "I'm glad she called back. I've been waiting to hear from her. I've been working really hard to put a stop to her situation. Totally intolerable, what that young woman is going through."

I agreed with Naomi. Every time this caller went to

work, she faced her asshole boss and his attempts to maul, grab, and pinch any available body part.

"All right," Naomi continued, "I'm going to go call her back right away. I am taking care of this situation before the year is done. Enough is enough! And I'm going to check in with Eliot Davis at the gallery. Have Josh there by five thirty tomorrow to start setting up, okay?"

I promised that I would, hung up the phone, and went back to staring at Josh, who'd barely spoken for the past two hours. Under normal circumstances Josh could carry on a full-blown conversation while cooking food good enough to make you shake your head in disbelief that you'd managed to live on anything else. Today was different. The food he was making today would be the public's first taste of his new menu, and the pressure was keeping him quieter than usual.

He was making Parmesan-panko-encrusted beef medallions served on crisp wafers and drizzled with an oregano vinaigrette. Panko, it turns out, is Japanese bread crumbs and not, as I'd feared, some sort of weird plankton. Because he was forced to work out of my little kitchen, Josh was playing it a little safe with this dish. He had wanted to do smoked bluefish with wasabi vinaigrette, but the odds of successfully smoking enough bluefish out of my beat-up oven were pretty bad. The amount of prep work for this beef dish wasn't too serious, considering that he had to make three hundred servings. Today he would clean and slice the tenderloins into half-inch-thick medallions, make the Parmesan-panko mix, blend up the vinaigrette, and bake herb focaccia, which is, of course, a somewhat flat and totally delicious Italian bread with olive oil drizzled all over the top crust.

"Hey, Red?" Josh was teasing. Every redhead in the world is cursed with the nickname, and he knew that I loathed it. Why do people think that they have the right to address redheads by their hair color? I spent my childhood cringing every time someone asked, "Red, where'd you get your red hair?" My redheaded friend Nancy used to respond, "From under my father's armpits!" She often shut people up, but I never had the nerve to answer with the same retort.

I smiled at Josh. "Sure, but if you call me Red ever again, I'll—"

"Could you take the oregano leaves off these stems for me? I need them for the dressing."

"No problem." I took a handful of the fresh herbs from his hand, pulled my chair closer to the table, pushed my computer aside, and began plucking leaves. That was fun for all of eight seconds. Then I realized what an excruciatingly annoying job this was.

2. *Removing oregano leaves from stems, even when helping hottie boyfriend.*

"I want a different job," I complained.

Josh came closer and peered at my piddling pile of

leaves. "Here, hold the end of the stem in one hand, then pinch it between the thumb and forefinger of your other hand, and glide down the stem to pull off the leaves."

"What about all these little branchy, twiggy things sticking out the side? Nope. Not doing this. Give me another job," I insisted.

"Some help you are," Josh teased. "Don't worry about it. You should probably finish your stuff for the booth tomorrow." He turned back to his cutting board. "I can't believe I finally get to meet the infamous Naomi. She definitely sounds unique."

Images of granola-crunchy Naomi swirling her many brown braids around, engulfing Josh in hugs, and spouting words about peace and love started to give me a headache. I appreciated her gung ho attitude about Josh and me—she was forever telling me about the benefits of having a loving, supportive partner when working in an "emotionally draining field"—but she and Josh were two very different personality types; he didn't have a Peruvian-knitted-cap bone in his body.

"Yes, well, she's excited to meet you, too," I said truthfully. "She asks about you all the time. Actually, I think she might have something romantic going on herself."

"Really? What makes you say that?" He began to assemble ingredients for the focaccia.

"She's been sort of giggly and even more high-energy than usual. She hasn't said anything, but I just have a feeling . . . maybe it's that lady who runs that AFL-CIO thing down the hall from us. She's always coming in to see if Naomi wants a chai tea from the café."

"Naomi's gay?" Josh asked.

"Well, I sort of assumed so," I said. "You know, she's always talking about women's rights and drinking weird beverages and 'forgetting' to put on a bra."

Josh laughed. "And that makes her a lesbian?"

"No. I mean, sometimes I drink chai iced teas or those funny smoothies with ginkgo and protein powder."

"Yeah, and I know *you're* not a lesbian," Josh winked at me. "And you better not let your classmates hear you talking like that. Aren't you stereotyping or oppressing or labeling or something?"

"True. Guilty, guilty, guilty. Okay, it's not those things, but I've never heard her talk about any men, and she's always referring to *partners* and *mates* and things. Anyway, the point is, I'm getting love vibes from her, and I think she's got some sort of romance going on."

Josh came over to me and grinned. "Well, I'm ready for a break, and I've got some love vibes going on, too." He leaned over and nestled his head in my neck, kissing me lightly.

"In that case, I think I'm ready for a break, too." I smiled and led Josh to the bedroom.

TWO

LOVE and food. I'd led Josh to bed, but what hauled him out was the focaccia dough, which really needed to be started. He stayed up late that night baking the bread and obsessing about Food for Thought. When I got up at ten on the morning of the twenty-eighth, he was dead asleep, so I tiptoed out of the bedroom and put on a pot of coffee. Fed up with my inability to brew a drinkable cup, Josh had bought me an ultrafancy coffee and espresso machine soon after we'd met. So far, I'd somehow managed not to break it, but success in steaming milk was still beyond me.

The kitchen was a disaster, so I took my coffee to the living room and sat on the couch to go over the material that Naomi and I were going to hand out. I'd finished preparing it only the day before and was convinced that I'd misspelled something or typed an incorrect phone number. Reading and rereading, I came across no catastrophic errors. Naomi had called me last night to say that she was very pleased with my work, was going to have everything photocopied this morning, and would meet me at the gallery around five thirty tonight.

Waiting for Josh to awaken, I took a gulp of coffee and surveyed the living room, which was almost as messy as the kitchen. Holiday cards, wrapping paper, and unwrapped presents were everywhere. I couldn't stand the thought of tidying up anything Christmassy until January first, at which time everything associated with Christmas would be banished. Especially the tree. Back when I'd been dating my ex-boyfriend, Sean, I'd made the mistake of becoming so attached to my Christmas tree that throughout January and February and into March, it had still been in my living room, the lights and ornaments pitifully dripping from its dry branches. At that point it was simply too embarrassing to be caught hauling the tree down five flights of stairs. In a two a.m. drunken fit, I'd persuaded Sean that in a stealthy manner suitable for Navy SEALS, we'd lug the beast out of the building. Although the building had an elevator, it seemed quicker just to let the tree surf its way down the stairs. Sean, who'd had about twenty-two beers, had been completely game, so we'd grabbed the tree and pushed it down the steps and into the back alley, where

Sean had lifted the dried-up Christmas tree and hurled it into the Dumpster. We'd then immediately raced upstairs and swept every single needle from my hallway and the stairs to give the impression that the tree in the Dumpster could have come from anywhere and that *I'd* certainly had nothing to do with anything so dumb as keeping a tree up until March. This year's tree would be gone on the first of the year.

But for now, I didn't mind the Christmas mess and was comfortably seated next to an indoor herb garden that I'd bought for Josh and then decided against giving him because it struck me as a ridiculous present for a chef. On those and other grounds, I'd also become the not-very-proud owner of a handheld stick blender, a two-year subscription to *Real Simple*, a bundt pan, and a set of see-through panties and bustier that I'd convinced myself were presents for Josh, since he'd get to see me in them. After realizing that the gift of *me* was disgustingly narcissistic, I had managed to buy something actually *for* Josh: a really expensive knife from his favorite store, Kitchen Arts. And since most of Josh's clothing consisted of chef clothes and of logo T-shirts given to him by beer and liquor distributors, I'd bought him a couple of plain pullover shirts that bore no reference to alcohol. As for his presents to me, I'd spent most of December fearing that Josh would give me something awful and corny, like a charm bracelet with miniature pans and spoons hanging from it. But Josh, knowing me as well as he did, got me a monstrous supply of paint rollers, masking tape, trays, and paintbrushes, and a gift certificate to Home Depot, where I could buy all the house paint I'd ever need. Now, this might not *sound* like a romantic present, but Josh knew that about every three months I repainted my apartment and was too goddamn lazy to wash the brushes or rollers and consequently left them, soaked in paint, to dry out and eventually end up in the trash. I still had an unsightly, crooked stripe painted across one wall of my bedroom, a wall that desperately needed help. Josh was a dream.

He'd also given me one of the Naked Chef cookbooks, a selflessly generous gift because he thought that most celebrity chefs stank. On Josh's accepted list were Julia Child, Jacques Pépin, Jamie Oliver, Gordon Hammersley, and Charlie Trotter. Oddly enough, he'd watch entire episodes of *Iron Chef* with me, but I could wear my Rachael Ray Yum-O T-shirt only in his absence. If he caught me indulging my addiction to the Food Network, his typical comment was, "What are you doing watching that bozo?" As though I were cheating on him by admiring another chef! But if you ask me, the reason he got all pissy about celebrity chefs was jealousy. His profession was highly competitive and underpaid. If Simmer succeeded, he could remain the executive chef there, have good reviews written about him, and maybe earn enough money to pay the bills. He might eventually open his own restaurant and hope that it survived long enough to make even a small profit, but as the owner, he'd have to deal primarily with the business aspects of the restaurant and would be able to do very little cooking, which was his true passion. If he got super lucky, someone famous might eat at his restaurant and give him his own show or create a line of Josh Driscoll cookware. Highly unlikely.

Impatient for Josh to wake up, I worked on Naomi's list, which was coming along:

3. *Attempting to put duvet cover on duvet without sweating to death.*

4. *Having shower curtains that refuse to stay on stupid shower curtain hooks and fall off while you are trying to take sexy shower with chef boyfriend.*

5. *Being given annoying hermit crab pet named Ken as gift from nephew.*

I glanced up from papers to stare at my worst present, Ken, who was hanging from the top of his cage as if trying to impress me and make me like him. My sister, Heather, was trying to teach her three-year-old son, Walker, about the "experience of giving" and had foolishly let him pick out presents for Christmas. Walker was in the stage of choosing gifts that he himself would like to be given, and I was pretty pissed at Heather for supporting his inability to take the perspective of another. Yet, who was I to talk? Looking around the room at the mass of gifts I'd purchased for others and kept for myself, I suspected Walker and I shared some sort of genetic family flaw and were therefore blameless. Anyway, I was now stuck caring for a damn hermit crab, one that Walker had already named, for Christ's sake. Still, I felt an obligation to keep Ken alive and not flush him down the toilet. I promised myself that I'd look up crab care on the Internet.

I grabbed the phone to call my best friend, Adrianna. Ade was an independent hairstylist who was building up a loyal and wealthy clientele. She'd just started representing a makeup line as well, and she was forever giving me awesome product samples. My social work school volunteer day was coming up, a day when students were required to help out at social service agencies other than their own field placements. I was taking advantage of Adrianna's skills. I'd hooked up with Moving On, a small house in Cambridge that provided temporary housing for women in what were euphemistically called "transitional situations." The director of Moving On, Kayla, was thrilled with my idea of bringing Adrianna along. The day after tomorrow, Ade was going to give some of the women mini makeovers—and with them, we hoped, boosts in self-esteem. Kayla said that a few of the women had job interviews coming up and could really use help with self-presentation and self-confidence. Besides, these women's lives were short on fun. New makeup and hairstyles would be a blast for them. Adrianna had even charmed the makeup company she represented into donating some products for her to give out.

I heard Josh open the bedroom door and head to the shower.

"Morning," I called.

"Hey, babe. Can you turn the oven on for me? To about three twenty-five?" He turned on the water. "I have to bake up the focaccia crisps."

"Sure." I went to the kitchen. As I set the oven, I felt proud to make a contribution to Josh's food. I was so excited about tonight that I could hardly stand it. This evening, Josh would be introducing his food to the rich and famous, and he'd probably become an overnight success and achieve national recognition as the hottest, most influential chef of our time! Okay, I was jumping the gun, but Food for Thought and the opening of Simmer really were excellent opportunities for Josh.

Now what was I going to wear again . . . ?

THREE

AT five thirty, Josh and I pulled his yellow Xterra up to the gallery and double-parked so that we could start unloading his food and equipment. Mercifully, it was not snowing or freezing. On the contrary, the weather was unseasonably mild. I hoped the warm temperature boded well for a high turnout this evening. Josh followed me up a set of cobbled steps to the first floor of a quintessential Boston brownstone and into the gallery, which had originally been the first floor of an almost palatial house. A generous and graceful bay window overlooking Newbury Street had been set up as a well-stocked bar. Most of the interior walls had been torn down to create a large front room with an archway that led to the back of the gallery. Everything was brightly lit from the amazingly high ceilings, and beautiful pine floors stretched all the way from the entrance to the rear of the gallery. With the exception of the floors and the artwork, every surface was almost overwhelmingly, even blindingly, white, as if the intention were to impair the vision of those who visited the gallery: white walls, white ceilings, white reception desk. In the case of some of the works on display, the effect was, I thought, a charitable one. A massive canvas depicted what looked like a close-up view of abdominal surgery, blood, guts, and all. An appendectomy gone hideously wrong? Another painting, also large, was probably titled something like *Study in Cobalt*: blue, blue, and more blue evenly and smoothly spread over the whole surface. Here and there, pieces of sculpture in bronze and stone sat on white pedestals, and under the archway was a monumental hunk of smooth granite in the form of a gigantic egg.

Well beyond the archway and the egg, at the far end of gallery, Naomi was tossing a white tablecloth over what I presumed to be our table. She was being helped by a frizzy-haired, lean man dressed entirely in black who fumbled awkwardly with the white fabric.

"Chloe!" Naomi called to me. "Isn't this exciting? Please, come meet Eliot Davis, the owner of this incredible gallery. Oh, and this must be your Josh?" She beamed at me in an uncharacteristically giddy fashion. I studied Naomi for a moment, trying to determine what was different about her tonight. Did she have on makeup? Yes, I definitely saw a pink hue on her cheeks and . . . was that lip gloss? I was even pretty sure that her chunky braids had been rebraided. Their usual stray hairs weren't visible. It suddenly hit me: Naomi was nervous! I'd seen her before only in the office or at the irritating rallies she was forever dragging me to. She was completely out of her element here in this upscale, sleek gallery where the visitors were going to reek of money and class and Botox. In her effort to dress up for the event, she'd put on a turquoise peasant blouse, what looked to me like karate pants, and seven thousand bracelets—an outfit she must have thought would help her fit in. Her adorned arms kept making a piercing, clinking sound every time she moved. She might as well have thrown some hideous, big poncho over the whole ensemble to complete the look. I couldn't resist peeking down to see that she had even put on simple brown flats instead of her usual Birkenstocks. Although her attempt at upping her fashion sense had failed, I still felt touched by it and hoped that she didn't notice the difference in our attire. I had on my most recent purchases from Banana Republic, a shiny brown Empire tank under a yummy off-white crocheted sweater, and dark suede jean-cut pants. I wanted to look good for this evening but knew that I needed to look somewhat conservative since I was, after all, working at the Organization's sexual harassment awareness booth, and any sort of provocative clothing might send an odd message.

When Josh and I reached the table, I made the mistake

of putting down a stainless steel tray of beef tenderloin in front of Naomi. Glancing at the meat, she visibly tried to avoid gagging. I'd forgotten that she was a vegan. Before she could open her mouth to say anything about cruelty to cows, I turned to Eliot. Lord, did he have big bug eyes!

"Hi, I'm Chloe Carter. I'm Naomi's social work intern. And this is Josh Driscoll, the executive chef at Simmer, which is opening a few doors down from you on New Year's Eve."

Josh placed a massive food processor next to the tray of dead cow, and we all shook hands.

Eliot smiled. "I can't wait for people to start arriving. This is fantastic that I get to help promote an organization like Naomi and Chloe's, and such a great restaurant with a fine chef such as yourself, Josh. Please let me know if you need anything at all. Consider this your home for the night. Can I get you anything to drink?"

"Nothing right now, thank you," I answered. Josh and Naomi shook their heads in agreement.

"I need to get moving if I'm going to get food out on time." Josh clapped his hands together, eager to start working.

"Okay, then. You can set up here." Eliot gestured to a couple of tables next to the one with the tablecloth. "Josh, I thought you might need two tables for Simmer, and I put you right here next to Naomi and Chloe. There's a large coatroom behind us, here, and a phone in there. Or feel free to use my office if you need to." In contrast to the front of the gallery, this area retained its interior walls. Eliot pointed to a room right off a hallway that led to a set of stairs illuminated by an exit sign. "And there are outlets here, too, if you need them. I see you've got a big food processor there, huh?" Eliot said, eyeing the industrial-sized piece of equipment, which Josh had put on Naomi's table. The heavy-duty machine, all steel and black and shiny aluminum, looked like a monstrous version of a Cuisinart.

"This is what we call a Robocoupe," Josh said. "Thanks to Gavin, I've got all new top-of-the-line equipment. And, yeah, I need to hook this up for the dressing. Okay, I'm going to go move the rest of the stuff from the car and find a parking spot, if possible."

"Please, park in the alley behind us. I own six spaces back there. Naomi's parked there. You'll never find a legal spot at this time."

"You know what? I'll take you up on that offer. And I'll just unload from there and come up these back steps if that's okay with you?"

"Absolutely," Eliot said.

Josh took off, and Eliot went to open the rear door. With Naomi's help, I covered Josh's two tables with the white tablecloths that Eliot had thoughtfully provided. Then, with considerable effort, I shifted the heavy Robocoupe to Josh's space. After that, Naomi and I worked on setting up the harassment table. Before long, Eliot and Josh returned, each carrying armfuls of culinary supplies, and then Eliot left to go to the front of the gallery to rearrange the bottles and glasses. I looked around the room as I worked, admiring the large canvases on the walls. The paintings here were much more appealing than those at the front, abstract works with bold colors streaked throughout.

Naomi leaned in and whispered to me as we spread out flyers. "Eliot has been extremely welcoming to us. And did you see how he helped out Josh just now? Not all gallery owners would do something like that."

"He seems very nice. And has very, um, distinctive eyes."

"He's really been quite helpful. And Josh seems very sweet, too."

Seeing Naomi so out of place made me feel more in place than I really was, and I felt determined to try hard to help her tonight. Her idea of art probably leaned toward objects made of gimp or woven on looms. But nutty as she often made me, I didn't want to see her embarrass herself. For the first time, I saw Naomi as slightly vulnerable.

"Here," I offered. "I'll do that." I took a poster from her and began to hang a list of unacceptable workplace behaviors on the front of the table.

I looked up to see Gavin Seymour, who made his way around the giant egg and headed toward me. I'd met Gavin a few times before and genuinely liked him. He usually dressed in fairly casual clothes, but tonight he was wearing a navy suit and gleaming black dress shoes.

In his late thirties and extremely handsome, Gavin attracted women easily and enjoyed bachelorhood. He was a tough businessman, but it still amazed me that someone his age had amassed enough money not merely to lease the high-end property that would house Simmer, but to renovate it. Ordinarily composed, even restrained, Gavin was clearly fired up about Simmer's first public appearance and practically skipped over to us.

Josh looked up from the table where he was busy lining up ingredients to make more dressing for the beef medallions. "My man, Gavin!" he called to his approaching boss.

"My man, Josh!" Gavin held a garment bag out to his new chef. "Look what I have for you." He ceremoniously unzipped the bag to reveal a bright white chef's coat for Josh. "All the coats arrived yesterday, and I just picked this one up from the dry cleaner. I know how you hate wearing new coats that haven't been washed yet." He removed the chef's jacket from the hanger and passed it to Josh. "It's your show now." He grinned.

"Hey, look at that stitching," said Josh, admiring the deep red thread that spelled out his name under the restaurant's. I left the harassment table to check out the jacket. "Feel the fabric, Chloe. That is one hundred percent Egyptian cotton. Absolute best. Don't think this coat'll stay white very long, so you better admire it now!"

The fabric was thick and soft, and I could tell this

was the kind of top-quality jacket that not every chef was lucky enough to wear. The buttons down the front and on the cuffs were covered in more white fabric, and the short collar had been pressed into place. Josh had been a little hesitant to ask Gavin for pure-cotton jackets, since not every boss was willing to spring for them, but Gavin had gone ahead and ordered these ultraexpensive ones for Josh. The cheaper coats were a cotton-poly blend—or, as Josh called them, "bullshit polyester pieces of crap"—that didn't breathe and made chefs and line cooks sweat even more than necessary in already overheated kitchens.

"Your Birkenstocks should be here tomorrow. Sorry I don't have them for you now," Gavin apologized.

"Not a problem. I think I can make it through the night," Josh assured him.

The first time I'd heard that Josh wore Birkenstocks in the kitchen, I'd had visions of him whipping up culinary masterpieces clad in sandals identical to Naomi's. Much to my relief, I learned that chefs often wore kitchen clogs rather than sandals suggestive of tofu and granola. Josh had explained that the long hours chefs were on their feet meant that they absolutely had to wear high-quality shoes or end up with terrible varicose veins, back problems, or other aches and pains. Chefs' catalogues carried a variety of kitchen clogs, but trial and error had taught Josh that the London-style leather clog made by Birkenstock was the only way to go. He went through at least three pairs a year, and he'd gotten Gavin to spring for the high-priced footwear.

Josh introduced Gavin to Eliot and Naomi.

"We're going to be neighbors, I see," Eliot said, shaking Gavin's hand.

"You bet." Gavin smiled. "I've always wanted a place on Newbury Street. This is where it's all at. I had to outbid that Full Moon Group to get the location, but it was worth the money. They're supposedly tough, and I never expected to outbid them, but I did. They're a big-money group. They certainly have more than I do, but I got lucky."

Eliot laughed. "I've heard they're tough. I know one of their restaurants has a table tonight at a gallery that belongs to a friend of mine. Anyhow, congratulations and welcome."

"Thank you. If you don't have other plans, we'd love to have you over to Simmer on New Year's Eve."

"Wonderful. I'll be there. I'll look forward to it."

Naomi was looking worried about our table's presentation and scurried off to hover over the flyers. Gavin wanted to go check out other galleries and restaurant tastings but promised to return to Simmer's table. Eliot said he'd walk Gavin to the door. And that's how Food for Thought began: with excitement, nervousness, generosity, and friendliness. I don't really believe in bad omens, but for what it's worth, there were none. I had no forebodings at all.

Four

JOSH surveyed his tables. "I guess I better make more dressing now since I might not have time later." He packed the Robocoupe full of herbs, oil, and lemon juice, and the noise from the big food processor prevented further conversation for the next few minutes.

Unable to resist the lure of food any longer, I walked over to Josh and took a good whiff of the dressing. "Oh, that is amazing," I said.

One of the many things I loved about Josh's food was that you were never overwhelmed by one particular flavor; the tastes and smells from his cooking blended seamlessly. I hated walking into a restaurant or eating a meal and thinking, *Yup, that's garlic,* or *Oh, lots of sherry in this.* Josh's food always consisted of some unidentifiable fusion of ingredients that left you wondering what made up that delicious flavor.

"Glad you like it." Josh smiled as he poured the dressing into a large stainless-steel container. He unplugged the Robocoupe, wrapped the cord around it, and lifted it off the table. "I'm going to move this beast out of the way for now. Hey, Eliot? Can I put this in your office?"

"Absolutely. Put it on the floor, desk, whatever you want," Eliot called back. He'd been pacing between the front of the gallery and our section at the back and was now heading to the front, probably to peer out onto Newbury Street, eager for people to start arriving.

By six forty-five, the gallery was packed with art lovers and food lovers, and Josh was working up a sweat to meet the demand for his beef medallions. He had turned on a butane stove and had a skillet heated to the correct temperature. I nudged Naomi every time I saw someone nod and smile while sampling Josh's food; I was beginning to fear that she'd end the night with a big bruise from all my elbowing. Our harassment booth had a few visitors, mainly people Naomi pounced on when they accidentally approached our table. Naomi's tactic was to try to engage an innocent person in a discussion of workplace environments and then to interrogate her victim about acceptable and unacceptable behavior.

I watched her in horror as she spoke to a frail woman of eighty or eighty-five who wore a rabbit-fur coat, a garment not designed to endear its wearer to Naomi, of course. Contemplating the probable ferocity of Naomi's attack, I mentally prepared myself to leap across the table and catch the poor woman should Naomi cause her to faint.

Naomi leaned over a mountain of flyers and spoke with urgency. "Do you think it is appropriate for your boss to ask you about what kind of panties you wear? Or what your favorite sexual position is?" That was my cue.

"Ahem, perhaps she would prefer to just take some informational packets with her." I shoved a folder at the surprised woman, who immediately and wisely limped off, leaning on a cane.

Naomi turned to me. "Employers and coworkers say things like that, Chloe, and it doesn't help anyone to pretend that it doesn't happen. I know you find my style to be somewhat aggressive, but, Chloe, we have got to make people of all generations and all backgrounds understand the reality of what can happen in workplaces across the country. We've got to be outspoken and make our voice heard. Give it a try."

A few moments later, Naomi lectured a young man on the requirement that every workplace have a sexual harassment policy in place. Would he like her to come to his office and give a presentation? I heard him respond that he was only sixteen and that the only job he had was shoveling his parents' driveway. So far, he insisted, the only unacceptable thing either of them had done was to refuse to buy him a snowblower.

I decided to take a short break.

I told Naomi that I'd be right back and made my way through the crowd to grab a drink. The unseasonably warm weather, combined with a steady crowd and Josh's butane stove, had heated up the gallery. The only relief came from a welcome draft of cool air in back of our tables. Someone, I realized, must have propped open the back door to cool down the room. I made my way past the sculptured egg and through the crowd, grabbed two bottled waters from the bar, and worked my way back to Josh's tables, where he had just refilled platters with beautiful focaccia crisps and was searing the thinly sliced beef in the skillet. Considering how popular his table seemed to be, I was surprised to see him looking stressed. He usually loved being the center of attention.

"Is something wrong?" I asked as I handed him a bottle of water.

"Mishti Patil is here." He frowned.

"Get out! That's excellent!" Mishti Patil was *the* restaurant reviewer in Boston. She wrote a weekly newspaper review and also did guest reviews for local magazines and online publications.

Josh shook his head and whispered to me. "No, it's not excellent. I don't want her here eating food I'm cooking off of a goddamn cafeteria table. Whatever. The beef is fine, but it's not the first dish of mine I want her to taste. And when she came over here, she told me Gavin had invited her to opening night. I mean, opening night! Can you believe that?"

"What's wrong with that?"

"Chloe, opening night is going to be crazy, and I don't want a reviewer there! It'll be the first night the whole staff has been on. Nobody will know what they're doing. It's going to be a mess. Opening nights always are. We should've just opened the restaurant quietly, worked out all the kinks, and *then* had an official opening where we invited people like Mishti. Now, she'll show up on New Year's and see chaos. This is ridiculous," he fumed while placing beef slices on focaccia. "I mean, Jesus, the kitchen isn't even ready to cook in yet. Don't get me wrong, I'm psyched that he gutted the place and that he's putting in all the new equipment and everything, but we haven't even had a real run-through. I still have to finish teaching my cooks how to make and plate all the dishes."

I hadn't realized how unready Josh felt for the opening. "Well," I said hopefully, "did she seem to like your food tonight?"

He sighed deeply. "I have no idea."

We were interrupted by Naomi. "Oh, it looks beautiful, Josh. Could I have one without the red meat, though?"

Josh managed not to roll his eyes and graciously made a plate of focaccia crisps and dressing for Naomi. Eliot appeared, looking more bug-eyed and frizzy-haired as the evening kicked into gear.

"Guess what? Randolph Schmitt, who's the organizer of this entire event, is going to give a toast *here* sometime tonight! I've heard he's going to do three or four toasts at different galleries tonight, but this will be his first stop." Eliot looked as if he intended to jump up and clap his feet together in a celebratory jig, but he just reached out and clutched Naomi's hands in his, evidently because she was the only one who appeared as excited as he was.

I'd invited my parents, together with my sister, Heather, and her husband, Ben, and spotted them in the big front room of the gallery. Heather and Ben looked relaxed and relieved to have a night out without their two children. I stood on tiptoe to wave to them. I caught Heather's eye, and she waved back excitedly as she pointed next to her.

What has she done?

My ex-boyfriend, Sean Blackett, was standing right beside my sister.

I am going to kill her! First, I am going to take back the expensive sweater from Ann Taylor Loft that I gave her for Christmas, and then I am going to kill her! What in God's name was Sean doing here? As far as I knew, he had no interest in art. I looked around in the hope of seeing that he'd come with friends but saw him surrounded only by my family members.

Mental note: Add to Naomi's list.

6. Having ex-boyfriend (brought by dumb sister) appear at new boyfriend's event.

"Crap, crap, crap," I muttered.

"What?" Josh asked.

Oh, God. Josh. There was no way I could avoid some dreadful introduction here. I mean, the gallery was only so big, and Sean might actually want to *eat* something at a food event, meaning that he'd end up right in front of Josh and me.

"It appears that my lunatic sister has unearthed my ex, Sean, and now we are all squashed together in this fricking art gallery celebrating the holidays together!" I was, perhaps, going to have some sort of anxiety attack.

"Well, let's get a look at the ex then, shall we?" Josh teased, standing on his toes to get a good view.

"Argh! This is a nightmare. I better go say hello and get this over with. I'll be right back." I walked toward Sean and my family and tried to think of polite things to say.

Sean had been a great boyfriend, but he just wasn't someone I'd wanted to spend the rest of my life with. Heather, on the other hand, thought Sean and I should've run off into a picturesque sunset and had forty babies together. And she knew damn well that when I'd broken up with Sean I'd been left with monster-sized guilt over dumping an altogether nice guy.

To top it off, Sean didn't look particularly good tonight. His whole body had thinned out. Not that he'd been heavy when we were dating, but now he looked sort of gaunt and pitiful. And he'd started wearing glasses. Look what I'd done to him! Maybe I'd upset him so badly that he'd barely eaten in the past few years? And I'd caused his eyesight to fail? I had zero interest in facing someone whose heart I'd crushed, but I forced an enthusiastic smile.

"Sean! What a surprise! It's great to see you," I lied. I gave him a brief hug and gave my sister the finger behind his back.

"God, Chloe. It's been a long time," Sean said. "I hope you don't mind I'm here. Heather called me and invited me to come out with everybody tonight. I thought it'd be good to see you again."

"No, of course I don't mind." But I did mind.

I hugged my brother-in-law, Ben, who whispered in my ear, "I cannot begin to apologize enough for this. I swear I had nothing to do with it." I loved Ben. He was always clean-cut and well-groomed, but tonight he looked especially put together. I could tell he'd recently had his monthly haircut, and his short, neat style showed off his high forehead and warm, green eyes.

"Don't worry. I know it was all Heather," I tried to reassure him, although I couldn't help wondering whether the whole family was engaged in some horrible reunite-Chloe-with-Sean conspiracy. "Hi, Mom. Hi, Dad." I turned to my parents. My mother was wearing a tremendously awful cape-like thing on which she had affixed patchwork squares. Her latest craft obsession?

"Hi, sweetie." Mom gave me a hug. I tried to avoid chafing my cheek on her cape. "Where's the food?" she asked.

"Yes, where's the food?" Dad chimed in, craning his head over the crowd. "Oh, yeah. Nice to see you, too, kiddo," he teased. But at least he gave me a sympathetic look that I took as a reference to the Sean problem. I was pleased to note that my father had not only run a comb through his graying hair but had traded in his usual jeans and flannel shirt for a pair of corduroys with coordinating jacket and dress shirt.

"Down this way." I gestured to the back of the gallery. "Mom and Dad, come with me. I have to get back to the Organization's booth, anyhow. Heather, why don't you stay here and get something to drink, okay? I'll see you guys in a little bit." I glared at her. I wanted to keep Sean away from Josh for the moment.

"What has your idiot daughter done this time?" I avoided screaming at my parents as we moved toward Josh. "Sean said Heather *called* him? She is a piece of work."

"I don't even know what to tell you, Chloe. I cannot imagine what she was thinking," Mom shook her head. "Oh, there's Josh!"

"Jack and Bethany! You made it," Josh said to my parents. My parents greeted Josh, whom they adored, and immediately asked him for a full description of the food he had prepared. I felt a little better realizing that my parents were complete fans of Josh. I left them hovering over their plates and returned to Naomi.

"There you are!" she said. "We had a rush of interested people here. This is such great publicity for us!"

"Really? That's good news." Naomi was so happy that I couldn't help smiling at her. Maybe she had relaxed enough to stop accosting everyone who stepped too close to our table.

Our piles of information had been significantly reduced, so I reached under the table and pulled out more brochures, fact sheets, and flyers from a box and restocked our table. Naomi was right; our table *was* doing well. I spent the next twenty minutes busily describing our organization to visitors. I was surprised at how much I knew about the Organization and wondered whether I'd been absorbing more information than I'd thought. When things quieted down, I realized that I hadn't even tasted Josh's food, so I excused myself and walked over to the good smells.

Josh was speaking with two sets of well-dressed couples who were standing at Simmer's table. "Hey, Chloe.

This is Oliver and Dora Kipper, and Barry and Sarka Fields. Oliver and Barry are from the Full Moon Group," Josh said, giving me a knowing look. Oh. The very same Full Moon Group that Gavin outbid for Simmer's location! "You know, they own Lunar, the Big Dipper, and Eclipse?"

Despite the fancy space-themed names, those places were pretty much bars and nightclubs, not restaurants. The Full Moon Group had just finished some sort of marketing blitz; you could barely go anywhere in Boston without hearing or reading something about its clubs. I'd been to Lunar a few times with Adrianna, but it was such a meat market that we hadn't been there for a while. For one thing, she and I both had boyfriends now. For another, it was . . . well, a meat market. Lunar served food of some kind, but it wasn't exactly known for gastronomic originality. I couldn't even remember its menu—and on the subject of food, I'm known for my total recall.

"Sure. Nice to meet you." I shook everyone's hand and had to refrain from squealing in shock at Dora. She had a forehead with the telltale tautness of too-frequent visits to doctors' offices for Botox injections. I suspected she'd had piles of other work done and guessed that any fat liposuctioned from her had been injected straight into Oliver's enormous stomach. The rest of him wasn't all that huge, but his gut made him look as if he'd deliver triplets at any moment. Everything about him was round; round face, round eyes, and round head.

I busied myself filling a plate and eavesdropped on the Full Moon Group. Barry had tight brown curls that clung to his head and deep brown eyes that exactly matched his suit. He was absorbed in commenting on the artwork hung in the gallery: "The artist's use of color in this one indicates his attempt to . . ."

Oh, blah, blah, pretentious blah, I thought.

Oliver burst out with a deep, raspy chortle. "Oh, shut it, Barry. What are you, some goddamn art collector now? You're not fooling anyone."

Barry's face reddened. "I know, I know. You don't care about art, but I really enjoy these galleries."

Oliver softened a bit and said, "Well, keep the business moving, and you can collect all the art you want, right? I know you're a food nut. What do think of what the cook has here?" With another chortle, he led Dora off into the crowd.

Cook? There is nothing more insulting to a chef than being referred to as a *cook*. In the culinary world, it's a slur, a derogatory term that devalues the professionalism of chefs. An executive chef has earned that title and expects to be called "Chef" by the kitchen staff. Sous chefs, second in line to the executive chef, are often called "Chef," too, although, depending on the restaurant, they're sometimes called by their first names. But even those outside the restaurant world should know that there is an important difference between the words *chef* and *cook*. Although the Full Moon Group's establishments offered nothing even remotely like fine dining, Oliver should have understood and respected the distinction. Indeed, maybe he understood it perfectly and was just a prick. I was glad that Josh hadn't overheard him.

Josh leaned into my ear and whispered,"Hello, my little snooper."

"I know. I can't help myself," I whispered back.

"So, Josh," Barry began, "you're going to be the executive chef at Simmer? What are your plans for the menu?"

Josh filled Barry in on some of his ideas. Meanwhile, I sank my teeth into the beef medallions. Oh, destemming the herbs had been well worth the work! The flavor was rich and complicated and amazing.

"Tell me, what inspires your cooking? Where do you get ideas from?" Barry helped himself to another appetizer. "These are wonderful, aren't they, Sarka?"

"Hm? Oh, yes. Wonderful," she murmured unenthusiastically. Her food was untouched, and she couldn't have looked less interested, and she was so thin that she probably never ate anything anyway. Sarka had a natural beauty that would have made even my beautiful friend Adrianna jealous. Her dark hair was slicked back into a simple ponytail. The severe style highlighted her gorgeous cheekbones and wide hazel eyes. It was impossible to stand next to someone like this and not feel horrendously unattractive. I yanked at my red hair, willing it to not succumb to the unseasonable humidity and frizz up.

In an effort at friendliness, I said, "Sarka! What a pretty name. And so unusual."

"Check," she said, as if we were going through some sort of to-do list together. Rather, that's what I heard her say.

Responding to what must have been my baffled look, she said in a flat tone, "As in the Czech Republic." Her face was as expressionless as her voice.

Feeling like a dope, I listened in as Josh and Barry continued to talk. It became apparent that Barry truly appreciated wonderful food. In view of the forgettable and, in fact, forgotten menu at Lunar and the reputation of the Full Moon Group's other places, I found his enthusiasm and knowledge surprising. Barry had traveled widely and had spent a large part of the past year in southern France, in various parts of Italy, and in a few countries in South America. "I went on a culinary tour of Italy that you wouldn't believe," he was telling Josh. "Sarka didn't want to come. She said she grew up having to travel all the time and getting lugged all over the place as a kid by her parents, and she was never touring anything for the rest of her life. So I had to go alone. But the meals I had were phenomenal. Our group visited a handful of cities and ate the regional specialties wherever we went. Same deal in South America. I really wanted to get some ideas for Full Moon's next location. Obviously, we didn't get the space we wanted"—he smiled—"but congratulations to you and Gavin. Fair is fair."

Josh nodded his thanks. "Gavin got the space. I just hope I can do it justice. Stop in anytime you want, and I'll show you around. And you should come in on New Year's for the opening."

Barry eagerly accepted Josh's invitation and took his bored wife off, presumably to listen to obtuse remarks about artwork.

"Josh?" I looked at him in disbelief. "Why on earth would you invite the competition to your opening?"

"Look, first of all, this guy, Barry, obviously cares about food. Second, it never hurts to show off. You don't ever burn any bridges in this business. The Full Moon has money, and you never know what they'll do in the future, right? How do I know Simmer won't shut down in six months and leave me without a job? You know Quasar in Kendall Square? Full Moon owned that, and they just closed. Probably because of its crummy location, but even so . . . you can't count on anything in this business."

Before I could ask Josh why he wanted a potential employer but not a reviewer present on opening night, Naomi interrupted. "Chloe! What are you doing?" I'd forgotten about her. Again. She was looking really irritated with me. For good reason. I did keep disappearing.

"I'm sorry, I'm sorry," I apologized. "I swear I'll focus from now on."

Josh saved me from further groveling. "Oh, my God. I don't believe it. Are you kidding me?" I looked at him and saw him staring at a young woman standing with Oliver, Dora, Barry, Sarka, and Eliot.

"Who's that?" I asked.

"That's Hannah," he answered.

"Hannah, your old girlfriend Hannah? The one who only liked turkey burgers Hannah?"

It made no sense to me that Josh had dated someone who cared nothing about food. Josh had told me that she'd never appreciated his cooking and had insisted that he make her turkey burgers all the time for dinner. After they'd been dating for almost a year, Miss Hannah Hicks had announced to Josh that she couldn't stand the hours he worked and that he'd better find a nine-to-five job if he wanted her to stick around. And that was the end of that.

"The one and only, Hannah."

7. New boyfriend's ex-girlfriend appearing on big night. Or ever.

Five

HANNAH had straight dark brown hair that hung just below her ears and razor-sharp bangs that cut across her forehead. She was so neat and tidy and put together that I wanted to squash her like a bug. I immediately hated everything about her: her minimal makeup, her tiny frame, and her simple, tailored clothes, undoubtedly bought in the petite section at Talbots. Worse, she was pretty in a pinched, uptight, naughty-secretary kind of way.

"Oh, good," I snarled. "Now we both have exes here. I'm just oozing warm fuzzies from every pore."

"I don't know what she's doing here." Josh shook his head. "Last I heard, she was living in New York."

"Well, she's not there now," I pointed out brilliantly.

"You don't need to be threatened by her presence," Naomi tried to assure me. "As uncomfortable as these situations are, you have the skills to handle difficulties such as this."

Social work wisdom was not what I needed right now. I needed a best friend. Oh, how I wished Adrianna were here with me! She'd know exactly what to do. I had no idea, and all I could think was that I was being punished for some unknown sin.

Hannah scanned the room in time to catch Josh, Naomi, and me all staring dumbly at her.

"Josh? Is that you?" she mouthed with exaggeration.

"I suppose I have to say hello," Josh said with resignation. He took a few steps forward, and Naomi and I immediately followed.

"Hannah," Josh said blandly. "What a surprise."

Hannah Banana cocked her head to the side and flashed my boyfriend a smile. "I never thought I'd see *you* again." She reached out and lightly thumped his chest with her hands. *And left them there, touching him!*

Josh took a step back and pulled me next to him. "Yeah. I didn't think I'd see you again, either. This is my girlfriend, Chloe Carter. And this is Naomi Campbell. They're here running the sexual harassment booth."

"Oh, yes. Nice to meet you, Chloe." Hannah gave me an icy handshake. "And, Naomi." Staring pointedly at Naomi, she probably had the same reaction most people did to the name that my Naomi shared with the notoriously unpredictable celebrity; the fear that Naomi might reach out and bite her or hurl a cell phone at her head.

"So what brings you to Boston?" Josh asked.

"I was hired by the Full Moon Group to head a marketing campaign for them to kick off the new year. I've been here for about six weeks, and I have another two to three months of work to do for them. Have you seen any of the publicity I've done for them? I've been killing myself, but the money is worth it."

"Then back to New York?" I wondered hopefully. I couldn't get her out of Boston fast enough.

"You know where I'm from? I see Josh has told you about me."

Dammit! "I guess he must have said something in passing," I said as casually as I could. I could've kicked myself for giving her any sign that Josh had even considered her worth mentioning.

"I'm not sure what my plans are." She eyed Josh. "It depends on a lot of things."

I obviously had to get rid of her as quickly as possible. After tonight, Josh and I would never have to see her again. As if to reinforce my hatred, Hannah reached into her purse and pulled out a small bag of what looked like dried snap peas—with Josh's beautiful food right in front of her. The barbarian!

"God, I'm starving," she said, crunching into a green crisp. "I can't get enough of these. Want one?" she offered us. Her fingers were covered in pale green dust, and I was afraid she'd stick them in her mouth and suck on them in shameless flirtation.

"Okay, well, nice to meet you," I said in the hope of ending conversation. Forever. Bad enough that she was still interested in Josh, but what kind of sick human being would choose dried snap peas over his food?

Even Naomi didn't like Hannah. I could tell. Naomi hadn't said anything to Hannah, which was very unlike my talkative supervisor. In fact, she seemed to be staring at Hannah with curiosity, wondering which evil planet had shot Hannah through space and beamed her down here. Naomi was on my side! I hadn't known she could feel such loyalty to me as I faced off against a horrible rival. I hadn't been the best social work intern, but I'd apparently been good enough to endear myself to her. Under other circumstances, I realized, Naomi would probably have gobbled up those snap peas, which were just the type of flavorless, natural food she liked. But she wouldn't take them. Not from Hannah.

"I should get back to work," Hannah said, as though I hadn't just kicked her out of our social circle. "Nights like this are all about networking, aren't they? Josh, let's catch up soon, okay? Here's my new cell number." When she handed Josh her business card, I was elated to see him carelessly fold it in half and put it in his pocket.

"Yeah, definitely," Josh spoke with what I heard as marked sarcasm.

Hannah gave him a close hug while I made juvenile gagging faces behind her.

When she finally left, Josh said, "I cannot believe I ever went out with her."

"Me neither," I agreed. "At least she's gone now."

Before I could add any other thoughts on Josh's dating history, a booming voice over a microphone asked everyone to gather at the front of the gallery for a toast.

"Chloe, I'm going to tidy up the tables in case anyone stops by during the toast, okay?" Naomi rushed off. God forbid anyone miss out on an important harassment fact for ten minutes.

"I think I've got enough food out to keep everyone fed for a little while." Josh put his arm around me, and we moved through the crowd. "Should we go hang out with Sean now?"

"Ha-ha. Actually, I'd like to talk to Heather for a minute if you can stand being near my family."

"I love your family. Heather included, even if she doesn't love me." Josh gave me a quick kiss and went to talk to my parents while I made a beeline for my sister.

I grabbed the back of her shirt and pulled her away from Ben. "Start talking," I ordered.

"Don't be mad at me, please. I just ran into Sean the other day and I thought you might like to see him again—"

"No, you did not run into him. He told me you called him! And why would I want to see him again?"

"I just want you to really think about getting involved with someone like Josh. Chloe, honestly, what kind of life could you have with him for the long term? He's a chef. He'll work long, late hours. He'll be gone evenings, weekends, holidays. What if you two get married and have children? He's not going to be there the way somebody like Sean would. And Josh is never going to make a lot of money. You know what most chefs make. Are you two going to live in your little condo forever?"

I was fuming. "You are so out of line, it is incredible we are related. First of all, I am *already* involved with Josh, and I don't need to think about it. I know what his career is like, and I would rather be with someone who is passionate and creative and dedicated, even if it means he isn't at home as much, than with someone I didn't love who works some boring, uncreative nine-to-five job," I spat out. "How dare you, Heather? Do I look unhappy to you? Did I ask for you to decide what I want? What I need? And what have you done to Sean? Did you tell him I want to get back together? God, you are unbelievable. I'm disgusted with you."

Heather had tears in her eyes. Oh, no! I'd gone too far and made her cry.

"I'm sorry," she said. "I am. I just want you to have what I have. But I didn't say anything to Sean, I promise. I just told him you wouldn't mind seeing him again, that's all."

"Heather, I don't need a goddamn picket-fence life

like you have. I'm glad you are happy and have a great architect husband and great kids and a big, fat house in snooty old Brookline. Really, I am. I want a great life, too, but I might do it differently." Especially if having Heather's life meant getting pregnant and being hit with the notion that wearing L. L. Bean and listening to Celine Dion made you some sort of Earth Mother. "Maybe I'll be with Josh, maybe someone else, but you have to stay out of it, okay? Please?"

Heather nodded rather pathetically. "I will try. I promise."

I gave her an exasperated hug. Static came over the loudspeakers, and I turned to the front of the gallery.

"Good evening, everyone. I'm Randolph Schmitt, and I'd like to welcome all of you to this year's Food for Thought!"

The distinguished-looking Randolph Schmitt was flanked by Gavin and Naomi on one side and Eliot on the other. After issuing a great many unsubtle hints about opening our wallets and donating substantial amounts of money to the Food for Thought charities, he introduced Naomi, who, he promised, would make some brief remarks about workplace harassment.

Having evidently overcome her anxiety about being surrounded by Boston's elite, Naomi practically leaped toward the microphone. Eliot looked so nervous that his frizzy hair seemed to pulsate with energy. He was, I assumed, appropriately afraid that Naomi would say something so bizarre that tonight's visitors would never again enter his gallery. He did, however, manage to clap politely as Naomi seized the microphone in both hands. She immediately thanked Mr. Schmitt, Gavin, Josh, and me for our hard work. "And a special thank you to Eliot Davis for his belief in our organization and for giving us the opportunity to spread the word about harassment in this phenomenal gallery of his."

Harassment right here in this gallery of his? Naomi, that's not at all what you mean!

Luckily, Eliot showed no sign of having heard her thanks as an accusation, and no one in the crowd laughed. Eliot, in fact, looked pleased as he modestly waved away her comments.

Eighteen minutes later, Naomi's audience was still suffering through a forceful speech condemning inappropriate workplace behavior, which is to say, a detailed lecture that could have been entitled "What to Do When Your Boss Tries to Lick Your Neck." Bored and restless, people began to talk among themselves. I glanced around the room, looking for Josh, and spotted him at the side of the room talking to Hannah, who must have lured him away from my parents. However terrible Naomi's lecture was, talking to Hannah had to be worse. The front door to the gallery repeatedly opened and closed as visitors escaped Naomi's fervent assertion that everyone here was "empowering harassers by remaining silent."

Oh, Naomi! She knew exactly what she was talking

about, and she held wonderfully strong beliefs. When I'd heard her speak at rallies in front of the State House, the crowds gathered there had cherished her every word. I knew how helpful she could be to women who called our organization. But she clearly had no ability to read her audience. The less attention tonight's speech received, the more flustered Naomi became and the louder she spoke. ". . . so you must document every step you take! You must make copies of every complaint you file with your human resources department! You must not let anybody get away with . . ."

A piercing, high-pitched scream from the back of the gallery cut Naomi off. Like fans in a football stadium wave, the mass of people, suddenly silent, turned as one toward the continuing shrieks that reverberated throughout the cavernous room. Turning with the crowd, I saw Hannah standing at the far end of gallery, by the back hallway. Every part of her body was motionless except for her mouth, which opened and closed with each yell.

During Naomi's endless talk, I'd apparently acted on a subliminal desire to distance myself from her by inching my way out of the front room toward the giant egg and the booths in the back area. As one of the people closest to Hannah, I started to step toward her when Barry brushed past me, rushed to Hannah, and grabbed her shoulders. "Hannah? What's wrong?"

She pointed behind her to Eliot's office. "He's dead! He's dead!" she said hysterically.

For a second, I wondered why Barry, the food-loving partner in the Full Moon Group, had taken it upon himself to be the first to rush to Hannah. Then I remembered that she'd been in Boston working for the group for—how long had she said?—six weeks. And the partners, Barry and Oliver, must have known her before that, or they wouldn't have gone to the expense of bringing her here from New York.

Barry took a few steps to the doorway and peered in."Oh, God! Oh, my God!" Barry disappeared into the office and immediately reappeared. "Oliver! It's Oliver!" he called out. "Call nine one one!"

By now, Josh was next to me. I caught his eye, and we silently agreed that he should get to Hannah before she had a total meltdown. I followed him. When he reached her, she fell into his arms and buried her head in his chest.

"I think someone hit him on the head with your food processor!" Hannah's voice was forced and had a strangely mechanical quality. Just as I was feeling worried about her and sorry for her, she did something so disgusting that I hate to report it: she used my boyfriend as a handkerchief. Josh, to his credit, made a face as she wiped her mascara-stained eyes and, yes, her runny nose on his brand-new chef's coat. "His head is all . . . bashed in," she stammered. To my relief, she did not go on to recite gory details.

The crowd that moments ago had been shocked into silence was now bustling about and reaching into Prada purses and Gucci suits to pull out cell phones. A man up front began shouting, "A doctor! Is there a doctor here?" Another man was supporting Oliver's wife, Dora, who had collapsed. She looked ghastly. Even from a distance, I could see that the stretched skin on her face, and especially on her forehead, had turned a peculiar shade of yellowish white. Oliver, I thought, wasn't the only one who needed a doctor, and he was apparently beyond help. Well, in this group, there was certainly no shortage of doctors.

Police, too, were available in large numbers. When Josh and I had arrived on Newbury Street, Food for Thought hadn't even begun, and there had already been cops on the street corners. Now, four uniformed police officers entered the gallery. One positioned himself at the front door and loudly announced that no one was to leave.

When I looked away from the front of the gallery, I saw Naomi rescuing Josh from Hannah. "Hannah, how horrible for you!" Naomi said, her voice shaking. She looked more freaked than Hannah did. Her face was pale, but I could tell that she was trying to gear herself into clinical mode and was determined to assess any psychological trauma that Hannah might be experiencing. I assumed that Hannah would resent Naomi's typical hand-holding, but within moments, the two were clutching each other and sobbing. Actually, Naomi was sobbing, and Hannah was simply looking frozen with shock, so it was hard to tell who was comforting whom.

But at least Naomi had detached Hannah from my boyfriend.

"Chloe Carter?" I spun around to see the only detective in the world I knew, Scott Hurley.

"Detective Hurley. How are you?" Not the smartest question. He looked even more haggard than the last time I'd seen him. I'd met Scott Hurley last fall and had immediately thought that he desperately needed a long vacation in Aruba. Tonight, his scraggly black hair and unshaven face assured me that he was as overworked as ever.

"Peachy," he said with sarcastic exhaustion. "Josh, how you doin'? Chloe, I'll talk to you first, then Josh. We're gonna need statements and contact info from everybody here before you can go."

8. Being questioned by police regarding revolting food-processor murder.

Hurley glanced up and called to an officer. "Connors! The docs are here. Help 'em through," he ordered. I decided to keep my back to the EMTs to avoid watching them wheel Oliver out of the gallery. Because of the thousands of hours I'd spent watching TV crime shows, I was relatively sure that the body wouldn't be moved for ages, but I wasn't taking any chances.

I followed the detective to the side of the room. My mother waved to me from across the crowd and smiled, as though watching her daughter being led off by a detective were the most normal thing she'd ever seen.

Hurley leaned against the wall and yanked a notepad and pen from his pocket. "Tell me what you know about tonight."

As much as I wanted to impress a law enforcement official by issuing dramatic statements about key events I'd witnessed, I had nothing useful to say, or so it seemed to me. I explained why I was here and said that I'd been up front when Hannah screamed. I had just met Oliver and knew almost nothing about him. I'd been paying no attention to what was happening at the back of the gallery.

Hurley looked down as he wrote. "The back door to the alley is open. Do you know who did that?" As I shook my head, I noticed that the high humidity tonight was making him sweat more than usual.

"It had been hot in here," I said. "So I noticed the cool breeze coming from back there, but I don't know who opened the door."

"You were here with your boss, Naomi Campbell?" He paused. "Is that her real name?"

I nodded and pointed her out.

"Was she with you, too? When you left your table? And when the screaming started?"

I shook my head. "No, she was still at our table when Josh and I headed up front. But she must have left pretty soon after that to give her speech. She was still speaking up front when Hannah started screaming."

"Who else did you see while you were up front?"

"Well, between you and me, Naomi didn't give the most scintillating speech I've ever heard, so people were kind of milling around and talking through most of it. Well, after Naomi had been talking for five minutes, maybe. People were bored. And they started to leave partway through, so I'm not sure who was where. Although I'm pretty sure my family was up front all night, since they knew I was irritated with them for bringing my ex-boyfriend, Sean, here tonight. My parents are here and my sister and her husband. My sister's the one who invited my ex-boyfriend. I mean, seriously, would you show up somewhere with your sister's ex while she is perfectly happy with her new chef boyfriend? Anyway, they were all here."

Uninterested in hearing about my family drama, Hurley took my phone number and asked me to get Josh.

I sent Josh to the detective, who, I was sure, wanted to know all about the Robocoupe that had been transformed from culinary appliance to murder weapon. Josh, I knew, hadn't had a chance to wash the Robocoupe, and I idly wondered whether Oliver's body was spattered with vinaigrette. Josh had poured out the dressing, but some of it must have remained in the bowl of the machine. And the murderer? Would traces of vinaigrette cling to the murderer's clothing? Or had the killer used only the heavy base of the Robocoupe, without the bowl?

I stood haplessly by myself watching the chaotic scene before me. Charity-goers were being interviewed by police officers, flashbulbs were going off near Eliot's office, and the heat and stuffiness in the room had everyone on the verge of melting. The police had obviously closed the door to the alley. Dora, Oliver's widow, was huddled on the floor, where she was being comforted by Sarka, Barry's wife. Both of them, it occurred to me, looked unhealthy. Dora's color was still a ghastly yellowish white. In any case, the bright overhead lights meant to show artwork at its best had the opposite effect on Dora. Instead of looking young, her overtreated skin looked stretched and thin. As to Sarka, she was what in some circles might be considered fashionably thin, but in my eyes she just looked malnourished.

A voice interrupted my morbid reflections. "Chloe." Ugh, Hannah. Shouldn't she be sequestered by someone for something? She'd found the body, for God's sake. Someone should be preventing her from escaping! Hannah, I might mention, looked like a model in an ad for multivitamins. In the brilliant gallery lighting, her hair was shiny, and her white teeth sparkled.

"Hello. Have you spoken to the police yet?" I asked in the hope of shoving her toward Detective Hurley and away from me.

"Just briefly. I have to stay here until they can take a more lengthy, formal statement from me," she said smugly. Little Miss Snooty seemed to feel quite the celebrity tonight, what with discovering the body and all. Christ, it's not like she was going to be whisked off to the Four Seasons and pampered while she narrated her torturous night.

"This might not be the right time," she started, "but you should know that Josh and I have a connection. He may be with you now, but you have to understand that doesn't change how he and I feel about each other." She must've been sniffing too many of those silly snap peas she'd been carrying around.

"Yeah, okay, Hannah," I said. Even I wouldn't stoop to picking a fight with someone who'd just found Oliver battered to death with a Robocoupe.

"I've been in Boston for a little while now, but I've been waiting to call him." She cocked her head to the side and blew her bangs out of her eyes. They fell neatly back in place and didn't stick straight up at freaky angles the way mine would have. "I saw he was going to be at this gallery tonight with Simmer, and I knew this would be the right time for us to see each other again."

I took a deep breath. *Think about your social work training, Chloe. People deal with trauma in very different ways. Her head is probably spinning, and she is trying to regain a sense of normality by going back to something familiar, namely Josh. Except that this little snot had been eyeing my Josh before the murder. She is a dirtbag!*

"I cannot believe Oliver is dead," Hannah continued as though she were talking to herself. "This completely fouls up all my work for the Full Moon Group." I expected her to stomp her feet and march off like a seven-year-old. Unfortunately, she remained where she was.

"I'm sure. It's so irritating when your boss dies and interferes with your marketing campaign, huh?" What a bitch this girl was! I was considering smashing *her* head in with a Robocoupe when Sean showed up.

"Hey, weird night, huh?" At least we now had a topic of conversation other than my dumping him and breaking his heart.

"Sure is. Sean, this is Hannah," I said dismissively. "Oliver was her boss." Would she just leave already?

"Nice to meet you." Sean held out his hand to monster girl and looked appalled at my insensitivity. "I'm sorry for your loss. What a dreadful night you've had. Are you all right? Would you like a glass of water or anything?" As usual, Sean was the epitome of caring and gentleness.

Hannah, suddenly demure, thought perhaps she should sit down for a moment. I rolled my eyes as Sean dashed off to find a chair for the damsel in distress.

Josh had finished with Detective Hurley and joined Hannah and me.

"They're taking my Robocoupe and everything from my table, can you believe that? The Robocoupe I can understand. I don't even want that thing back after what happened. But the platters? My butane burner? What a pain in the neck."

"Chloe! They've confiscated our flyers!" Naomi had appeared, enraged that the police were collecting all of the Organization's materials from the evening. I silently thanked the Boston Police Department for saving me from having to sort, file, lug around, and otherwise deal with the countless posters and papers from our table.

Eliot appeared, looking totally bedraggled and defeated by the night's events. I couldn't imagine how upset he must feel that his gallery had become a crime scene. Would the murder really hurt his business? Maybe it would attract ghouls and drive off the kinds of people who bought gigantic granite eggs and oil paintings of operations.

"Folks," he said, putting one hand on Naomi's back and one on Josh's, "this is obviously a terrible way to end the evening. I know we all had high hopes for publicity and fund-raising tonight, but that all takes a backseat to Oliver Kipper's murder." Eliot's protruding eyes produced a few tears, and he shook his head a few times as if to gather himself together. "I need to stick around, but I'm sure you can all go home."

"Not all of you." Detective Hurley interrupted. He peered down at his notebook. "Hannah Hicks? You'll need to stay."

Six

THE next morning, I woke up to Josh's cell phone shrilly echoing throughout my apartment. Ugh. I was on school vacation and was not to be disturbed while catching up on post-crummy-evening sleep. By the time Josh and I had managed to slip past my parents and our exes without formal, awkward good-byes, it had been pretty late. Our drive home had been full of sighing and head-shaking and the unspoken agreement that there was no need to pick things apart: not the reemergence of both Hannah and Sean on the same night and not the grotesque murder that had been committed with one of Josh's kitchen appliances. I think both of us felt embarrassed by our disappointment that the evening had obviously been less about Josh's food than one would have hoped, so we had kept repeating things like, "How awful!" and "Poor man!"

Josh had left early to go in to Simmer and had obviously forgotten his cell phone, a lapse that showed how tired he must've been when he'd left. But with only two days until New Year's Eve and the opening, he had a mountain of work to tackle. His phone had been ringing constantly over the past few weeks as he set up purveyors to handle the restaurant's food supply and searched for kitchen staff. I'd better pick up the phone and give whoever was calling Simmer's number.

"Josh's phone," I murmured, still half asleep.

"What? Who is this? I need Josh!" a woman shrieked insanely.

I completely hate it when someone calls me and then demands to know who picked up the phone. "Who is this?" I asked calmly.

"Who is *this*?" she repeated even more hysterically. "Give Josh the phone now!"

"This is Chloe. Josh can't come to the phone. Can I take a message?"

"What? No, you can't take a message. This is Hannah, and I've been at the police station all night, where I've been terrorized by a bunch of idiots who want to know everything about the Full Moon Group and what happened last night, where I was and what I saw! What is wrong with this city? Josh needs to come get me. Please!"

Oh, God. Even I felt sorry for her. Since she'd spent

the entire night at the police station, it was no wonder she was coming unglued. But didn't she have anybody else in Boston to call besides her ex-boyfriend? Still, there was a limit to how nice I was going to be to Hannah, who'd just threatened to steal Josh back. Not that he'd want her. Even so.

"Are you still at the police station?" I asked.

She whimpered. "Yes, and I don't have a car and I don't even know how to get home."

"All right, give me the address. And then go wait outside."

I vaguely recognized the address she gave me, but never having been held for questioning, I had no picture in my mind of exactly where the police station was. Josh knew nearly every single street in this city and would've known exactly how to get there. As he explained it, he'd been lost in every possible location while driving around looking for undiscovered markets where he could buy unusual ingredients and ethnic specialties. But there was no way I was going to call him and send him Hannah's way. I just hoped I knew where I was going.

Josh had told me last night that Hannah was a tough, independent woman who usually got weepy and needy only when her tears and pleas served a purpose. He had said that even *he* had thought she'd looked pretty shaken up after finding Oliver's body. At a guess, Hannah had sensed his sympathy, and this morning phone call of hers was an effort to play on it.

Although I was willing to drive into Boston to get Hannah, I was hardly going to roll out of bed in my pajamas and race downtown without making an effort to look at least semidecent. Even after a night of what I hoped had been relentless interrogation under bright lights, Hannah probably retained her neat-as-a-pin look, and I was not about to be shown up by Josh's ex. Besides, rescuing Hannah, I told myself, was a test of social work professionalism; I was off to meet with a traumatized client and had an obligation to look professional. As it turned out, my professionalism translated into a tight shirt over a heavily padded bra, skintight pants, and tall black boots, not to mention the twenty minutes with a flatiron needed to calm down the effects of last night's humidity on my hair. It had cooled off today, but it was still abnormally warm for December in Boston.

I then spent six minutes staring at Ken the hermit crab in an effort to determine whether he was alive or not. There did appear to be some crab tracks in the sand, so I hoped he'd been taking midnight strolls across his cage. I changed his water dish, scooped up something gross that must be crab poop, and sprayed the tank with a water bottle. Heather had told me that misting the hermit crabs was supposed to increase their activity level, but Ken seemed as outraged by humidity as I was and stayed hidden in his shell.

Since I couldn't pick Hannah up in the pigsty I called a car, I spent ten minutes tossing embarrassing CDs into the glove compartment—six volumes of *Now That's What I Call Music*, two *American Idol* compilations, and a few other horrors—and throwing out Dunkin' Donuts cups and half-eaten candy canes. I displayed Josh's CDs on the passenger seat to give the impression that I frequently drove around listening to System of a Down, Mudvayne, Drowning Pool, and Papa Roach and was quite possibly the *coolest girlfriend in the entire world.*

I found Hannah outside the police station and turned up "Let the Bodies Hit the Floor," as though it were quite possibly my most favorite song ever. I pulled up in front of Josh's ex and cooly waved to her. She must have been looking around for Josh's bright yellow Xterra and took no notice of me. I kept waving, and Hannah kept ignoring me. I couldn't have been more than ten feet from her, double-parked in front of a pissed-off driver in a monstrous Durango, but Hannah stood oblivious to my increasingly wild gestures. I rolled down the window.

"Hannah!" I yelled above the music.

Turkey Burger Girl finally walked to my car, bent down, and peered through the window as though I were some tourist asking for directions. "Oh. Chloe, it's you. Is Josh coming?"

Yeah, Josh was coming, and we'd taken separate cars to pick up this fool.

"No, he's at work. Do you want a ride or not?"

Hannah looked around, as if to make sure nobody saw her getting into a car with me, and reluctantly opened the door. I slowly and dramatically gathered Josh's CDs off the seat saying, "Here, let me get these out of your way." She showed no sign of recognizing me as *the coolest girlfriend in the entire world*, sat down, and promptly turned off the music. "Do you have any coffee?" she demanded.

"The coffee machine in the car is out of order today," I said dryly.

"Do you at least have a tissue?" Without waiting for a response, she opened the glove compartment and unleashed a flood of my hidden CDs. I hurriedly grabbed them off her lap and cast them into the backseat. Goddamn Heather and her stupid birthday gifts. Who wanted a remix of Jennifer Lopez's greatest hits? The sound of that woman's voice made my ears bleed, and now Hannah Banana thought I spent my time singing along to musical catastrophes.

"No," I said trying to control my blushing, "I don't have any tissues." Not that Hannah seemed to need one. She was pretty composed, especially by comparison with the way she'd sounded on the phone.

"What took you so long? I need to go to the Whole Foods near my apartment, okay?"

Clearly an order, not a question. She was testing my professionalism, I decided. I'd need to watch myself, especially if I wanted to hear the details of her night at the station. I was itching to learn what Detective Hurley knew about her that I didn't.

"Which store do you want to go to? I don't know where your apartment is." I was driving aimlessly around and now almost turned the wrong way onto a one-way street.

"I go to the Whole Foods on Westland. Right by Symphony Hall. Turn here." Hannah gestured left, visibly smug that she got to tell a Boston resident where to go. "Oliver and Barry put me up in a condo off Boylston Street." More smugness oozed from her pores; condos around Boylston Street didn't run cheap. Gone was the hysterical Hannah of the phone call, and back was the Hannah I'd met last night, bossy and superior.

"So, what did the police ask you about?" I was hoping, of course, that she'd say something terribly incriminating. "Are you officially a suspect?" She was at the gallery last night and did work for Oliver, after all. Besides, she was a horrible person. And my competition. With any luck, she'd soon be arrested, convicted, and locked up for the rest of her life!

"They wanted to know all about the Full Moon Group, how long I've been working for them, what kind of employers they are, stuff like that. I said I didn't really care what kind of people they are. They pay me well, and that's what I'm interested in. Barry and Oliver didn't always get along, but I stayed out of their problems. I was there to do a job. Oliver runs . . . well, ran," she corrected herself, "a tight, moneymaking business. He was practical, knew what made money, and he wanted to keep on doing what brought it in. That's where I came in. I was keeping them on track and pushing ahead with what had been working for them. You should go into one of their clubs and see how packed they are."

Careful to voice no opinion, I said, "I have."

"Barry, on the other hand, is so full of himself and his grandiose ideas about fancy food and art and culture. He's always going on about wanting them to open a fine-dining, ritzy restaurant. I mean, come on! That's not what the Full Moon Group does. They've got highly successful clubs, and they make a killing. Why would they mess with that? And, actually, I don't think Barry does want to mess with it, considering how much money he and Sarka spend."

"Do you know anything about Oliver's wife? Dora?" I asked, figuring now that I had Hannah talking, I should get what I could out of her.

"Oh, that stupid woman. Like I told the detective, Oliver and Dora fought all the time. She is a self-entitled bitch, and I don't blame Oliver for being fed up with her. Basically, her role in life is to be a pain in the ass and spend lots of money."

"So why was Hurley so interested in you?"

Hannah practically *harrumphed* at me. "Because I work for them, Chloe. I have insight into who might have wanted Oliver dead. And his business partners, obviously."

"So was Barry being questioned last night, too?" I wondered aloud. I didn't get an answer. By waiting for one, I almost missed the turn into Whole Foods.

"Here! On your right!" ordered Hannah, irritated that I was not performing my chauffeur duties adequately.

I parked in the lot and trailed into the store behind Hannah. She grabbed a shopping cart and headed into the produce section. I caught up with her as she pulled a folded piece of paper from her purse. She whipped her perfect hair around to look at me. "Josh is cooking for me this week, just so you know. He wrote me out a list of what to buy. He's not sure what night yet because he's so busy with the new restaurant, but he's got it all planned out."

I reached out and snatched the paper from her hand. *Shit, she wasn't kidding.* I saw Josh's familiar writing on the back of a harassment flyer. Right there on the back of one of *my* flyers was a list of ingredients and directions in his chef slang:

Chkn., bone in

bunch leeks, rough chop

mixed root veg. (pot., swt. pot., parsnip, etc.), lg. chop

1 lg. onion, rough chop

mixed frsh. herb, rough chop (oreg., thyme, etc.)

Looking up from the list, I was at first ready to *rough chop* Hannah, who didn't give a rat's ass about good food. How *could* Josh be cooking for her? I refused to make a scene. The best thing to do when faced with bad behavior was to be a class act, right?

"Wonderful!" I proclaimed, forcing a huge smile. "Let me help you gather all these items for your romantic dinner!" I reached next to me and started grabbing red bliss potatoes and hurling them into the cart without bothering to put them in a bag. I yanked the shopping cart from Hannah's hands and pulled it ahead ten feet. "Look at these beautiful root vegetables! And butternut squash!" I tossed five in. "How about some rutabaga? Or parsnips?" I didn't wait for an answer and added eight of each to the growing mountain of ingredients. At the rate I was going, there'd be enough to feed a battalion of old girlfriends. I added twelve gigantic onions to the mound and reached in to mix the whole mess up. "There. Are. Your. Mixed. Root. Vegetables!" I hollered, garnering stares from the shoppers around us. "Follow me! You'll need fresh herbs! Lots of them!" I was just plain old shouting now.

So much for my class act.

Hannah at least had enough sense to keep her mouth shut during my tirade and said nothing when we got to the checkout, where she paid $86.29 for her supposed dinner for two. The four overpriced organic chickens I'd insisted on hadn't helped with cost control.

I leaned in to the checkout person and whispered conspiratorially, "She's having a romantic dinner with an old boyfriend. Keep your fingers crossed!"

Hannah watched me like I'd completely lost it. Granted, I *had* lost it, but for good reason, and once the crazies had kicked in, there was no stopping them. For the sake of my mental health, Detective Hurley should've placed Hannah in solitary confinement for the duration of her miserable life.

As we walked silently back to the car, with Hannah carrying all the bags, I tried to regroup. I was acting as badly as Hannah. I racked my brain to come up with a smooth social work way to handle this situation and heard snippets of class lectures whip through my mind. *Victim of trauma . . . resulting defense mechanisms put in place to protect the fragile ego . . . compassion for troubled client . . .* Hannah's controlling and obnoxious behavior could be the result of finding herself in an out-of-control situation. I needed to cut her some slack.

Oh, yes. While making her feel guilty and ashamed.

I drove to her apartment complex and planned my words.

"Right here." Hannah pointed to a posh four-story building surrounded by a wrought-iron gate. I put the car in park.

"Look, Hannah," I started, finally calm, "I know you had a horrible night, and I apologize for the way I acted. But how would you feel if your boyfriend's ex-girlfriend said the things that you've said to me? Probably not very good. I haven't done anything to you that warrants this kind of treatment. It is unacceptable and needs to stop." There. Simple and to the point. I had set my boundaries and made it clear that they were not to be crossed—just as Naomi had taught me to advise our sexual harassment hotline callers!

Hannah stared at me, expressionless.

"So," I continued with a little less confidence, "I understand that there can be leftover emotions from past relationships, but, um . . ." Why was she staring at me like that? "You see . . . Josh . . . Josh has moved on from the past and is looking forward to the future, you know, with me, and . . ."

"You have parsley in your hair," announced Hannah, reaching out and plucking a green leaf off my head. "Tell Josh to call me." She collected her bags and slammed the door before strutting up the walkway.

I was beginning to doubt that running interference between Josh and his ex had been worth the embarrassment. But I had to keep trying: until Oliver's murder was solved, Hannah would keep trying to persuade Josh to rescue her from supposed police persecution. The ideal solution to the murder would, of course, consist of absolute proof of Hannah's guilt. But even if someone else turned out to be the murderer, the police would stop questioning Hannah, and she'd lose her excuse for playing on Josh's sympathy.

I drove a few blocks and then used my cell phone to call Adrianna, who was the only person capable of preventing me from phoning Josh at work, demanding to know why he'd ever gone out with a psychopath, and threatening that if he actually cooked for her, I'd shred his Gordon Hammersley cookbooks to paper cole slaw with his best knives.

"Hi, Chloe. I feel like I haven't talked to you in weeks!" Adrianna said.

"I know. I missed you. It's been what? Two days?" I laughed. We usually talked two or three times a day, but between holidays, murder, and Hannah, I'd been busy. I gave Adrianna a detailed account of everything that had gone on last night and this morning, and waited for her advice. With luck, she'd urge me to call in an anonymous tip to the police to pinpoint Hannah as a savage murderer.

What she said was,"Do nothing."

"What? Please tell me you're kidding," I said, peeling a corner toward Brighton.

"Chloe, do not say anything to Josh about this dinner. You'll just be acting like a jealous girlfriend. Besides, aren't you and Josh having dinner at your parents' house tonight? He's going to be there with you, not with her. So, you have some time."

"I wish she would just disappear," I whined.

"Do you trust Josh or not?" Adrianna answered for me. "Of course you do. The only thing you have to do is start acting more dignified and block Hannah's moves. Let her crash and burn on her own. Girls like that always do."

"Fine. But I'm going to have to tell him about picking up his ex from the police station."

"Yes, that's true, but he'll thank you for saving him the hell himself. Based on what he said about her last night, he's no big fan of Hannah's. He's probably mortified that he ever went out with her."

I agreed that if I had to see Hannah again, I would restrain myself from lobbing any more vegetables her way.

"I want to hear more about this murder. I don't think you know this, but I do Dora Kipper's hair, so I've met Oliver a bunch of times. The Kipper Compound, as I call it, is a monstrous house. Every time I've been there, Dora's had some huge renovation project going on."

"Really?" I was surprised, not by the information that Dora kept renovating her house, but by the news that Adrianna did her hair and makeup. Adrianna is a genius at making people look great. Her clients don't just have fabulous hair and makeup; they have hair and makeup that make the most of their looks. Adrianna obviously hadn't done the plastic surgery or Botox injections or whatever it was that had given Oliver's widow, Dora, the ravaged appearance I'd noticed. But Adrianna had a knack for undoing the mistakes of doctors and nature, and I hoped she would talk to Dora about changing her foundation color.

"Oh, yeah. Huge house, huge attitude. Dora treats me like a servant and acts like she's some celebrity getting done up for the red carpet. She made me get separate products just for her, so whenever I go there, I have to bring my 'Dora duffel,' which is a bag of hair treatments and shit that have her seal of approval. The only reason I put up with her is because she'll pay me whatever I ask. Truly, they are disgusting people. The classic money-grubbing, shallow couple."

"Let me guess. Two kids raised by nannies and cooped up in private schools?"

"Are you kidding?" Adrianna said. "Dora is too selfish to even consider the possibility of ruining her body or her purse pockets with children. Anything that might intrude on her lifestyle is out."

"So far, I haven't heard anything positive about those two. Not that Oliver deserved to be smashed over the head with a food processor. Listen, I'm going to the store myself now, but why don't you and Owen come to dinner at my parents' house tonight? They'd love to see you guys."

"We'd love to. If it's okay with Bethany and Jack. What time?"

"Sevenish. I'll let them know you'll be there. One thing about my parents is that they love company, and they always have twice as much food as we need."

"Okay. Are you feeling better now?" Ade asked me.

"Yeah, I'm just irritated. But I'm going to bake a

hazelnut tart for tonight, and that'll take my mind off this Hannah disaster."

I hung up, called my parents, and left a message on their machine to say that Adrianna and Owen would be joining us for dinner. Then I ran into Shaw's supermarket and picked up what I needed for the tart. I had a limited repertoire of things I knew how to bake, but this hazelnut tart was always delicious, and it was perfect for the winter season. Sweet, rich, gooey, syrupy filling covered the bottom of the piecrust. The chopped hazelnuts rose to the top of the tart and took on a glistening sheen from the sugary ingredients. I'd never made the dessert for Josh but felt confident that it was a surefire way to impress even a chef.

Cooking for a chef is scary. The week before Christmas, I'd tried on three occasions to make lace cookies. I could swear that I followed all three recipes to the letter, but my globs of dough had never melted into gorgeous, bubbling, lacy disks, and each time I'd had to throw everything in the trash can. Although I know what good food tastes like, I can't always cook it myself, so when I cooked for Josh, I usually stuck with a few dishes that I trusted myself to make. There is nothing more embarrassing than serving icky food to a chef. Take the time I concocted what I thought was going to be a wonderfully rich and flavorful pasta dish made with tagliatelle, summer squash, zucchini, grape tomatoes, Calamata olives, garlic, onions, heavy cream, a splash of chicken stock, tons of fresh herbs, and Parmesan cheese. The thing had *no* flavor. None whatsoever. In fact, it had an outright absence of flavor. Josh was completely nice about my failure and even rescued the meal by tossing in a little balsamic vinegar, but I was still humiliated. Once in a while I came up with a recipe on my own that turned out to be delicious, but it never looked as attractive as Josh's food did. My reliable consolation when I made an ugly-looking dish was a memory of a Martha Stewart Christmas special that had been on years ago, long before she was sent to Camp Cupcake. Martha and her guest, Julia Child, stood side by side erecting towers of cream puffs to form Christmas-tree-shaped desserts. Martha's was a two-foot-tall piece of confectionary perfection, and Julia's was so far beyond lopsided that it threatened to fall over. But Julia Child was Julia Child, and you just knew that even if her cream puffs toppled onto the floor, they'd still taste a million times better than Martha's. I was no Julia, but I did trust myself with a hazelnut tart.

I arrived home to find an unfamiliar car parked in my space. Just what I needed. My condo was on the third floor of a house that had been converted into individual units, each of which came with an assigned parking spot in a little paved area next to the building. Since there is practically never any on-street parking available in the neighborhood, I assumed that the strange car belonged to some desperate soul who hoped no one would notice its presence. I parked temporarily in a neighbor's spot and headed upstairs. I was climbing the steep steps that ran up the back of my building when I ran into Noah. Ick!

Noah lived on the second floor. I'd made the mistake of having a fling with him last summer, just before I'd met Josh. Cocky, arrogant, slick, and good-looking, Noah had somehow tricked me into thinking he might be worth my time. Our short-lived relationship, if it could even be called that, had ended when I'd discovered that Noah felt the need to share himself with every twenty-something in the greater Boston area. The pig! Today, seated on the landing reading the paper, he was wearing nothing but sweatpants. It was a warm day for December in Boston, but it was not *that* warm. Any excuse to show off, and he was all over it.

"Hello, Ms. Carter." Noah grinned saucily.

"Hello, asshole." I kept walking. Noah showed no reaction to my usual greeting. I probably wasn't the only woman who said hello to him that way.

"I didn't realize you were around," he said. "My friend is parked in your space, but she's leaving in a minute anyhow." He flipped the paper over and let out a contented sigh obviously meant to suggest satisfaction with his morning romp.

"Of course she is. God forbid she hang around too long, right? Tell her to move it now, or I'll have her towed to Quincy." I got to my back door and fumbled for my key. "Aren't you supposed to be at work?" I yelled down at him.

"Day off," he called back.

So I'd had a crappy night and crappy morning. Big deal, right? I'd spend the rest of the day in domestic bliss, baking away and listening to music.

I walked into my living room to catch my cat, Gato, peeing in my yucca plant. "Get out of there, you freak!" I shouted at him. He finished his business, stared grumpily at me, and hopped off to find other mischief. Ah, domestic bliss.

I turned on the oven and dumped the hazelnuts onto a baking sheet. First, you roast them, and then you peel off the skins. I set out the rest of my ingredients and put the store-bought piecrust into the oven to brown. I couldn't be bothered to make my own piecrust, and the ready-made was always better than my homemade, anyhow. I changed into comfortable sweats and big fuzzy socks and pretended it was a cold New England winter day. I was grateful there wasn't a bitter ice storm raging outside, but a gentle snowfall would've felt more festive than this unseasonable warmth.

I mixed up the filling for the tart and tried to think about something other than that pain in the ass, Hannah, who was clearly going to keep running after Josh. He just wasn't mean enough to tell her to buzz off and stay out of his life. In fact, he wasn't mean at all. I, on the other hand, could tell her to go to hell, but I couldn't exactly spend twenty-four hours a day driving her away from my boyfriend. And as long as she was caught up in

Oliver's murder, she'd take advantage of Josh's kindness to try to lure him back into her life. Not that he'd fall for it, I assured myself. But I didn't need the aggravation.

Stupid Hannah, I thought. I measured out a third of a cup of corn syrup and whisked it in with the eggs. Was she officially a suspect? I hadn't even asked if she'd been fingerprinted, and I'd been too busy launching produce into her cart to notice whether her hands were covered in ink. Anyway, she'd probably washed her hands. Had anyone else been taken to the police station along with Hannah? Gavin hadn't spent much time in the gallery last night, but he still struck me as a good suspect. Although he had outbid the Full Moon Group for Simmer's location, maybe he'd wanted to make sure that the group wouldn't remain a threat; with one partner dead, the Full Moon Group's ability to compete with him was weakened, wasn't it? On the other hand, when Oliver was alive, Gavin had already had what he wanted: the ideal Newbury Street location for a restaurant that was about to open.

I pulled the browned piecrust and the hazelnuts out of the oven, spread the nuts between two dishcloths, and rubbed them around to peel off the skins. These were exceptionally big hazelnuts, and, as I realized when I peeked under the top dish towel, they'd already been skinned. *Dummy,* I said to myself. I threw half of them into the blender and pulsed the machine to chop them coarsely. The chopping created quite a racket, and I worried that the blender would overheat and start emitting smoke signals. I didn't remember such a violent noise erupting the last time I'd used it, but if this blender was on the fritz, I'd have a good excuse to buy a new, fancier one! I transferred the hazelnuts to the bowl with the other ingredients, mixed everything, poured the whole mess into the pie shell, put it onto a baking sheet, and gently carried the wobbly tart to the oven. I set the timer and started to clean the kitchen. Josh always cleaned as he cooked, whereas I usually made a disaster of the kitchen and ended up having to scrub every surface. This time, I was trying to follow his lead.

Has Hannah called a lawyer? I wondered, as I loaded my tiny dishwasher. Maybe a lawyer could solve all my problems with her. He could advise her not to discuss the case with anyone—especially ex-boyfriends. Why were the police so interested in her, anyhow? And what had she been doing at the back of the gallery last night? Why had she even been near Eliot's office? Had she been demanding even more expensive living accommodations from Oliver? And when he refused, she'd clunked him over the head with a Robocoupe?

I curled up on the couch and tried to distract myself with DVD episodes from season four of *24*. When the timer went off, I pulled the tart out of the oven and admired its golden color. The smell was so yummy that I couldn't resist pulling a small chunk of hazelnut goo off the top. I mean, I had to test it before serving, right?

Something was horribly wrong.

I bit down and practically cracked a tooth. Why were these hazelnuts so hard? Instead of a lovely, tender bite, I had just chomped down on what felt like bits of rock. I stared at my beautiful hazelnut tart in disbelief. What a complete idiot I was! No wonder the hazelnuts had looked so big!

I had not removed the shells.

I had chopped up and baked *goddamn shells*.

My ridiculous error was clearly Hannah's fault. If I hadn't been so busy figuring out how to get rid of that fool, I'd never have made such a stupid mistake. I threw the tart into the garbage.

What if I had gone ahead and proudly served the shell tart to Josh and my family? I'd have been mortified. Thank God I was alone and could simply make a new one.

At least I had enough hazelnuts . . . if not enough common sense.

Seven

JOSH picked me up that night, and we spent the ten-minute drive to my parents' house in Newton trying to catch up. I confessed everything about the Hannah fiasco except the unflattering details about vegetable warfare.

"I'm sorry you had to deal with her. She really wasn't this bad when I was with her. I'm not even sure what I saw in her, but I guess sometimes you just end up in relationships and don't even know how you got there." We rode up a hill on Commonwealth Avenue and drove past the deserted Boston College campus and into Newton. "Thank you for taking care of her, Chloe. I really appreciate that. I won't forget my cell phone again, I promise." Josh winked at me.

Adrianna and Owen, together with Heather and Ben and their kids, Walker and Lucy, were already at my parents' Spanish-style house at the top of Farlow Road. "Whose car is that?" I pointed to a beat-up blue Chevy parked behind Adrianna's car.

"Snacker is here!" Josh's face lit up. Snacker's real name was Jason, but like most of Josh's friends, he'd acquired a nickname that obliterated the need for an actual real name. Josh's new sous chef, Snacker, had been visiting his family in Colorado for Christmas, so he had a lot of catching up to do in Simmer's kitchen to get ready for the opening, which was only two days away. Snacker and Josh had gone to culinary school together, and Snacker had spent the past few years traveling from chef job to chef job all over the country. He'd been in Florida, Atlanta, Saint Thomas, Hawaii, and Seattle, among other places, and Josh had convinced him to come to Simmer and settle down for a while. Somehow, Josh and Stein were going to squeeze Snacker into their little apartment in Jamaica Plain.

"I can't believe he showed up!" Josh said excitedly. "He called the restaurant this morning and said he might not make it to the city by tonight. I told him where we'd be, though, in case he made it."

I'd never met Snacker and was happy finally to meet one of Josh's best friends. We walked into the living room and were hit by the smell of fir. My parents (well, more specifically, my mother) had done their usual excessive holiday decorations. Once again this year, my mother had somehow managed to cram three Christmas trees into the house, each absolutely covered in tiny white pearl lights. Curly willow that she'd grown in their big garden last summer had been dried out, and the stems were wrapped in thin red ribbon and arranged in silver vases throughout the house. Garlands with ornaments were draped across every available space, and candles were nestled in nooks throughout the room. No matter how overdone, the house always looked magical at the holidays, especially because the need to make room for Christmas decorations forced my mother to remove her vile little crafts projects from the walls. She suffered from some terrible affliction that caused her to knit, crochet, glue gun, and weave weird-looking materials into weirder-looking crafts projects that were prominently displayed on the walls of the otherwise lovely house. I was particularly relieved to see that her hand-painted birdhouses had been hidden away.

Everyone was gathered by the fireplace in the living room.

"There's my friend Josh!" A dark-haired guy in his late twenties rose from his chair and threw his arms around Josh. Josh hugged Snacker back, a big grin on his face. Wow, Snacker was pretty cute! Tall and muscular, with olive skin and . . . not that I was looking.

Even Adrianna, who rarely took a second look at anyone but Owen, seemed to notice how hot he was.

Ade removed her lavender mohair cardigan to reveal a simple, sleeveless black dress. As usual, she looked like she'd just come off of a *Vogue* photo shoot; her blonde hair cascaded onto her shoulders in soft waves, her nails were manicured, and a hint of makeup highlighted her natural beauty. There was a tiny, evil part of me that hated her for looking so damn gorgeous all the time.

"Hi, Mom. Hi, Dad," I said, giving them each hugs. My parents both looked half their age, cause to hope that I had a genetic predilection for a youthful appearance. Mom had pulled her hair back with a ribboned barrette I'd made for her at camp fifteen years ago, and Dad wore pressed jeans with sharp creases. Thank God I had Adrianna in my life to counteract the defective fashion gene that ran rampant in my family.

I greeted everyone and then scooped up my adorable nephew, Walker. "Hi, buddy." I spun him around and then hung him upside down, a trick that never failed to make him laugh.

"Is he going to throw up?" Adrianna asked over Walker's giggles.

I laughed at her horrified face. Adrianna thought of children the way most people thought of nuclear bombs. "No, he's not going to throw up. But if he does, I'll be sure to aim him in your direction."

She moved her feet out of the way.

"Come on, Ade." Owen snuggled up to her on the couch. "He's a cute little guy. Aren't you, little man?"

Owen was dressed in his usual quirky attire. As fashion-forward as Adrianna was, she had somehow paired up with the most fashion-backward guy. Tonight, Owen was clad in bright red pants and a matching jacket over a T-shirt I recognized. It was unfortunately emblazoned with the words *Beaver Liquors*. I hoped he'd keep the buttons on his coat done up. With his ruffled black hair and blue eyes, he was as adorable as ever, even with the inappropriate shirt.

Walker marched sternly over to Owen. "I'm not a man, and I'm not little. I'm a boy. I'm three, and I have a penis. Want to see?"

"Walker!" Ben lurched out of his seat in time to stop his son from yanking down his Jimmy Neutron underpants. "Sorry, guys. He's been interested in, well, his manhood, so to speak." Ben looked down at Walker. "Kiddo, remember how we talked about the fact that some things are private? This is one of those things."

"You have a penis, though."

I seriously thought Adrianna might faint.

An hour and a half later, everyone except Walker was seated at the dining room table. He was in the living room watching Thomas the Tank Engine and eating macaroni and cheese.

"I can't believe I have a child that won't eat anything interesting," Heather complained as she returned to the table after checking on her son.

"Ha!" My mother said to the rest of us. "This from a

child who drove me crazy the year she was eight and would only eat Middle Eastern food! I sent her to school every day with baba ghanoush and tabbouleh rolled in pita. He'll grow out of it, Heather. You did. Pretty soon he'll be demanding you make him Armenian food every day for lunch."

Despite the garish and unappetizing porcelain elves that occupied most of the dining space, my parents' guests enjoyed the delicious dinner: pork loin stuffed with fresh apricots and sage, sautéed spinach, and roasted fingerling potatoes. Josh had advised them on the menu for tonight, but they were both excellent cooks in their own right.

"Who needs more wine?" my dad asked everyone.

"Not for me," Heather said sadly. "One more month of nursing, and I'm done," she sighed. Lucy was in her lap at the table, passed out asleep after nursing for what seemed like hours. "Eight months of this is more than enough, right?" She looked around for reassurance.

"Absolutely," Ben said, leaning over to kiss her on the cheek. "You've done great."

"So, to Josh and Snacker!" My mother raised her wineglass. "Best of luck with your new job." We all drank to their success. "So, now, tell us everything. Is the menu set? Is the kitchen finished? Are you both going to become rich and famous and start your own television show?"

Josh laughed. "Well, I don't know about rich. I had to

take a small pay cut from my last job to work at Simmer." Heather gave me a knowing look, and I willed her not to say anything. "But," Josh continued, "it's costing Gavin a fortune to renovate this place. And he did a stupid thing, which is to pay his contractor by the day instead of getting a price for the entire job. He's getting royally screwed, if you ask me. But at least, as of today, we have electricity, and the stoves and all the other equipment are hooked up and working."

Heather adjusted Lucy in her lap and reached for her water glass. "I would've thought any chef job on Newbury Street would guarantee a high salary." Heather had the nerve to act all innocent while pointedly criticizing Josh's career!

"You'd think, huh?" Josh wasn't easily thrown by my sister. "Once the restaurant starts doing regular business and making money, Gavin is going to give me bonuses every three to four months based on my food cost. If I keep that under control, I'll get a percentage of the profits. And once Simmer takes off, which I'm sure it will, I'll get a raise."

"Really?" I said, surprised. "I didn't know that. That's excellent. Do you have everything in writing?" Naomi had taught me the importance of a paper trail in practically everything you did. I noticed my mother glaring at Heather and me for discussing money at the table, behavior she found rude and classless.

"Nah." Josh shook his head, evidently not minding

our lack of manners. "Chefs don't usually have contracts and formal arrangements, unless they're working for a larger corporate facility, like a hotel or a chain restaurant. Gavin is a good guy, though, and he's got the attitude that if he does well, I do well, too. He knows what I can do for Simmer, and he's going to keep me happy. But I have to earn his respect. I can't just ask for too much without proving myself. It's an investment. I take a pay cut now, and it'll come back to me later. But the food is all mine, and he's trusted me to pick out everything from the kitchen equipment to the plates and serving dishes. Not that I could do this without Snacker, though." He and his friend did some mysterious little handshake that involved funny finger waves accompanied by what sounded like yodeling.

"When you were interviewing with Gavin, did you have to cook for him?" my dad asked. "Or did you just show him your résumé and old menus from other jobs?"

"No, I had to audition. Some employers will hire you without having you cook, but that always makes me worry about what kind of place it is. Most restaurant owners have you audition with a mystery box."

"What's a mystery box?" Ben scooped the sleeping Lucy from his wife, who had been struggling to transfer food to her mouth while holding the baby in both hands. I gestured to Ben to hand the little bundle over to me. I needed a good baby fix once in a while, and there was nothing like holding a warm, blissful sleeping baby. I snuggled Lucy in my arms and gave her a soft kiss on her forehead.

"Oooh, I know what a mystery box is!" piped up Adrianna, who'd been unusually quiet tonight. "That's where they put secret ingredients together for you to use in dishes. You have to use whatever's in there, even if it's gizzards or something, right?"

"You got it," smiled Snacker. "Tell 'em what you had, Josh!"

"Oh, God, it was a weird mix. Pumpkinseed oil, a whole leg of lamb, a whole salmon, foie gras, veal cheeks, and something called farrow." Josh looked at our confused faces. "Yeah, I didn't know what farrow is either. I think it's some kind of hulled wheat. And because the restaurant wasn't open when I auditioned, I went to Gavin's house and cooked, so I didn't have that many fresh vegetables and herbs to use. Usually you're cooking a mystery box with more traditional items and enough other supplies around, but I had, like, parsley, chives, potatoes, carrots—just your basic staples. To make matters worse, Gavin watched me pretty much the whole time."

"Don't they always?" asked Owen.

Snacker answered for Josh, who had his mouth full. "No, not very often. Usually they give you the mystery box and say, 'See you in three hours.' Gavin did the smart thing, which is to watch how your potential chef uses his time, how clean he keeps the kitchen as he works, his culinary skills, and all that. For instance, that's why

Gavin gave him a whole leg of lamb and a whole salmon. Not because he expected Josh to cook all of it, but because he wanted to see him break them down."

"So what did you make?" asked Owen.

"I used the veal and lamb for one dish. I cut the lamb into steaks, grilled it, and served it with a warm corn and fava bean relish and a caramelized onion polenta. The veal cheeks, I seared those in the pumpkinseed oil and then braised them in verjuice and chicken stock. Verjuice is like a grape juice, and you can use it instead of vinegar. I put the polenta in the center of the plate, the veal on one side, and the lamb on the other, and I ran the corn and fava bean relish across the top."

"And what about that farrow stuff?" asked Heather, who was for once showing interest in Josh.

"Well, I cooked it risotto style and served that with steamed salmon and a fennel-orange salad. I didn't really know what to do with the food Gavin gave me. A mess of food like what he gave me doesn't give you any freedom. It doesn't let you show how good you really are. It shows what you can do with a restrained list of ingredients, but it really limits you. If you're cooking in a restaurant, you won't be working under those conditions, so I'm not sure how useful a mystery box like that was. But he obviously seemed happy enough with what I did to hire me. He'd seen my résumé and where I'd worked, so he knew I could cook. This was a way to see what I could do in unique circumstances, I guess."

"It sounds like you did a superior job, considering the food you were given. I love this concept of 'auditioning' for a chef position," Mom said. "One thinks of 'auditioning' for the theater, but that's really what you *are* doing. Trying out for the lead. And in order to get the part, you have to show off your performing arts talent! It's wonderful!" Mom needed to lay off the wine; she was becoming a little too enthusiastic.

"And so what will your schedule be?" Heather asked.

Josh and Snacker looked at each other for a moment before Josh answered. "Probably six days until things get steady." I guess they'd been trying to figure out who would deliver the bad news. "I'll be off Mondays, and Snacker will be off Tuesdays."

My stomach dropped. *Six days a week?* What's more, when classes were in session, I was cooped up with Naomi all day every Monday for my field placement. When was I ever going to see Josh?

"That'll just be temporary," Josh said, mostly to me. I looked at him and tried to smile as though I completely understood and was prepared to be the ultimate trouper. "Gavin wants us both to have two days in a row off, but I know myself, and I won't be comfortable until everything is running as cleanly as possible."

Noticing that I was likely to start wailing more loudly than even Lucy ever did, Dad jumped in. "Well, so, how is the menu coming? Are you all set?"

"The New Year's Eve menu is going to be a set menu

with dishes from the regular menu, which is basically done, too. It's a pretty big one. I think it's too big, but Gavin wants it like that. Mostly he let me do what I want, except for what I refer to as the *obligatory steak.* Every restaurant I've worked at has insisted that there has to be some form of steak and potatoes on the menu. I love a good steak, but chefs everywhere are bored silly by having to cook it all the time. Anyhow, we'll be open for lunch to get the shopping and business crowd, so we've got half of the dinner menu cut down into lunch-size dishes, plus sandwiches and stuff like that."

Crap. *Open for lunch* meant Josh would have to be there early. No more long mornings lounging around together. As much as he trusted Snacker, I knew that Josh would be there every day to prep for lunch. And wouldn't be home until well after the last plate had gone out at night.

"God, we have so much to do," Josh said, leaning back in his chair. The weight of what he had taken on seemed finally to be hitting him. "Snack, do you know how to use that scheduling software I was telling you about?"

Snacker shook his head. I knew Gavin had been installing all sorts of restaurant software on the computer that he and Josh would share. There seemed to be a program for everything: purchasing, recipes, inventory, and so on. Next to Ade, Josh was the least computer-literate person I knew.

"With everything that goes on at a restaurant, how do you guys get breaks?" Ben asked, reaching for more of the delicious pork loin.

"We don't," Josh said with some weird form of pride. "Most chefs don't. You work from the minute you get there until after service. If things are slow, you take a few minutes to regroup and grab something to eat. I never eat a normal meal when I'm working. It's just eat while you cook. Or sometimes you can make food for yourself and the staff around four o'clock or so, before the dinner rush, or after we close at night. The more you feed the staff, the happier they are, and the better job they do for you when you need them."

Josh was the kind of chef who worried more about his staff than about himself. He had the worst eating habits and would often eat nothing until late at night after he'd finished work. By then he'd be so hungry that he'd have a huge meal of food from the restaurant, or he and some friends would meet up in Chinatown and binge at Moon Villa. From what I could tell, most chefs ate terribly and lived with chronic heartburn.

"So what about staffing?" Owen asked with his mouth full. "How many seats are there anyway?"

"About eighty seats, with another twenty at the bar," Josh told us. "And in the summer, we'll open up the patio out front and fit another twenty-five there. The kitchen staff is basically me, Snacker, five other guys to work the line, and two dishwashers. Then there's front-of-the-house staff. Cole, the general manager, three bartenders, two hostesses, and a bunch of servers."

This whole picture started to make me nervous. I was worried that I'd hardly ever see Josh and that when I finally did, he'd be exhausted and destitute. I reminded myself, though, that this job was an emotional and financial investment for everyone involved and that between Gavin's drive, Josh's food, and the unbelievable location, there was no way that Simmer could fail.

Was there?

EIGHT

HOPING to get off the topic of the work that Josh and Snacker had ahead of them, I changed the subject to the comparatively neutral topic of Oliver's murder. "So, has everyone seen the news today? There's been a lot of coverage about what happened last night at the gallery." I adjusted Lucy so that her head rested in the crook of my other arm. For a six-month-old baby, she was feeling pretty heavy.

Josh jumped in. "Oh, yeah, Chloe. I forgot to tell you. Detective Hurley stopped in to Simmer today."

"Really? What did he want?"

"He asked me a lot about the ingredients I was using last night. And, get this, he wanted to know if I'd been using any prepackaged food. Can you believe that? Like

I had a box of frozen dinners I was heating up? I guess you could count the panko crumbs as prepackaged," he admitted. "But nothing else. He also wanted to know if I'd seen anyone eating food other than what I'd been making, particularly snack foods. I think there must've been traces of some kind of food on Oliver's body."

Prepackaged food. Hannah had been eating those silly snap pea snacks. Hurrah! She'd thrown the Robocoupe at Oliver's head and then rubbed her green hands all over his body. I should've just left her in front of the police station to make her return trip there easier. She *had* killed Oliver! Hannah in the role of murderer was fine with me, even though I had no idea why she would've wanted to kill her wealthy employer, who was clearly taking good care of her. Or had someone else deliberately left trace evidence of green snap pea powder to implicate Hannah? Or the murderer was someone else who liked terrible food? If so, Barry, the victim's partner, was off the hook. Barry had traveled all over the world in search of fine food, and at the Eliot Davis Gallery, he'd appreciated Josh's beef medallions and the accompaniments; he certainly hadn't helped himself to Heather's nasty snap peas. Barry's wife, Sarka, was emaciated. At the gallery, I'd wondered whether she had an eating disorder or a serious illness. In either case, it seemed unlikely that she'd been carrying around prepackaged snacks. Then there was Oliver's widow, Dora, who looked yellowed and ghastly despite Adrianna's efforts.

Could an addiction to junk food account for her unhealthy appearance?

Before I could begin to mull over possible motives, I was drawn back in to the dinner table conversation. My parents, Heather, Ben, Josh, and I simultaneously told the tale of last night's murder to Owen, Ade, and Snacker, all of whom had had the good luck not to attend the ill-fated Food for Thought. I'd already given Adrianna some of the details, but my family loved narrating their own versions.

"And then this young woman began shrieking . . ."

"I did my best to recall where everyone was . . ."

"Naomi was droning on and on . . ."

"I spoke to one officer who wanted to know . . ."

"Damn, I should've driven faster!" said Snacker. "Look what I missed! Could I have some more of those potatoes? This dinner is incredible."

"Well, thank you." Mom passed him the dish. "Although we can't take all the credit. We had to consult with Josh, who was kind enough to tell us in excruciating detail how to put the pork loin together." She smiled at him. Cute! I didn't know Josh had done that. At least my parents approved of Josh. Who cared what Heather thought?

"Do we know what happens to the Full Moon Group now that Oliver's dead?" my father asked the table.

"Presumably Barry Fields takes over everything, right?" I guessed.

"They probably had an insurance policy to cover this situation," Owen said. Owen has tried out many jobs, including his most recent stint working on a blimp, and a few years ago worked for about six months at an insurance company. "It's called a key man policy. You use it when you've got a relatively small business and you want to cover yourselves in case you lose a 'key man,' a crucial person without whom the business could collapse. They probably had key man insurance to cover the owners. You can use the insurance money to hire a replacement for the person who died, or you could buy out the shares of a business that were left to a family member. In some ways, it's a pretty general policy, but it's separate from regular life insurance." Blah, blah, blah, boring, boring, boring. Thank God Owen didn't work in insurance any longer. He did tend to change jobs faster than I could polish off a plate of Josh's risotto, but at least most of his jobs were in fields more scintillating than insurance.

"Speaking of jobs I've worked," Owen added, "I wanted to announce that I accepted an offer today. I interviewed today to be a puppeteer's assistant. Doesn't that sound interesting?"

Ade nearly choked on her food and looked at Owen as though he had utterly lost his mind. *"Anyhow,"* she said pointedly, obviously not wanting to discuss Owen's latest radical change of career in front of everyone, "this Full Moon Group can keep everything going, and we can still go out for bad food and expensive drinks at the clubs."

"Unless Oliver was killed for this key man insurance money," Josh added, "and Barry gets caught. Hard to run a bunch of clubs from a jail cell."

The idea of Barry as the murderer was an extremely disappointing one because it left Hannah completely out of the prison picture. But at least she wouldn't have a job in Boston anymore and would move far, far away, not, as I envisioned it, back to New York, but to Tahiti, maybe, or South Africa or, ideally, Antarctica, where she might freeze to death. Yes, Hannah in Antarctica. I could live with that.

But there was no reason to think that any of us at the table would be able to solve Oliver's murder or that any of us had even seen his killer last night. The gallery had been crowded. Most of the people there had been strangers to all of us. Besides, anyone could have snuck into the back of the gallery through the back door that had been left open. The murderer might have slipped in and out without being seen by anyone at all.

I finally returned Lucy to my sister and we wrapped up dinner. My hazelnut tart, which was topped with fresh whipped cream, got glowing reviews from the two chefs at the table. Obviously, I did not reveal that this was the *second* of two tarts I'd baked that day.

We said our good-byes, and I reminded Adrianna that our visit to the shelter was tomorrow at one. In the morning—since "harassment doesn't break for the holidays"—I'd have to face Naomi and hotline calls, but after lunch, I'd meet Adrianna at the shelter.

Josh drove us back to my apartment, and although I was thrilled about his new job, I was still pretty worried that the fifteen minutes it took to drive from my parents' house in Newton to my condo in Brighton would be the last time we'd be alone together until . . . well, until I didn't know when. But we would have tonight. Snacker had insisted that Josh spend the night at my place, since the two of them would see plenty of each other at work. Snacker knew where his new apartment was, and Stein would be there to welcome him.

"Josh," I said when we got into bed, "I am really happy for you. Simmer is going to be so perfect. You've worked so hard, and you deserve this. Gavin obviously knows what he found in you, and he appreciates how talented you are." I set the alarm to five thirty for Josh and turned the light off.

"Yeah, we'll see how everything goes. I wish we weren't opening on New Year's, because that adds more pressure to a first night, but it'll all work out. Forty-eight hours from now, the opening will be over. Gavin's a good guy. But he can be tough, and he definitely has set ideas about certain things." Josh let out a big sigh and rolled over in bed to cuddle me.

"Like what? The 'obligatory steak'?" I asked. Then I kissed him.

He kissed me back, slipped my T-shirt off, and moved on top of me.

"You don't want to know." He slipped under the covers.

I didn't. No, not right now.

Nine

AH, the Boston Organization Against Sexual and Other Harassment in the Workplace! My home away from home. It was December 30, the morning of the day before New Year's Eve. Why was I stuck spending school vacation here? I looked around at the dreary office, which showed evidence of my failed efforts to organize the Organization. I had arranged and rearranged the few pieces of furniture, attempted to file the millions of papers floating around the room, and lined up the shoe boxes that Naomi used for the few office supplies we had: four staplers, two tacks, seven thousand rubber bands, and a green pen. The monthly budget for office supplies was about three cents, and the board of directors had not approved my lively proposal to renovate the depressing two-room office. *Envision an inspiring decor . . . tropical colors and accent lighting . . . Consider the research that demonstrates a strong correlation between the physical environment and emotional health . . .* The board, however, had evidently decided that cheesy industrial felt carpeting, concrete walls, and battered cafeteria tables provided a work setting suitable for an agency devoted to helping the harassed. The board must have felt that since our hotline callers never saw us, the office could continue to look like a disaster area, and no one would be the wiser. In the hope of hanging one of my mother's wreaths, which were hideous but colorful, I had tried to force a nail into the concrete. After many failed attempts with a power drill, I'd left a bent nail, sans wreath, hanging sadly from a concrete block.

I scooted my chair closer to what served as my desk. The folding chairs and folding cafeteria tables gave the impression that we were some kind of covert agency that might suddenly need to pack up quickly and disappear. I picked up the phone to check for messages, found that there were none, and flopped back in my chair. As much as I griped about social work school and this internship—pardon me, *field placement*—I really did want to accomplish something while I was here and consequently found myself wishing that somebody would call for help. It seemed to me that very few people knew about this organization, whereas I was pretty sure that throughout Greater Boston, women were being harassed at work and needed help. Nobody deserves to be frightened or, in some cases, terrorized at work. It occurred to me that if I didn't loathe Hannah so much, I could pick her brain for marketing ideas to let women know that we were available. The one request of mine that the board had granted was for high-speed Internet access for the computer, so I speedily searched the Web for ways to "get the word out."

I had a few hours to kill before I had to go meet Adrianna, so I called Josh, who said I could pop into Simmer on my way.

Just after I hung up, Naomi burst in the door. "Good morning, Chloe!" she said breathlessly, her arms laden with binders and notebooks. What she did with all these materials was beyond me.

"Morning, Naomi," I said, quickly looking for something on my desk to suggest that I was engrossed in work and not fantasizing about what Josh might make me for lunch.

"We obviously need to have a staff meeting after the horrible evening we experienced together. Let me put my things down, and then we'll talk." Uh-oh. I was in for one of Naomi's "staff meetings," which meant that the two of us would sit practically on top of each other and bare our souls.

The phone rang. I hoped it was someone who'd need my help for the next hour. "Hello? Boston Organization

Against Sexual and Other Harassment in the Workplace. How can I help you?" It had taken me months to get that greeting down pat. I'd suggested to Naomi that we simply call ourselves the BO, but, reasonably enough, she'd vehemently objected to the abbreviation. At least Naomi put up with my calling us the Organization. In return, the BO remained strictly my own unspoken name for our agency.

"Good morning. Is Ms. Campbell in, please?" a male voice asked politely.

"One moment, please, and I'll connect you." I always liked to give the impression we were a huge company and that I would have to transfer the call through a complicated phone system to track down the person being called.

"Naomi, it's for you," I called into our only other room, the office where Naomi kept her desk. Hers, much to my annoyance, was actually a desk and not a folding cafeteria table. Maybe one day I would qualify for real furniture, too!

"Oh, hi!" Had she just giggled? "One minute." My supervisor had the nerve to shut the door between our two rooms. I knew it! She had a romance brewing! And with a man! Maybe I would use our staff meeting to investigate Naomi's love life.

Moments later, Naomi reentered the main room, attempting to hide a smile. "Okay, let's get going here."

She pulled a chair up next to mine. "I think it is

important that we process what happened at the Food for Thought event. Although we hear about violent crimes in the paper and on television, we were present at the scene of a terrible tragedy, and I'd like us to use each other as sounding boards to express any emotions we are experiencing. Chloe"—she paused and looked at me hard—"how *are* you?"

I knew that if I said, "Fine," the single innocuous word would lead to a lengthy discussion about my repressing unbearable emotions, so I lied and blathered on for a bit about how I was coping and leaning on Josh for support. "And how about you, Naomi? Do you have someone special you can lean on?"

"Thank you for your concern. I have a very good support system in place. Now, moving along, let's talk about the current cases we're dealing with. In particular, there is a young woman I've spoken to a number of times. The same woman who left that message on your voice mail the other day, remember? She has chosen not to give any identifying information about herself, which is fine, but I think that it's because she is so terrified of her employer. I spoke with her a few days ago, and her situation was unbearable. Her contact with one of her bosses disgusts me. He continually makes sexual advances, touches her inappropriately, and uses explicit language when speaking with her. Every caller we get deserves our full commitment, but no one is more needy or deserving of our help than this woman."

I knew exactly the caller Naomi meant and had to get her off the subject of this woman because, when I'd taken her first call, I'd given my usual unorthodox advice about fending off jerks by eating stinky foods. In answering the hotline, I tried to begin by following the standard recommendations from the manual, but I sometimes had to move beyond the book in ways that would have infuriated Naomi. For example, I didn't want her to find out that I frequently suggested that women take self-defense classes and practice their moves on abusive bosses.

"You know, Chloe," continued Naomi, "I cannot stand to think of another woman waking up in the morning, frightened to death about having to go to work. I've never told you this, but I've been through this firsthand."

I stared at Naomi. "What?"

"The year before I went to graduate school, I was working in a bank. I just had a teller job, and I was trying to save money that year for school. It was the worst year of my life. The bank manager seemed like a really wonderful guy. Married, pregnant wife, a real family man who was well liked by everyone I worked with." She took a deep breath and went on. "I thought he was really nice, too, until the harassment started. I was young and insecure, and at first, his comments seemed like compliments, and I'm embarrassed to say that I was flattered by some of the things he said. It seemed like harmless flirting, I guess, at the time." She paused. "And then his comments became more suggestive. He started touching me in passing and pretending his touches were accidental. Asking me out, wanting to be alone with me . . . well, it became terrible and scary. I didn't know how to handle it, and I felt partially responsible because I'd been stupid enough to like some of his initial attention. When I'd ask him to stop, he'd ignore me. By the time I finally got around to speaking to the HR people, I was miserable. And you know what HR did? Nothing. Not a thing. They told me I had no proof and that this man had been an exemplary employee for all his years with the bank and it was highly unlikely that he was doing any of the things I was describing. I could fill out some paperwork if I wanted, and they could look into it, but it was my word against his, and perhaps I'd better just find another job." Naomi had tears in her eyes.

I reached out and touched her leg. "Naomi, I'm so sorry you went through that. I had no idea."

"And so I left the bank. I didn't know what else to do. There was no one to give me advice and tell me what to do. The sexual harassment policy seemed like a token paragraph thrown into the HR manual. No one there had any training in how to implement the policy or how to handle complaints. I felt alone and frightened. I knew what he was doing was wrong, but I didn't know what steps to take to protect myself. That's when I decided that this is the kind of work I'd get into. I had planned on working with teen mothers after school, but this work became my calling. After my own experience. That's why I'm so driven by my work here."

I immediately felt horrible for all the times I'd made fun of Naomi behind her back. It made me queasy to think of anyone terrorizing her. As much as her outspoken, overly dramatic style and her use of social work catchphrases ("Provide access for the disenfranchised!") drove me crazy, she had grown on me. And now I was proud that Naomi had transformed her terrible experience with her manager into a motivating force to assist other women who needed help.

"And this young woman who's been calling reminds me of myself in some ways. When you work for a small business like she does, it's even worse. She's got nobody to help her except us, Chloe. She doesn't deserve what she's had to put up with!" Naomi was vehement. "And just because this Full Moon Group has money and power over her doesn't mean they can get away with this!" Naomi clapped a hand over her mouth. "Oh!"

"She works for the Full Moon Group?" No way! My mind raced. Finally, a motive to implicate my favorite suspect! If harassment occurred at the Full Moon Group, maybe Oliver had harassed Hannah, who'd murdered him in self-defense! Or in a vengeful rage! On second thought, I realized that the Full Moon Group must have lots of female employees besides Hannah and that the sicko harasser could be someone other than Oliver. It could be Barry, for instance, or someone in charge at one of Full Moon's locations.

"I shouldn't have said that. I can't believe I violated her privacy like that. You're a coworker, after all, but this caller has been so secretive. She only revealed her employer to me accidentally in one of our conversations. I'm not even sure she's aware that she did so. I was just letting her talk and vent some of what's been going on for her, and it came out. So, obviously, we need to keep this information to ourselves, as with all of the information we get from hotline callers."

"Absolutely," I assured her. Confidentiality was no joke here. Women who called were not only desperate to stop harassment but desperate to hold onto their jobs, and they were usually too scared to give us much information about where they were calling from. When the women called from work, they sometimes whispered so nobody would hear them talking. Another sad fact was that we often had no way to return calls, since many women didn't give us their home phone numbers because they didn't want their husbands or partners to know what was going on. Although it was the harassers who should have been ashamed of themselves, it was the victims who felt embarrassed and guilty.

"Do you want to show me your list of things that cause you anger?"

Uh-oh. "Um, I'm still working on it. Can we review that later?"

Naomi agreed but reminded me of the importance of this insightful exercise. When we'd wrapped up our meeting, I jumped on the Internet to search for anything I could find about Oliver's murder. Most of the links led me to pages with brief accounts. Nowhere could I find new information. One page, from the food section of a newspaper, mentioned the murder but focused on Simmer and "its up-and-coming young chef, Josh Driscoll." The article included details about Josh's background and sample menu items, and the number to call for reservations. A lengthy description of the design and decor of the new restaurant, together with polished quotes from Gavin, made me suspect that he'd had enough clout to persuade someone to include the material.

I did find Oliver's obituary, which appeared with a photo, but was surprisingly brief. It stated that he was survived by his wife, Dora, and that a private memorial service was planned for a later date. After everything Adrianna had said about Dora's extravagance, I wondered why she wasn't giving her husband a lavish funeral.

"Chloe?" Naomi said as she put on her winter coat. "I've got to run out and drop off this thank-you present to Eliot for welcoming us so graciously to his gallery. Be back in an hour or so, okay?" I wondered what the gift was. Probably New Age candles or a book on speaking openly with your inner child.

"Sure. I'll see you later."

Back to the important work of surfing the Web. I searched for information on hermit crabs. My goal was to learn how to keep Ken alive. In minutes, I'd discovered an entire population of people out there frighteningly devoted to their pet crabs. I learned that Ken would need a bath once a week. I'd have to dump him into a bowl of water and let him slide around for a few minutes while he washed out his shell. I could handle that.

What I could not handle was that Ken was going to molt. Yuck! He would burrow himself in the sand and look dead for a few days, and then would move from his shell into another, slightly larger, shell. I immediately concluded that Ken's cage would have to be shrouded during this process. The sight of a shell-less Ken would make me puke. But I'd have to buy him some alternative shells. The site I was looking at even sold a large number of hand-painted hermit crab shells in various sizes. For eight ninety-five plus shipping, Ken could sport a Spiderman, tie-dye, or bull's-eye shell. And here I was dressing (housing?) him in plain brown! I decided that if Ken decided to actually *move* in my presence, I'd reward his good behavior with a decorative shell or maybe with a decorative cage background or the toys and fancy lighting the site also sold.

I read a long paragraph on how to determine whether or not your hermit crab was dead, and I silently cursed Walker for having given me a pet that required study to determine whether he was even alive. And should the crab, in fact, be dead, I could click on the link that took me to the Hermit Crab Memorial Page. I went ahead and clicked on the assumption that Ken wouldn't make it much beyond New Year's. Oh, this had to be a joke! Should Ken pass on to "Hermie Heaven," I could go and post a eulogy on the site. Pages and pages of memorials to dead crabs loomed in front of me with wistful words from their owners. "Oh, Bingo! You were the best little guy. It's so hard to lose a pet, and you will be missed more than words can say. You will always be loved. See you again . . ." Oh, good God. "Only a tiny bit of time with a tiny bit of a crab, but a giant hole in my heart." And my favorite: "I never had the chance to name you. I took you home, but it seems the car ride was too much for you to handle. When you hardly moved and then your leg fell off, I knew." The other crab forums were filled with pleading messages from owners seeking help from other hermit crab fanatics: "Hermit crab missing legs!" and "Can I use a hamster ball with my hermit crab?" and "Something has gone dreadfully wrong!" and "Traveling with crabs?"

Some hermit crab owners, I concluded, were more devoted to their pets than Dora had evidently been to Oliver. He'd rated nothing better than a short obituary. Where was his wife's loving eulogy to him?

After learning more than anyone should want to know about the hermit crab world, I took a quick look at the Full Moon's locations. Lunar, Eclipse, and the Big Dipper all had Web sites boasting the best evening entertainment Boston had to offer. Eclipse's site showed a calendar of guest DJs, theme nights, and drink specials, and a link to the menu, which had wings, potato skins, and nachos: bar food and nothing else. I knew from Josh that food like that was all purchased frozen and in bulk, tossed in a Frialator or oven, and plated to serve. Nothing challenging here for a chef, that was for sure, and I could see why Barry might have the itch to do something more creative. Lunar's food was slightly more upscale and pricey than Eclipse's. Its Web site showed pictures of young, drunk women with overly waxed eyebrows and spray tans hovering above elaborate appetizers and clutching colorful cocktails in their French-manicured hands. Yawn. This place was a meat market for the young and wealthy. I was ashamed to remember that in the days before Josh and Owen, I'd been in Lunar a few times with Adrianna and that we'd gone there to toss ourselves into the singles scene. Worse, I had to admit to myself that I'd had a pretty good time knocking back grapefruit cosmopolitans and Long Island iced teas. Would I go there for dinner? No. But for a good time with friends? Maybe. But I realized that I'd love to go poke around Full Moon's so-called restaurants with Josh to check out the employees and see whether they knew anything about Hannah the Horrible. But I'd never get Josh into one of these places. And I didn't think he'd be overly supportive of my desire to prove his ex-girlfriend guilty of murder. Maybe I could get Adrianna to go with me.

I checked my e-mail, deleted four messages suggesting that I enlarge my penis, and shut down the computer. It was already eleven. I couldn't believe how much time I'd spent reading about Ken. I wanted to see Josh at Simmer before I met Adrianna at Moving On. I threw on my coat and was locking the door to the office when Naomi's voice rang down the corridor.

"I'm back! Just leave it open," she called breathlessly. "Sorry I took so long. I wanted to catch you before you left for Moving On. I'm really proud of you for spending the afternoon there. I know you'll do great work today!" I had a feeling she was going to lean in for a hug, so I busied myself with the buttons on my coat. Naomi was the most touchy-feely person I'd ever known. She attributed the need to hug all the time to the emotional heaviness of our work. She was forever spouting positive messages of empowerment ("We are strong enough to give ourselves to others!" and "Reach beyond your self-imposed limits!") while gripping me in a tight embrace. Although I really did like Naomi and was learning a lot from her, there were only so many times a day I wanted her arms flung around me.

"I'll call you later," I promised her as I headed off to Simmer.

One smelly T ride later, I exited the subway at Newbury

Street. Outside Simmer, a man on a ladder was putting the finishing touches on a glass panel with the restaurant's name etched through the opaque sign. I walked through an area with a low wrought-iron fence—the outdoor patio for use in warm weather—and entered through the unlocked front door. When I'd been here two weeks earlier, I'd been alarmed to see the unfinished state of the restaurant. The unpainted drywall, the cords dangling from the ceiling, and the concrete floors had worried me. On New Year's Eve, would the customers be eating off paper plates while perching on folding chairs? Now I could finally see what the finished Simmer would look like. For a start, there was an actual floor. Better yet, it was beautifully tiled in rich browns with thick grout lines between each tile. The grout would be hard to clean, but the rustic style gave the restaurant a homey feel. The plaster walls had been textured using brushes swept vertically and horizontally to suggest linen, then painted a warm beige and framed with dark wood molding. Wall vases, paintings, and mosaic panels decorated the large room. As I watched, a man was installing dramatic, ultramodern light fixtures. Except for calculating that the expensive remodeling was contributing to Josh's low salary, I felt relieved to see that Simmer was coming together. Josh had told me that Gavin wanted the restaurant to have a "worldly" feel in its decor and its food rather than to have a single ethnic theme.

Gavin was clear that he wanted the menu to reflect many different culinary influences; what mattered to the owner was the quality and variety of the dishes. There would be Asian-style sashimi plates as well as Southwestern-influenced soups and gourmet Italian pasta dishes. Josh loved the freedom. The challenge, Josh had told me, was to avoid dishes that couldn't be paired with any others and to make sure that there was some sort of cohesive quality to the menu as a whole.

The square tables and high-backed chairs were in place, and the bar at the front of the room was well-stocked with high-end liquor. Matt, the bartender Gavin had lured away from a South End restaurant, was behind the stone counter feeding glasses into racks suspended from a high shelf.

"Chloe?"

Gavin walked toward me, all smiles. "So, what do you think?"

"It's beautiful. It really is. Congratulations."

"You here to see Josh?" he asked.

I nodded, and he pointed to the back of the restaurant. "He's in the kitchen with Snacker. Make yourself at home. I've got to make some calls, if you'll excuse me. We're missing half of our goddamn bowls that were left out of our dishware order. They charged us for them but forgot to deliver them, so now I have to yell at some poor schmuck and make sure they get overnighted to us. Ah, the joys of being a business owner." Even with last-minute problems, Gavin couldn't conceal his excitement about Simmer's impending opening; he was practically glowing. "But there's nothing like Newbury Street. I can't wait until that patio opens up. The people watching, the atmosphere, the food . . . I can't wait! We've already had a bunch of curious neighbors pop in to check us out. Hair stylists, store owners, they've been stopping by wanting to see what kind of food we'll be doing. Everybody wants to get an in with us before we open. So, anyway, I've got make this call, but I'll walk you back to the kitchen."

I followed Gavin to the back and then through the large wooden doors that swung into the kitchen.

"I'll see you at the opening, right, Chloe?"

I nodded, and Gavin headed off to the left to his office.

Josh and Snacker were hovering over one of the gigantic gas stoves. "Perfect, perfect, perfect," Josh was saying happily. Both chefs were wearing their spotless new white coats, baggy black pants, and shiny black leather kitchen clogs. Give it a couple of days, and those sparkling outfits would be saturated with odors and marred by splotches that no detergent could remove.

When Gavin had started construction on Simmer, I'd hoped that Josh would have a magnificently generous workspace. Giving the chef a big kitchen, however, would have meant reducing the amount of space at the front of the house and consequently decreasing the number of tables available to paying customers. Not that this kitchen was cramped, but on a busy night with a full staff, things might get tight. Three huge tiers of stainless-steel shelves held sauté pans, stockpots, and roasting pans. The stoves, ovens, and other major pieces of equipment hogged space, of course, and small appliances were everywhere: blenders, food processors, stick blenders, and a giant mixer.

"Hello, Miss Chloe," Snacker greeted me, shaking a skillet hard and tossing its aromatic contents.

Oh, he was still adorable! Again, not that I was looking. Well, not looking for *me*, but I could admire, right?

"Hi, babe!" Josh stopped stirring a bubbling pot and waved me over. "Come taste this stock." He held out a teaspoon and fed me the most unbelievably delicious beef stock. At that moment, right there in my mouth, the whole concept of bouillon cubes met its dried-up, prepackaged maker.

A man said, "If that's what they do to stock, I can't wait to try an entire meal."

I spun around to see Barry in the corner of the kitchen. He was leaning so comfortably against one of the stainless counters that he looked almost at home. I hadn't even noticed that anyone else was here. Why? I had eyes only for Josh.

"Chloe, you remember Barry Fields? From the other night?"

"Yes. I'm so sorry about your partner."

Barry's brown curls had been severely gelled against

his skull to create the effect of a shellacked swim cap, and his rumpled sport coat was, I thought, the same one he'd been wearing the other night.

What could Barry be doing here? Josh had told him to stop in, but I thought that he'd been issuing the chef's version of "Let's get together for lunch sometime." Barry, however, had taken Josh literally. I peeked at my boyfriend and raised an eyebrow.

"Thank you." Barry nodded. "It's a rough time right now. Thought I'd stop in here for some comfort food, as they say."

"Yup," Josh agreed. "We just whipped up something for him."

Oh, I got it. Josh was being cocky; he was showing off for the guy who'd lost this location. He might as well have stuck out his tongue and yelled, "Ha-ha!" Or maybe his tactic was to keep his friends close and his enemies closer. As Josh had pointed out, this "enemy," Barry, could one day be a good connection. Or maybe Josh and Barry were just two food afficionados sharing their common interest?

"Snack, how's the veg doin'?" Josh asked his sous chef.

"Just done now, Chef." Snacker pulled the skillet off the heat and poured what Josh loosely referred to as a "hash" onto a plate. When Josh said *hash*, he didn't mean some unidentifiable mess you'd find next to two fried eggs with a side of bacon. He meant a delicious combination of vegetables he'd pulled together, sautéed over high heat, and seasoned with a rich broth, a sauce, or just salt, pepper, olive oil, and maybe fresh thyme.

Josh reached into an oven and, using only a thin dish towel, pulled out a tray to reveal a gorgeously browned game hen. He picked it up bare-handed, gently placed it on a cutting board, sliced off a beautiful portion, and added it to the plate with the hash.

"Here you go, sir." He carried the dish over to Barry. "And fresh rosemary bread, too," he added, turning to another counter to cut a thick wedge from one of four loaves. "You're next, Chloe," he promised me with a wink, having probably seen the drool dripping down my chin.

Barry took a mouthful from his plate and, when he finally swallowed, put down his plate and fork. "Superb. Really, Josh. Losing Oliver is miserable, and this is just what I needed." Was he going to cry? "No wonder Gavin won't part with even a share of this place. With you two here, Simmer is going to do well. It's a dream."

Barry had come here to attempt the impossible feat of convincing Gavin Seymour to let him in on a restaurant that Gavin had just put oodles of money into? A restaurant on the verge of opening? And, more than everything else combined, a restaurant that he loved? What an idiot Barry was.

"It's just been a terrible few days. I've known Oliver most of my life, and to have him suddenly gone . . . well, it's just unimaginable. We grew up together and started Full Moon together. Even with the disagreements we had, he was one of my best friends. Practically family." He rested his head in one hand, but with the other hand, he kept eating. Barry looked positively heartbroken. I hoped that Josh's comfort food fulfilled its mission by soothing some of Barry's sadness.

We'd just met Barry. Josh could at least offer the condolence of a delicious meal. I racked my brain to come up with something to say to a stranger who'd lost a best friend, but Barry was now focused on his food. Besides, he did have a wife and, presumably, friends who could help him deal with this loss, so I tried not to feel horribly inadequate. I have to admit that I was aching to ask him about Hannah, but it seemed cruel to push him to discuss Oliver's death.

Josh and Snacker looked as uncomfortable as I was with the silence that had now fallen, so I changed the subject. "So, tell me what's been going on here today," I said to the two chefs as I dug into the plate Josh had made up for me. It was identical to Barry's: game hen with glorious hash and fresh rosemary bread.

"Josh has been running me through the menu," said Snacker, "and we've been cooking up some of the more complicated dishes so he can show me how he wants them plated. And, more importantly, I've been asking Josh if you have any single friends in need of some male companionship."

I laughed. I'd be surprised if Snacker didn't get clubbed over the head and dragged back to some woman's house by the end of the day. "I'll work on it for you. I promise."

Josh groaned. "Hey, hey. Snacker's got plenty to do around here to keep him busy, so don't get him all distracted with one of your friends this early in the game."

After Barry and I had finished our food, he thanked Josh and Snacker and promised to return on New Year's Eve. "I know how much you two have to get done, so I'll leave you to your work. Thanks again for everything. This really did cheer me up a bit."

We waved good-bye, and I was ashamed of how relieved I was to have him gone. It's awful, but there is something intolerable about being around someone else's pain when you can't do anything to help. Maybe next semester I could sign up for a class on coping with grief?

I watched Josh while he worked in the kitchen. He was looking particularly sexy today, what with the sparkling white coat and all, and I was hoping for some alone time in one of the storage rooms, even though it was probably some enormous health code violation to fornicate near the dry goods. Besides, I really had to get going if I was going to make it to Moving On to meet Adrianna.

I did manage to pin Josh against a wall for a few minutes of groping while Snacker stepped into the office to make some phone calls and confirm orders with purveyors. "Am I going to see you tonight?" I asked in between kisses.

He sighed. "I don't know. I don't think so." He slid both his hands into my back pockets and pulled me in close. "I've got too much to do, and I'll probably be busy all night. I'll call you later, though, okay?"

What Josh meant, I knew, was that he wouldn't have even one day off for the next two weeks. I already missed him.

I dragged myself out of his arms. "Okay, I'll talk to you in a bit."

Just one more kiss—

I heard the kitchen doors swing open and shut.

"Oh, excuse me. Sorry to interrupt."

I pulled away from Josh to see Eliot Davis standing by the door looking embarrassed to have caught us glued to each other. "I just wanted to see how the restaurant was coming along." His physical features, especially his peculiar eyes, were unattractive, but he wore a boxy, trendy-looking sport jacket and somehow exuded an air of sophistication appropriate to the owner of a Newbury Street gallery. I hoped that Naomi's thank-you present hadn't been some god-awful macramé wall hanging or the stinky handmade candles or pop psych book I'd imagined.

"It's okay." I laughed. "I'm on my way out anyhow.

Nice to see you. And thanks again for your hospitality the other night at the gallery."

"Nice to see you, too, Chloe. Bye."

Josh squeezed my hand, and I left for another dreaded T ride, this one to Cambridge.

Ten

MOVING On was located in an adorable yellow house on a quiet street off Mass. Ave. outside Harvard Square. Adrianna's car was parked out front, and I hoped she wasn't going to kill me for being a few minutes late. The program director, Kayla, let me in and showed me into the combined kitchen and dining room. I don't know what I was expecting, but Moving On looked like a normal house, with real furniture, hardwood floors, pale green walls, and white trim. Three windows in the kitchen gave a view of a back patio with a grill, covered for the winter to protect it from the snow. After working at the Organization, I'd assumed every nonprofit would be barren and depressing. This was a cheery, comfortable environment; it was a home.

Adrianna stood in the kitchen, wrapping a nylon cape around a young woman seated in a chair.

Adrianna greeted me by saying, "Hi, Chloe. This is Isabelle, and she's ready to chop off this mane of hair."

"Hi, Chloe." Isabelle spoke in a whisper. She looked about twenty years old and probably weighed all of one hundred pounds, not including the ten pounds of frizzy black curls that overwhelmed her tiny frame. She was either frozen in her seat or ready to fly off it; either way, here was a young woman terrified of what was about to happen to her hair. And to make matters worse, Ade looked even more beautiful than ever with her artistically colored blonde hair blown out to its fullest in an homage to early nineties' supermodels. She looked so glamorous that poor Isabelle must have felt dowdy by comparison. Anyone would have. I did.

"Hi, Isabelle. Don't worry about anything. Let me just talk to Adrianna for a second before we get started." I grabbed my stylist friend by the elbow and led her off to the side for a moment.

"Ade, what did you say to her? She looks petrified!"

"Nothing, I swear. I just suggested that we cut off all of her damaged hair, try a more flattering cut, and get her using better products. What's the problem?"

"The women here do not exactly have piles of money floating around with which to maintain highlights and dye jobs, okay? And I can guarantee you that Isabelle isn't in a position to buy high-priced shampoo! The point of being here is to make her feel good about herself, not make her feel inadequate, okay?"

I knew from talking with Kayla the other week that Isabelle had been kicked out of her house at sixteen and hadn't had a permanent place to live since then. She'd bounced around, staying with friends and living on the streets for years, until her room at Moving On had become available. Kayla had said that she had no idea how someone as shy and withdrawn as Isabelle had toughed it out on her own for so long.

For once, Adrianna had the sense to look sheepish. "Oh, God. I'm sorry. I don't know what I was thinking. I'll take care of her."

Thirty minutes later, Isabelle's hair had been washed and conditioned in peppermint-scented products, and Adrianna was finishing a chin-length cut with chunky layers that would help her curls fall softly.

I scooted my chair close to Isabelle, who looked near panic as strands of her hair continued to fall to the floor. "So, Kayla told me you have an interview tomorrow morning? What's the job?" I asked.

"Well, um, it's in Westwood, at a medical building. They need someone to do some office stuff, I guess. You know, filing and making copies, I think."

"Westwood? That's quite a hike from here." How this girl was going to get from Cambridge to Westwood on public transportation five days a week was beyond me. That was at least a forty-five-minute drive by car, barring traffic jams.

"Well, I worked out a route. If I get the job, I'd have to be there at nine, so I think if I leave here by five thirty, I should be okay."

"What?" Adrianna stopped her styling. "Five thirty in the morning? You wouldn't even get back here until late at night! Are you kidding me?"

Isabelle clasped her nervous hands in her lap. "I'm not really qualified for a lot of jobs 'cause I never finished high school. I'm trying to get my GED, though. Kayla is helping me and a couple of the other girls here with that when she has the time. I've had a few other interviews closer to home, but I don't have much work experience, so no one will hire me."

"No, no. Chloe, do something," Adrianna instructed me. "We can't send her off with this great new hair to spend her entire day commuting to frickin' Westwood!"

"Oh, uh, okay. Let's see." I glared at Ade. I wasn't exactly a headhunter. "You're looking for office work? Or is there something else you might like?"

"It might sound silly, but I've always wanted to work in a bakery. I love the way it smells—sort of homey and safe. I never really had that when I was growing up, but I used to go into this bakery near my house when I was a kid, and the owner would give me a cinnamon roll every afternoon on the way home from school. She'd let me hang out there for a couple of hours if I needed to when my parents . . ." She broke off for a moment. "It seemed like a nice place to be."

Adrianna smiled at me. "I bet Chloe could help you out with this."

"Let me make a phone call. I might have something better for you, Isabelle." I pulled my cell phone out of my purse. "I'll be right back."

I dialed Josh's number, and he picked up quickly, sounding significantly more harried than he had when I'd left Simmer.

"Hey, Josh. Sorry to bother you. What's going on there? You sound busy."

"Oh, Christ. It's havoc here," he groaned. "I've got a big staff meeting so we can prep the front and the back of the house and try to make this opening go as smooth as possible. And I forgot I have to go out later to take care of some other stuff."

That *stuff* better not have to do with Hannah.

Josh continued. "Just becoming one of those days, you know? What's up with you? How's it going with you and Adrianna?"

I ignored the possibility that Josh might be seeing Hannah later. Well, I ignored it for now. "Good. Only I'm wondering if you can help me with something."

I begged Josh to find some way to hire Isabelle to do something in the kitchen. Anything! Simmer wasn't a bakery, of course, and the hours would be horrible, but the commute would be easy. Mainly, I thought that what Isabelle needed was a work setting with a family feeling. Restaurant kitchens were hot and demanding and sometimes chaotic, but Josh always took excellent care of his staff.

"Does she have any restaurant experience?" Josh asked hopefully.

"I'm not sure, but I don't think so," I confessed. "She's always wanted to work in a bakery, so she's interested in cooking on some level. And she needs a break. If you don't give her a job, she's going to have a long commute and be miserable." Guilt, guilt, guilt!

"All right, you got me. Send her in, and I'll give her a kitchen job. The money won't be wonderful, and I don't know how many hours I can give her, but send her in if you want. Can she be here for the staff meeting today?"

If I could've hugged Josh over the phone, I'd have done it.

When I shared the news, I couldn't tell who was happier about it, Adrianna or Isabelle. Adrianna started maniacally blow-drying Isabelle's hair with a diffuser, shouting above the din, "Oh, my God, this is so great! Are you so excited? Do you have anything to wear?"

Although Isabelle didn't say much, she couldn't stop smiling and must have said thank you a hundred times. Moving On had provided her with some outfits for interviews. Since there was no need to be formal with Josh or Gavin, we helped her to select plain black dress pants and a pretty yellow sweater. Working in Josh's kitchen, she would be provided with chef pants and a kitchen shirt, so she wouldn't be spending hard-earned and much-needed money on work clothes. All she'd have to buy would be a pair of good shoes.

Adrianna rummaged around in one of her bags and pulled out hair and makeup samples to leave with her new client. While she did Isabelle's makeup, I wrote down directions to Simmer. When we finally got our protégée out the door, we were beaming like proud parents and waved overzealously as she walked down the street to the T station.

"Okay, we've got to keep moving," I reminded Adrianna as I swept up hair from the floor. "We've got four more women here who need to get ready."

I stayed with Adrianna for another two and a half hours while she worked wonders with more residents of the house. Now that she understood where these women were coming from and the challenges they were facing, she dropped her normally brash, outspoken, and headstrong style and showed remarkable compassion and sensitivity.

"I can't believe we're done," Ade said, rolling up the cape and beginning to pack away the mountain of supplies that had accumulated on the table. "That was great."

"You were wonderful!" I commended her. "You about ready to go?"

"You go ahead. I want to stay and talk to the director.

I was thinking I might volunteer here whenever they need me."

Would wonders never cease? I hugged Adrianna and left for home. When I arrived, it was almost five, and Gato yet again welcomed me by urinating in a plant. I took off my uncomfortable shoes and then threw on some sweatpants and a T-shirt, and sat down at my computer to check my e-mail. I deleted even more copies of almost the same letter that had snuck through my spam blocker earlier today, a version now *urgently* suggesting I get my penis enlarged.

A bunch of e-mails were from my lawyer friend, Elise, who lived in Chicago with her husband. To judge from the number of e-mails I got from Elise each day, being a lawyer primarily involved surfing the Web for entertaining stories and interesting sites. She'd sent a bunch of links to sites with music clips from Kevin Federline—in Elise's opinion, listening to him never ceased to be violently amusing—and one link to photographs of celebrities caught with wardrobe malfunctions. Elise also forwarded me an e-mail from her ex-boyfriend, Alex, with a picture of himself, his wife, and their new baby and a pretentious note detailing how happy he was with his family life and his snooty academic professorship. Elise was pleased to see that his wife was quite possibly the homeliest creature on the planet and that their baby was a squished, wrinkled little blob who looked remarkably like a cross between

Winston Churchill and a bulldog. Elise and I took a sick pleasure in creating an imaginary life for Alex based on the scant details she received from his sporadic e-mails. Our latest was that he'd taken up knitting bulky, brightly colored Argentinian-style sweaters and was forced to work summers in Alaska catching crabs from boats that sailed through high storms.

Next I checked voice messages. The first was from the lawyer in charge of Uncle Alan's estate, and *this* lawyer apparently had time to do things other than send e-mails to friends making up stories about his exes. His message was an unamusing lecture reminding me yet again that the credit card I had been given was strictly for the purpose of buying myself school-related items. He remained irrationally convinced that Williams-Sonoma, Gap, and J. Crew sold nothing related to social work.

The next message was from Sean. "Chloe, I really need to see you. It's important. Can you call me back as soon as you get this?" I jotted down his number on the back of a gas bill and sighed. Clearly, Sean had seen me and was bowled over by an intense desire to reunite with his past love. Did I really want to call him back? I decided to start dinner and mull over the question.

I opened the fridge to see what I could throw together and had to fish through a whole mess of other food to find what I wanted. Josh had stocked my fridge with what seemed like hundreds of free samples of food he'd been given by purveyors. When restaurants need food, they don't go to supermarkets; rather, they get deliveries from meat, fish, vegetable, dry goods, and alcohol companies, among others. And even when a restaurant was all set up with its purveyors, representatives from rival companies stopped in periodically to try to win the restaurant's business by dropping off packaged samples of products. Some samples were ordinary things like chicken breasts and sirloin steaks, but others were fancy cuts of meat and various high-end products that Josh didn't need. I now had ten individual-sized packets of gourmet pasta, including one of black-and-white-striped ravioli stuffed with lobster, and another of Gorgonzola and roasted red pepper tortellini; two sealed bags of ground lamb; a Cornish hen; venison sausage; a package of pork chops; and an unidentifiable duck part. When Josh gave me samples, I usually threw them into the freezer, which was now crowded with them. Once I'd sorted everything out, I happily realized that I had all the ingredients for one of my favorite winter dishes.

I started to assemble ingredients: kielbasa, onions, garlic, white beans, canned tomatoes, kale, chicken broth, and a variety of dried herbs from the spice rack. "That Kielbasa Thing," as I ineloquently referred to it, was a thick, delicious, hearty, comforting stew. It was not named something like Kielbasa Surprise, because I avoid cooking or eating anything called a festival, a carnival, a medley, a party, or, especially, a surprise. In my experience, Pasta Surprise all too often means *Surprise!*

There are jelly beans in your macaroni! Furthermore, festivals, carnivals, surprises, and such reminded me of the disaster known as *Recipes and Memories of the Carter Family*, which was a nightmare collection of supposedly touching stories and secret recipes gathered by some distant relative of my father's. My parents, Heather, and I had each felt obliged to fork over twenty-five dollars for the small three-ring binder that contained mysteries of the Carter clan. When the book arrived, I opened the binder and immediately found a hint of problems to come. Paper-clipped to the title page was a small sheet with the heading, "Errors Discovered After Cookbook Returned from Publisher." When making the King Ranch Chicken, I should not use ½ cup of chili powder, but 1 teaspoon. The Popcorn Cake recipe required an *angel* food cake pan and not an angle food pan. The Bundt Cake Supreme-O needed ¾ cup water, not the "¾ bunches of water" called for in the book. When I made Outdoor Cooking Banana Boats, I was not to be confused by the phrase "with o cutting," which should be read as "without cutting." Whew!

The book included the following gastronomic calamities: Magic Marshmallow Crescent Puffs, Centipede Surprise, Pretzel Salad, Dishpan Cookies, and Old-Timer's Soggy Cherry Cake. Million Dollar Salad was made from canned cherry pie filling, canned crushed pineapple, Cool Whip, condensed milk, and, anomalously, a fresh ingredient, namely, bananas. When I bravely showed Josh the cookbook, he was admirably tactful. His only comment was that Fritos did not belong in a cheesecake.

A chapter devoted to cooking tips and household hints advised the reader to dress up buttered, cooked vegetables with canned French-fried onions and never to use soda to keep vegetables green because it destroys vitamin C. I learned that instant coffee mixed with a little water makes a great paste for cleaning wood furniture and that ice cubes will help sharpen garbage disposal blades. The latter was actually a useful idea. The garbage disposal was exactly where most of the food from the book belonged. I began to worry about my lineage and to wonder how my father escaped the familial craving for something called Stuff (a combination of hamburger meat and canned mushroom soup) and a genetically determined longing for ham loaf containing ground ham, ground pork, oatmeal, fruit juice, and ketchup. His food-snob genes, I decided, must have come from his mother's side of the family. I'd inherited them, of course. Even so, no snooty food queen, I loved homemade casseroles, soups, and good old-fashioned lasagne. I just didn't want Jell-O in my casserole, Red Hot candies in my soup, or canned peas in my manicotti.

I went ahead and sliced the kielbasa and onions, put them in a big pot over low heat with some olive oil, and threw in some dried herbs. While I waited for the onions to soften, I smashed four cloves of garlic with the flat of a knife and opened the canned tomatoes and cannellini beans. In other words, I avoided returning Sean's call. I still could not believe that he had called me. And wanted, no, *needed* to see me. It felt wrong to go off and see Sean while I was involved with Josh. Not that Sean had invited me to a pay-by-the-hour motel or anything, but the prospect of having any contact with him made me a little uncomfortable. Plus I had all that leftover baggage and guilt that comes from a breakup, and I had no interest in getting together to rehash the past, or worse, hurt Sean again. On the other hand, if Josh could go running off to cook dinner for Hannah the night before Simmer opened, why should I feel guilty about a friendly visit with Sean? Especially because I was willing to bet that I could get Sean to go to one of the Full Moon restaurants with me. Maybe I could get a feel for how the employees were treated and whether or not Naomi's anonymous caller was telling a credible story. That Kielbasa Thing would keep nicely. In fact, it always tasted best on the day after it was made.

I picked up the phone and called my ex back while I tossed the garlic into the pan.

"Hey," Sean said, "I'm really glad you got back to me. Can you meet me somewhere so we can talk?"

"Sure. What about Eclipse? Can you be there at seven?"

Sean agreed. I hung up and finished cooking. I added the tomatoes, the beans, and some chicken broth, waited for the stew to reach a slow simmer, crammed two huge handfuls of kale on top, and put the lid on. When the kale had wilted, I stirred the pot and turned the temperature way down to let the dish cook gently.

I didn't have the energy to go through the whole blow-drying thing, so I took what I called a half shower, which meant tying my hair up in a knot and dodging the water spray while sudsing up. A raid on my closet yielded a fuzzy pale blue scoop-neck sweater and simple pants. When I'd finished redoing my makeup and flatironing my hair, I pulled the kielbasa off the stove and filled the sink with cold water. I dumped four trays of ice cubes in and set the hot pot in the water bath to cool for a few hours until I got home. Josh had taught me never to transfer hot food directly to the refrigerator, where it became a haven for bacteria, and he'd warned me that if I covered a hot dish and then immediately refrigerated it, I might just as well inject myself with the evil-sounding *Bacillus cereus*. Safe temperatures for perishable food were very hot and very cold. I hoped I was following his directions correctly. I had a nagging feeling that I should've divided the stew into small portions to make sure it cooled rapidly, but there was a limit to my supply of Tupperware.

After delivering a lecture to Gato on peeing nowhere except in his litter box, I left to meet Sean.

It was finally getting cold in Boston, so cold that I was happy to step into the warmth of Eclipse. The seasonally brutal winds had numbed my ears and cheeks, and I cursed myself for not having bothered to wear a hat and scarf. For the night before New Year's Eve, Eclipse was quite busy; I'd expected everyone to be home saving money and building energy for the big night. Good Lord, this place was tacky! The solar system had apparently exploded in it. Three-dimensional neon planets hung on the brick walls, a planetary mural had been graffitied behind the bar, and the ceiling was littered with tiny lights meant to look like stars. Even with all the neon business everywhere, the room was so dark that I could barely find Sean. I eventually located him at the bar nursing a Guinness. In a simple pullover and khakis, he looked remarkably, and even irritatingly, well-dressed. When we were dating, he'd been a notoriously poor dresser.

"Hi, Sean," I said as I removed my coat and sat down on a barstool next to him.

"Hi, Chloe. Thanks for meeting me. I hope I didn't interrupt your night."

"No, not at all. I'm just starving though. Can I borrow your menu?" I felt suddenly nervous, as if at any minute Sean might confess his undying adoration and propose. "Have you eaten? Do you want something?" I was trying to avoid whatever topic Sean had in mind. The last thing I wanted to do was rehash our past or discuss our nonexistent future.

"Sure, I could eat," Sean said, picking up his menu. "But, listen, the reason I called you—"

I cut him off. "Look, it's Barry." Eclipse's owner was

at the other end of the bar speaking with one of the bartenders. He caught my eye, smiled, and came over to our seats.

"I didn't expect to see you again so soon, Chloe," he said, shaking my hand. In my eagerness to find a strong motive for Hannah to have murdered Oliver, I was almost disappointed that Barry failed to attempt any inappropriate touching, thereby confirming that Full Moon establishments were rife with sexually aggressive behavior. Did I really expect him to just reach out and grab my boob as confirmation?

I introduced Sean and Barry to each other and got a puzzled look from Barry, as though he'd caught me cheating on Josh.

"Sean is an old friend of mine," I said. "He was at Food for Thought the other night," I explained, meaning that Josh knew of Sean's existence and that I was not some horrible tramp involved in clandestine meetings with other boys in nightclubs.

"We just stopped in for a bite to eat," I said. "To catch up."

Barry nodded. "Everything is on the house for you two. Frankly, I couldn't ask someone with your taste to pay for the food here. It's garbage, if you ask me. Oliver really wanted standard bar food here, so that's what we did. I don't know how you can eat here when you're used to Josh's food. I don't know if you know, but I used to go to Magellan all the time."

Magellan was Josh's old restaurant, where he'd run a very successful kitchen. He was reusing some of his best dishes from his stint there by putting them on Simmer's menu.

"I'm sure everything will be fine," I assured Barry. "Not all food has to be totally upscale all the time, right?"

Barry shrugged. "Yeah, I suppose. Well, anyhow, go ahead and order whatever you can stomach and consider it covered. Sean, it was nice to meet you." He shook Sean's hand, smiled at me, and left.

We looked at the menu and, after Sean had proclaimed that everything looked great, the bartender took our order for spinach and artichoke dip with tortilla chips, buffalo wings, and loaded potato skins. It wasn't exactly a high class selection, but that kind of food definitely had its place.

"I've got dinner plans later," Sean said, "so I probably shouldn't eat too much, but I'm starved." From what I remembered, Sean was always hungry.

I reached across him for the three-page laminated descriptions of Eclipse's bar offerings. "I think I'm going to get a drink." I scanned pictures of neon-colored concoctions.

"Chloe, the reason I called you is about what happened the other night," he began again.

"Uh-huh," I nodded, searching for the bartender. "Oh, excuse me. Could I have a Global Warming, please?" I'd just ordered the most politically incorrect drink I'd ever seen, but it had lots of rum.

"When I was at the gallery the other night, I was looking for the restroom, and I accidentally came across one of the office rooms back there. I saw a man and a woman in there. And the man had himself pressed up against the woman, forcing himself on her. I was about to step in, but the woman didn't seem to need my help. She pushed him away and said every four-letter word I'd ever heard. Then she started hitting him with a bag of chips. I'm not sure how much good that did, but it did seem to surprise him. I didn't realize it until later that night, but the woman was Hannah. And when I saw the newspaper the next day, I figured out that the man was the guy who was killed: Oliver."

I knew it! "So Oliver was after Hannah?" I asked excitedly. "Wait, could she have been holding a bag of dried snap peas? And not chips?"

Sean took a sip of his beer. "I guess. There was some green on the bag, now that I think about it. I wasn't really paying attention to what brand she was using to batter the guy with. Maybe I should've gone in to help her, but I guess I was afraid of embarrassing her. I didn't know exactly what was going on, but then Oliver was murdered, and it wasn't until the next day that I made the connection. And I'd seen Hannah fighting with him. I'm not sure whether or not to tell the police about it."

My Global Warming arrived. I took a long drink and

then remembered that I was driving and shouldn't drink much of it. Before responding to Sean, I pretended to be studying the contents of my glass. *Okay,* I thought, *so the anonymous woman who'd been calling Naomi worked for the Full Moon Group, as did Hannah. The caller was being harassed, as was Hannah. At least one time, that is. So, was Hannah, in fact, the caller? Was Hannah driven to kill the man who was harassing her?* As overeager as I was to throw Hannah in the slammer, it sounded as if she'd defended herself pretty effectively against Oliver. From what I knew of her, she was outspoken and tough. I wasn't sure she would've put up with routine harassment from her boss.

Then I caught myself. I had just blamed the victim. As Naomi was forever pointing out, harassment was not something that women allowed or didn't allow. Strong, independent women were victims of harassment all the time.

Our food arrived in all its deep-fried, high-calorie glory. "Ooh, this looks good," Sean said, grabbing a chicken wing. Sean's culinary preferences seemed to have deteriorated since we'd dated. In those days, he hadn't displayed a marked craving for frozen appetizers. "So, what do you think? About calling the police?" He had a large glob of buffalo sauce on his cheek.

"I'm thinking," I answered, scooping up dip with a tortilla.

If Hannah was the anonymous caller, she certainly

had the support of the Boston Organization. More to the point, at the Eliot Davis Gallery, when Oliver had forced himself on her, she'd known that she was not alone in dealing with harassment—if, of course, she was our caller. And Naomi had been right there in the gallery. A terrible thought entered my mind: If the anonymous caller was Hannah, Naomi, who had spoken to her quite a few times on the phone, would have recognized Hannah's voice when they met at the gallery. Naomi, herself the victim of harassment, had a passion for defending harassed women and had a particular interest in this case since she had formed a relationship with the caller. Seeing Oliver at the Eliot Davis Gallery, had Naomi connected Hannah's description of her harasser with Oliver, who was also there that night? Maybe Naomi had even witnessed a scene like the one Sean had just described and had taken radical action to end Hannah's victimization. With all of her yoga muscles, Naomi could easily have lifted up the Robocoupe and slammed it down on Oliver's head. I had a clear image in my mind of Naomi leaving the office this morning for the Eliot Davis Gallery, supposedly to deliver a gift to Eliot. But didn't criminals often return to the scene of the crime?

"Chloe?" Ugh, Sean still had the sauce on his cheek. Couldn't he feel it? Should I shove some napkins at him or just reach over and clean him up? Or would he take that the wrong way?

"No, don't call the police." The last thing I wanted

was for Naomi to be implicated, and if the police heard about the harassment Sean had seen, they'd inevitably follow the new lead to my supervisor. "I don't think the Hannah and Oliver incident has anything to do with his murder," I lied.

"Good," my ex said. "I still feel like I should've done something when I saw them fighting. I didn't really want to have to tell the police about Hannah because—"

"Look," I interrupted. "It sounds like Hannah handled it." I was done talking about Hannah the Horrible.

Relieved that Sean obviously had no interest in reviving our failed relationship, I asked him about his life and caught up on his family. Twenty boring minutes later, I had heard every detail of his parents' cruise to Alaska and of his nephew's rise to stardom on the local T-ball team. Sean hadn't been dating anyone seriously but was still looking for that special someone. Yawn.

We finished eating. I felt bloated and gross. Whenever I gorged myself on Josh's food, I felt full, but I never had the disgusted and disgusting sensation that this food was giving me. Barry had warned us that the food was garbage. He hadn't been kidding. But I had to admit that I was really enjoying my drink, and drinks were, after all, what the place was about. I stretched my back, which was cramped from sitting on the uncomfortable stool.

Even with the dim lighting, I spotted Hannah right away.

She was not at home! Not at home having my boyfriend prepare dinner for her! She was not with my boyfriend at all! What had I been thinking? There was no way Josh was going to leave Simmer the night before the opening to cook for Hannah Banana! On second thought, it was still early enough for her to meet up with Josh later. Watching Hannah, I realized that she was at Eclipse because she was working. Standing at the back of the bar, she held a clipboard and was scanning the room and making notes. If I were Hannah, I thought, I'd be writing, *The terrible food should be updated with refreshing new cuisine. Lose the circa 1980 neon, and install comfortable seating.*

Coming to my senses, I realized with a jolt that I definitely did not want to be caught by Josh's ex while out with my ex. Hannah would love to let Josh know that I was at a bar with Sean. I had to escape before she saw me.

Sean had his back to Hannah, and I tried to angle my body so she wouldn't see me. I did my best to crouch down in my seat, which was, of course, a barstool and consequently didn't lend itself to crouching. The result of my effort was to make me look as if I had early-onset osteoporosis. "Sean, I've got to run, but I'm glad you asked me about calling the police, and it was good to see you again." I reached for money to cover my drink, of which I'd had only half.

Sean stopped me. "Don't worry. I've got it. I'm meeting

someone anyway, but it was good to see you, too." He didn't seem offended by my eat-and-run attitude, so it was easy to avoid an awkward good-bye. I gave him a quick, polite hug and left Eclipse.

I was halfway home before my car finally warmed up. I thought holiday thoughts and admired the preparations for First Night, Boston's annual New Year's Eve celebration. Ice sculptures were taking shape. Banners had been hung over the streets, and strings of lights were strewn across trees. Feeling the residual effects of Global Warming, I succumbed to maudlin reflection: it was all so beautiful, and I was in a rotten mood.

I was glad that Sean had sought my opinion instead of going directly to the police to report on the altercation between Hannah and Oliver, but the possibility that Naomi might also have witnessed it left me with a terrible feeling. Had her passion for her work become violent passion? Naomi was admittedly eccentric, but there was a beautiful purity about her fervent devotion to her cause. The image of Naomi behind bars was horrifying. On the one hand, Oliver's murder was an inexcusable offense. On the other hand, I couldn't let Naomi, of all people, go to jail.

Eleven

I arrived back at the condo to find Noah once again on the wooden structure on the back of the building that served as a fire escape and outside stairway. On the night before New Year's Eve, he was belatedly stringing lights. Clad only in a pair of workout pants, he looked ready to provide bodily services at any moment to any interested woman who happened upon him.

"Oh, for Christ's sake, put on some clothes," I snapped as I brushed past him. "This weather we're having? It's called winter."

"Aren't we cranky tonight," he commented, smirking.

"Yes, 'we' are." Stomping up the stairs, I hoped I was accidentally-on-purpose kicking wet slush down on top of him. "And having to look at your ass isn't helping."

"That's not what you used to say," he hollered.

Must he constantly remind me of last summer's indiscretion? I reached my landing, jumped up and down, and mashed wet snow between the cracks in the floor boards. Then I dumped an old window box full of ice water down on him.

"Hey, cut it out! You're not very full of the holiday spirit!"

I slammed my back door. If only it'd been cold enough earlier this week, I could have sent icicle spikes through his head.

Suddenly exhausted, I flopped down on my bed and grabbed the cordless phone from the nightstand. Three messages: Doug, Adrianna, and Josh. I kicked off my shoes and listened to the first one, from my friend Doug, who confirmed that he would pick me up at six forty-five tomorrow night to go to Simmer. Doug was so much fun that I was embarrassed to realize that I'd completely forgotten he was coming with me tomorrow night. He was a doctoral student at my graduate school and a teaching assistant in a couple of my classes. I'd met him the previous September, on my first day of social work school, when he'd rescued me in the bookshop by tossing most of my so-called required reading back onto the shelves, thereby saving me hundreds of dollars and thousands of hours of boredom. Adrianna, who was extremely envious that I had a gay friend, had been bugging me for months to ask Doug to hook her up with one of his gay friends. Since she'd started working on her own and was out of the salon scene, she'd lost touch with "her boys," as she phrased it.

I dialed her number. "My gay friend is escorting me to Simmer tomorrow. Guess you're stuck with a plain heterosexual to bring you, huh?"

"Damn you!" she snapped back at me. "Where's mine?"

"Gay people are not like Halloween candy. He doesn't have a stockpile that he just goes handing out to whoever asks!" I insisted. I couldn't very well go to Doug to request that he fix up one of his homosexual friends with one of my straight friends as if he ran some backwards dating service. Still, having a good gay man in her life was every woman's dream, so I felt a little selfish about not wanting to share Doug. At the same time, I felt possessive; Doug was mine. Ade would have to go find her own.

Ade said, "Well, Owen will just have to do. Anyhow, I had a great time today, and Kayla set me up to go in and do some volunteer stuff with the women at Moving On. I'm so psyched to do this, so thank you for bringing me today."

"Ade, that's great! I'm so glad this worked out." I'd taken Adrianna with me to Moving On mainly because I'd gone into a panic when I'd been informed that we social work students were required to volunteer somewhere for the day. Other students were reviewing mental, and maybe even written, lists of their own talents and figuring out ways to put those gifts to good use. My friend Julie, for example, decided to help remodel the common room in a subsidized apartment building. I was barely able to hammer in a nail without fracturing my hand, and it took only one glance around my condo to know my painting skills had never advanced beyond the preschool level. Bursting with enthusiasm, I had no capacity to paint within the confines of pesky walls and floors. Having no discernable talents, I'd decided to volunteer Adrianna's services.

"So, Chloe, guess who called me today? Dora! Oliver's wife?" she reminded me.

"Why did she call you?"

"Remember? I told you. I do her hair. She called to see if I could come over tomorrow to get her ready for New Year's Eve. Typical. It's just like Dora to call at the last minute. But can you believe that it's been only a couple of days since her husband died, and she's worried about her hair? God. As much as I like hair, if Owen were murdered, I'd have other things on my mind besides whether or not my roots were showing." She paused. "Probably."

Dora, the happy widow, thrilled to be rid of her nasty husband, celebrates by glamming up for the night? Dora killed her husband and was now celebrating? Aren't most murders committed by the family or friends of the victim? Maybe Oliver hadn't been harassing Hannah but had just been hitting on her, and if that was the case, it probably hadn't been the first time he'd gone after another woman. I could see it all: Dora, fed up with her husband's philandering, or attempted philandering, had whacked him! Naomi was thus off the hook. Unfortunately, so was Hannah. Unless the two of them had conspired . . . ?

"Can I come with you?" I begged. "I'm kind of curious about her. We can say I'm your assistant."

"Didn't she meet you the other night at the gallery?" Adrianna pointed out.

"Oh. Good point. Well, she probably won't remember me. And if she does, who says I can't be a social work student interning as a stylist-in-training? She's not going to care. Just let me come with you."

"Fine. I think this is ridiculous, but whatever you want. Just be prepared to stand there and hold hairpins for an hour. Dora likes weird updos with complicated twists."

Next, I called Josh back at Simmer.

"Yeah?" he said into the phone, obviously swamped.

"It's me. Just returning your call. What's up?" I asked.

"It's mayhem here. I'm going to be working all night. And get this. I found out Gavin is bribing that restaurant reviewer, Mishti Patil, to write a glowing preview review of the restaurant. Can you believe that? I don't need some pity review. She's coming tomorrow, and she'd see on her own how the food is. This is bullshit," he vented to me.

"Oh, my God. I can't believe Gavin did that. That is so insulting, Josh! And I can't believe Mishti could be bribed. I thought she was a straight-and-narrow tough reviewer. That's why she has so much clout, isn't it?"

"I guess she' not so straight and narrow after all."

"How did you find out? I assume Gavin didn't just tell you. Or did he?"

"No, one of my dishwashers, Javier, heard it. Gavin probably thought he didn't understand English, and he must've mouthed off about what he was doing when Javier was nearby."

"What are you going to do?"

"Nothing. What can I do? Anyhow, that Isabelle girl is here. She seems like a good kid. She doesn't know how to do anything, and she's probably wondering what you got her into, but she's working tomorrow just because I need the extra set of hands. Let's hope we don't scare her off."

I hesitated. "What are you going to have her do?" What had I done to poor Isabelle? She was going to be caught in a kitchen storm with Josh and Snacker yelling at everyone, screaming for orders to be put up, and generally behaving like psychotic chefs on an opening night. I hoped she would understand that would not be the norm at Simmer. Or I hoped it wouldn't be the norm.

"Oh, she'll be busy doing whatever I need done. I'm

going to show her how to prep some of the vegetables for me in the morning, and then at service, I'll have her fill in wherever she can. And she'll probably help keep the kitchen clean while we're working. I'm going to give her a quick tour of the kitchen tomorrow morning, and then I'll keep her with me to go run and grab anything I need. She'll be okay. I'll take care of her, so don't worry," he reassured me.

"Okay. Just give her my number if she needs anything. I'll let you go. I miss you already," I confessed.

"I know, babe. I miss you, too. I'll call you in the morning, all right?"

"Hang in there."

I clicked the phone off and sulked for a few minutes. Josh's schedule was going to leave little time for love.

TWELVE

WHY Dora needed her hair done at nine in the morning was beyond me. I hit the snooze button on the alarm clock and pulled the blanket over my head. It was still dark out. To my mind, no one should be forced out of bed to cater to the whims of the widowed rich. If I was this grumpy about waking up, Ade, morning person that she wasn't, would be twice as cranky.

I hit snooze two more times until I finally convinced myself that it was absolutely necessary to pry myself out from under the covers if I wanted to look relatively awake when Adrianna picked me up. It took me twenty minutes to pick out what I thought a hair stylist's assistant should wear. I ended up settling on simple black pants and a white top: universal employee attire.

I opened the fridge to check for something to eat and found nothing that interested me. I wasn't a fan of most breakfast food, and unless I could arrange for fresh pastries and muffins to be delivered to me daily, my interest in breakfast wasn't going to increase. I did love eggs Benedict and overstuffed omelettes, but the odds of my making hollandaise sauce or whipping up an omelette early in the morning were slim. Besides, my homemade omelettes were never as good as the ones I got eating out or the ones I used to get at my college cafeteria. As absolutely terrible as most of the food was in college, the omelettes were outstanding. Unfortunately, hot breakfast was served during the week only until eight thirty—eight thirty in the *morning*—and since I never scheduled a class before ten, I had to be desperate for food to get up early. Lunch and dinner had bar themes: a gas-inducing taco bar, a dried-out baked potato bar, an overcooked-pasta bar, and sometimes a who-the-hell-wants-waffles-for-lunch-or-dinner bar. The food was so bad that I started going to the salad bar and microwaving weird combinations in the hope of creating something edible. My greatest success, or so it seemed at the time, was cold rice mixed with ranch dressing, curry powder, and peas, the whole concoction microwaved to a blazing temperature to suggest an Indian dish. In retrospect, it sounds pretty gross, but at the time, it wasn't half bad.

Adrianna beeped her horn at eight forty-five, just as I

was fitting the top on my to-go coffee cup. I raced downstairs.

"Morning," Ade grumbled.

"Too early for you?" I asked as I settled into the passenger seat.

"You're not kidding. What's Dora going to do after I do her hair? Sit around all day and pose? Stupid woman." Oh, she was grumpy. Not that I enjoyed being roused at an early hour, but Ade was resentful; she was working at this hour only because she needed the money. "Anyhow," she said, grabbing my coffee out of my hand, "what'd you do last night? And is this caffeinated?"

I cleared my throat, ready to be reprimanded. "Yes, it's caffeinated, and I saw Sean last night."

Since my dear friend was, at best, a terrible driver, I should've known better than to break the news about seeing my ex-boyfriend to her while she was behind the wheel. While she stared at me, I stared at the road with the intention of alerting her to the presence of random obstacles, like other cars or human beings. "It's not a big deal. Could you just try to drive, please?"

She swerved to avoid barreling into a parked car and turned right onto Beacon Street. Thank God, there was barely any traffic. On the morning of New Year's Eve, the whole city seemed like a ghost town.

"Why would you see Sean?" she demanded.

I explained his Hannah dilemma and why he'd called me.

"He couldn't have talked to you over the phone? He had to see you in person? Please, Chloe, he's still hung up on you."

"What? No, he is not," I insisted. "He just, well . . . Oh, shit. Do you really think so? He wasn't acting like it."

Adrianna smiled and raised her eyebrows. "Why wouldn't he be, right?"

"Shut up. Anyhow, it doesn't matter. I don't think I'll see him again, and I'm glad we can at least be friendly after I dumped him so hard."

"Hm-hmm. Should Josh be worried?"

"No, Josh should not be worried! How can you even ask that?" Now I was getting grumpy.

"I'm just checking. Relax. Josh is great. I'm just making sure there are no lingering feelings. Oh, I forgot to tell you. I stopped into Simmer last night."

"You did?" I grabbed the dashboard as we peeled a corner.

"Yeah. I got a little tour. It looks great."

"Where was Owen?"

"He had a *gig*, as he said. A puppeteer gig, if you can believe it. Some show for kids or something. It's ridiculous. So I wanted to get out of the house, and I figured I'd go down and check out the new place."

"And Josh was there?" I asked hopefully.

"Of course he was there. Where else would he be?"

"I don't know. Cooking a late-night dinner for Hannah?"

"You're crazy. He was working like a dog when I was there. Oh, here's Dora's street."

We got to Dora's house—or should I say palace?—and parked next to a Bentley. Yes, I swear to God, a Bentley, which mercifully, Adrianna avoided hitting. She popped her trunk and grabbed the two bags with her styling supplies. I followed her up a cobbled walkway to a medieval-revival monstrosity complete with steep roofs and half-timbering that had patterned brick in between dark beams. Even on the last day of December, it was obvious that the grounds were heavily manicured. Evergreen shrubs had been pruned into lifeless-looking cones and orbs. Ick. My landscaping parents would have turned up their noses at the display of vegetative geometry.

As if reading my mind, Adrianna turned to me and said, "Is this not the ugliest house you've ever seen in your life? Money does not buy taste. Wait until you see the inside. You're going to want to throw up."

"Hello, dear," Dora said as she opened the oversized front door. Dora's face was as taut as it had been at the gallery the night Oliver had been murdered. As a budding social worker, I felt a strong desire to sit this woman down to discuss her need for incessant Botox treatments, but I reminded myself that I was here as Adrianna's assistant.

"Hi, Dora. This is my new assistant. She'll be helping me out today."

Dora barely glanced at me and didn't seem to recognize me or to care that Adrianna hadn't told her my name. Her lack of interest was going to make my undercover operation easy. "Let's go to our suite. My suite now, I guess."

As we followed Dora up a winding staircase to the second floor, my stomach churned at the gaudy decor. The dominant colors were nausea-inducing mauves and greens. Pastel furniture filled the large rooms. Dora wore a hot-pink silk robe with a lacy negligee peeking through the top, and slippers with miniature feathery boas fluffing out of the straps. Ade turned to me and covered her mouth as she made silent retching motions. I smacked her arm away and willed myself not to have an attack of the giggles.

We settled in the master bedroom, which was all pale chartreuse and at least the size of my entire condo. Dora seated herself in a chair she'd placed in the center of the room so that it faced the television. To keep myself out of Dora's eyeshot, I stood behind her—not that she noticed people like me.

"So how are you doing, Dora?" Adrianna said with fake concern as she wrapped Dora in a nylon cape. "I am so sorry to hear about Oliver. You must be devastated, you poor thing." I loved watching Ade kiss some ass.

"It's the worst week of my life, without a doubt," Dora agreed. "I've been with Oliver forever, and now he's just gone."

She grabbed the remote and started flipping channels. Oh, good. *Perfect Strangers* was on. And coming up next, Shannen Doherty's brilliant made-for-TV movie *Friends 'Til the End*, in which Shannen stars as the lead singer of a rock band who acquires her very own stalker. Unbeknownst to the other women in the room, I'd seen this movie a few times and considered it one of the *best* guilty pleasures of all time. By exerting superhuman self-control, I might be able to refrain from humming along to ex-Brenda singing the idiotic "Does Anybody Hear Me?" I seriously hoped that Dora wasn't planning to start flipping channels again.

Adrianna began combing Dora's hair and clipping up sections in preparation for foiling in highlights. "What's going to happen to Oliver's business now that he's gone?"

"Oh, the Full Moon Group will be fine. All their businesses run themselves at this point. Truthfully, I'm a little relieved that I don't have to listen to any more talk about Oliver's unfailing sense of brotherhood with that goddamn group. I loved him, but I didn't love his work. Especially Barry and his ridiculous desire to convince people that he's some kind of aristocrat. A gourmet restaurant is nothing but a silly, expensive hobby. Oliver was the one who knew how to make the money, and all Barry wanted to do was throw it away by opening a fancy new place with great food and no profits. Don't get me wrong. I like to eat out at nice restaurants as much as the next person, but I don't want to *own* one. But they'd known each other for years, so Oliver could take Barry's irritating whims better than I could. I don't know how Oliver was so patient with Barry, but he thought of him more like a brother than a partner, so those two had a sibling love-hate relationship. They'd be fighting one minute, and the next, everything would be fine."

Adrianna held her hand out, and I handed her more hair clips. "Can you grab the foils out of the bag while I finish this?" Her tone of voice was meant to make her sound like a master speaking to an apprentice.

"So you're going out tonight, Dora? I'm glad you're getting out of the house."

"Yes, Sarka insisted that I join her and Barry tonight at some new restaurant." Oh, great. She was going to be at Simmer for the grand opening. "I'm only going because Sarka is truthfully a very nice woman, and she doesn't want me to lock myself in the house forever." In this case, "forever" meant the entire three days since her husband had been murdered. Three days, and this woman was actually going out to dinner to celebrate New Year's Eve!

"Dear," Dora continued. "I've forgotten to ask you. Would you be able to stop at Sarka's to do her hair for tonight? Barry called me last night to see how I was doing, and when he found out I was having you come by today, he thought it might be nice for Sarka to have some pampering, too. She's been upset about Oliver as well."

"Not a problem," Adrianna assured her. "I've got some time before my next client. Does she live far from here?" Ade eyed me, silently asking if that would be okay. I quickly nodded a yes.

"No, they only live a few blocks from here. She won't want anything too fancy, so it shouldn't be a long appointment. I think Barry just wants to do something nice for her. Sarka's expecting you. I said that you'd go there as soon as you were done here."

Ade showed no reaction to Dora's high-handedness. She quickly mixed up a smelly bowl of hair color and started weaving a comb handle through thin sections of Dora's hair, separating strands into the foil sheets I was now handing her. "I'm glad you have friends to help you out. What restaurant are you going to?"

"Some place on Newbury Street. Simmer, I think it's called."

"Oh, how funny! We're going to be there tonight, too," Adrianna said.

"Oh." The fact that mere folk like us would also be at Simmer seemed to lessen the upscale factor. "Well, we just wanted to go somewhere simple for the evening. I'm not really up for much more, obviously."

I refrained from kicking Dora for referring to Simmer as "simple" and kept quiet as Dora and Adrianna made small talk. I disliked this woman, but I couldn't find any obvious reason to think she'd killed her husband. She wasn't a sobbing wreck right now, but her composure wasn't proof of guilt. And why kill off the man who was supporting her and her awful taste? Unless she was unimaginably tired of dealing with the tumultuousness of the business? But if she was going to get rid of half of the Full Moon Group, why not destroy the partnership by taking out Barry? My reasoning made no sense, even to me. In searching for motives, I was inventing weak possibilities.

That still left Naomi as a likely suspect. Would she have done something so stupid? And so violent? The Avenging Harassment Angel, she'd be called in the headlines. And when I needed a job reference, what would I do? Have her compose one from prison?

When Ade went to the bathroom to mix some more color, I followed her. "Ask her if she killed Oliver," I demanded.

"Are you nuts? I'm not asking her that. Besides, she's obviously in a state of shock and trying to go about her life as though nothing has happened."

"Okay, well, ask her about Oliver's life insurance policy. And the key man thing Owen told us about. Maybe she's getting a huge settlement of some kind."

"Fine, I'll try," she agreed, going back into the bedroom. "But I'm not saying *key man*. She'll think we're investigating her."

"Well, we are."

Adrianna waited until Dora was bent over the sink having the color rinsed out before broaching the subject. "So, are you going to be fine moneywise, Dora? I don't mean to be nosy. I just want to make sure you'll be okay."

Dora shouted above the noise from the faucet. "Oh, I'm fine. Oliver had a standard life insurance policy and all that."

I nudged Adrianna, and she nudged me back harder before asking, "What about the business? Do you get anything from that?" she asked.

"Barry is signing over that part of the insurance money to me." Before I could shout *"J'accuse!"* and point my finger at the murderer, she continued, "But I don't need it. I have my own money. I'm going to donate all the money from the business somewhere. I don't know which of my charities needs it most, though. Maybe I'll divide it up and give some to each."

I couldn't keep quiet any longer. "Why doesn't Barry want to keep the money and put it back into the business?"

Adrianna glared at me for overstepping my bounds.

"He says he just can't keep money that came from Oliver's death. All their places will keep making money, and Barry and Sarka are well enough off. They just don't need it."

With all these people tossing aside large sums of extra money, I was starting to feel slightly bitter that no one was handing any over to me. Or to Josh, whose salary was barely going to cover his bills.

It took most of *Friends 'Til the End* to finish Dora's hair. Adrianna wasn't kidding when she'd said Dora liked elaborate updos. Her newly highlighted shoulder-length hair seemed to take forever to pin up with individual sections twirled and then rolled into flattened circles and with the rest of her hair pulled tightly back into a mess of curls that stood in a perky mound on the top of her head. The style, perfect for a prom, was by no means suitable for a middle-aged widow, and the new light color seemed to mirror and even to mock the yellowish hue of the woman's skin.

"Okay, just how you like it," Adrianna announced after jabbing one final bobby pin into Dora's hair disaster. I couldn't understand how Ade could stoop so low until I saw how much cash Dora handed her. And me.

After getting directions to Sarka and Barry's house, we left Dora alone in her cavernous mansion and packed up the trunk with Adrianna's bags. As I walked to the passenger door, I noticed a tremendous trash pile by the driveway. Next to a mountain of garbage bags was an oversized aquarium tank complete with a screened lid and a fluorescent light fixture.

"Hold on!" I stopped Adrianna before she got into the car. "Look what Dora is throwing out! A perfectly good tank. This would be perfect for the hermit crab Walker gave me. Help me move it into the car."

"You are not trash-picking from one of my clients, Chloe! That is disgusting. What if she's looking out the window and sees us rooting through her trash? No way. Get in the car."

"Fine. But there's no reason that I shouldn't take it if she's getting rid of it." I buckled my seat belt and sighed. "Dora's husband just died, and apparently her pet something just died, too. She's not having a good week at all."

"I can't believe it's already eleven fifteen." Ade sighed as she started up the engine. "So what did you think of Dora?" she asked.

"If she did kill her husband, it obviously wasn't for the money. But that is certainly a lot of trash outside today. I wonder if she's throwing out some of Oliver's stuff. Seems pretty quick to be cleaning out his closets, don't you think?"

I avoided telling Adrianna that Oliver had been after Hannah. To pass on Sean's account would have been to raise the specter of Naomi as an avenging angel. Out of loyalty to Naomi, I didn't want anyone, even my best friend, to know of my fear that my supervisor had radically violated the principles of the Code of Ethics of the National Association of Social Workers by murdering a harasser. Still, I might be able to glean a little information about Dora and Oliver without betraying Naomi. I wondered whether Oliver had made a habit of pushing himself on other women and whether he regularly had affairs. Could Dora, like Sean, have caught Oliver and Hannah together in the gallery office? But we could hardly have probed by asking Dora whether she'd enjoyed Food for Thought: *Other than that, Mrs. Lincoln, how did you enjoy the play?*

"Do you think they were happy together?" I settled for asking. "I mean, you've been in their house a bunch of times, so you must have a feel for their relationship, right?"

Adrianna nodded. "Well, Dora is stuffy and snobby and not my most favorite person, but she's always spoken highly of Oliver. She seemed very off today. I almost feel bad leaving her by herself in that mansion. She and Oliver had been together for years, and she must be totally lost. Like I said, I think she's in a state of shock and has no idea what to do with herself."

Throughout the short drive to Sarka's, I continued to press Adrianna about Dora and Oliver's marriage, but nothing I heard suggested a motive for Dora to have murdered her husband. Oliver had clearly been an ass of some sort, but whether or not Dora knew it was questionable.

"Why are you so interested in her?"

"No reason. Just wondering about the lifestyles of the rich and widowed," I said innocently. "And we'll see about Sarka."

"So now you think Sarka killed Oliver?"

"No, but maybe we'll get some juicy information from her," I said.

THIRTEEN

AS Dora had said, Barry and Sarka Fields lived nearby. After a four-minute drive, we arrived at what turned out to be my dream house: a traditional two-story colonial painted gleaming white, it had black shutters, an attached garage, and a white fence topped with latticework. Christmas lights and garlands were strung around the bright red front door, and on the door itself was a big fresh wreath. There was even smoke billowing out of the chimney! I was ready to move in.

Not knowing what Sarka wanted done with her hair, Adrianna and I unloaded all of her bags again, went up the brick walkway, and rang the bell.

The door opened, and there was Barry, dressed in an expensive navy suit, clearly ready for a workday. "You must be Adrianna. Thank you for coming on such short notice." He reached out and shook Ade's hand and then realized that I was standing there, too. " Chloe? What are you doing here?"

My cover had been blown. "Adrianna is a good friend of mine, and I'm just tagging along with her today to get a feel for the business. I'm writing a paper," I said vaguely. "On, you know, self-employed women who . . . work." I'm not always quick on my feet.

Barry, however, apparently accepted my feeble explanation. "Oh, well, great. Ladies, please come in out of the cold. It is finally starting to feel more like winter around here, don't you think?"

We stepped into the warm house and hung our coats in the entryway. The look and the ambiance here were completely different from what I'd noticed at Dora's. The living room walls were a rich red; the trim, a warm ivory. Everything was cozy and comfortable and totally livable, as if the *Extreme Makeover* team had just left. There were two big, soft couches and a matching chair and a half (one of those oversized, cushiony armchairs I'd been wanting and for which I lacked the funds and the space). The rest of the furniture was, I guessed, from Restoration Hardware or Pottery Barn. A fuzzy rug covered the center of the room. A real wood fire burned in the fireplace, and the mantel held lighted tapers in a natural honey color. In a corner of the room a Christmas tree was smothered in ribbons, bows, vintage-looking ornaments, and string after string of lights. I sighed. I'd have given anything for a living room like this. These people had somehow leaped into my brain, extracted my fantasy house, and set it up for themselves.

As if reading my thoughts, Barry said, "Make yourself at home." He gestured to the comfy couches, and I somehow controlled the urge to hurl myself onto the overstuffed pillows. "I'll go find Sarka. I've got to go do some work today, and she didn't have any plans, so I thought it might be nice for her to do something for herself while I'm gone. I hope it wasn't inconvenient for you to come over today?"

"Not at all," Adrianna said. "Dora is a regular client of mine, and I'm more than happy to see one of her friends."

"That's great. Thank you. I'll be upstairs on the computer, and I've got tons of phone calls to make. There are still so many people who haven't heard about Oliver, and Dora is really not up to making those calls."

When Barry left the living room, I was tempted to trail behind him to sneak a look at the rest of the house.

Adrianna was as awestruck as I was by the beautiful room. "Well, this definitely looks nothing like Dora's house, that's for sure."

"You're not kidding. There isn't one smidge of bad taste in here, is there?"

Sarka appeared a few minutes later, her hair wet from the shower, her face bare of makeup. If she hadn't been so scrawny, she'd have been stunning. She wore a matching white zip-up sweatshirt and pants that mercifully covered what must have been visible bones.

"Hello, I'm Sarka. It's nice to meet you. Dora says wonderful things about you." She smiled softly at Ade. "And you must be Chloe? Barry says we met briefly the other night at the gallery. I'm so sorry I don't remember."

My memory of Sarka that night was that she'd looked exceedingly bored, so I wasn't surprised that she'd forgotten our introduction. "That's okay," I said. "There was a lot going on that night."

Adrianna lifted up her bag. "Where would you like me to set up?"

Sarka waved her hand around the room. "We can stay in here if you like. I'll just pull a smaller chair in from the dining room, and we can sit by the fire."

The suggestion astounded me. My graduate-student living room was nothing by comparison with Sarka's, but when Adrianna did my hair, we used my bathroom or kitchen. The chemicals she used for color were, by definition, designed to tint what they touched, and I didn't want a hennaed couch or highlight-splotched pillows. Furthermore, there was already more than enough of Gato's fur everywhere without the addition of the trimmed-off ends of my own hair. Even though Sarka could clearly have afforded to replace anything that was stained and ruined, and even though she undoubtedly had cleaners to vacuum up hair, why use the living room? Even if she merely wanted Adrianna to put up her hair without tinting or trimming, it struck me as odd and inappropriate that she wanted us to stay here instead of moving to her bathroom or bedroom, or even to her kitchen. Was she in the habit of blow-drying her hair in the living room? Did she brush her teeth here?

"Would either of you like some coffee or tea?" Sarka offered. "Or there's some frittata left over from breakfast, if you'd like."

"Actually," said Adrianna, "I'd love a piece of frittata and some tea, if you don't mind. I didn't get a chance to eat breakfast."

"Oh, you must be hungry. I'll bring out food for all of us, then, okay?"

I nodded happily, and Sarka left for the kitchen.

"I can't believe she wants her hair done in this gorgeous room," Adrianna said. "I hope she doesn't want color, because I might have a panic attack if I spill anything. I wonder if I have a plastic sheet I could put across the floor." Adrianna rifled through her bag.

"You can't do color in here! We'll have to move to the kitchen or bathroom."

Moments later, Sarka returned with a tray that she set down on the coffee table. "The frittata has Cheddar cheese, jalapeños, sun-dried tomatoes, and fresh basil. I hope that's okay? Have a seat and help yourself to whatever you want."

"It smells delicious. Thank you," I said, sitting down on one of the plush sofas. The frittata was spicy from the jalapeños and had a hint of sweetness from the tomatoes that cut the heat. "It's incredible. Where did you get this?" I wondered aloud.

"Oh, I made it. I love cooking, and this is a new recipe I found in a magazine. The secret is that you add some of the liquid from the pickled jalapeños to the beaten eggs. I never would have thought to do that, but it really works, I think."

I wouldn't have pegged Sarka as a cook, since she'd snubbed Josh's food at the gallery and looked as if she subsisted on water, with the occasional bite of celery stalk as a special treat. So far, however, she was much warmer than the icy woman I'd met the other night.

"So, what would you like done with your hair today?" Ade asked between mouthfuls of the egg dish.

"Oh, I don't know. I don't get my hair done very often. I usually just tie it back in a ponytail, but Barry wanted to cheer me up. He thought it would be fun for me to have something new done for tonight. I feel sort of silly having someone come to the house just for me, but it was really sweet of him. Because of Oliver, we're coming a bit unraveled. Whatever you want to do is fine." Sarka helped herself to a thin slice of the frittata. So she did, in fact, eat!

Adrianna took a good look at Sarka. "Well, if you usually wear it pulled back, why don't we let your hair down. It'll still be simple, but something a little different from what you usually do."

"Sure. But nothing too fancy, okay?"

I took her to mean nothing remotely like Dora's elaborate updo.

When we'd finished eating, Ade set Sarka up in a chair close enough to the fireplace to enjoy the warmth without roasting. She combed through Sarka's long, dark hair with a wide-toothed comb. "I'm just going to trim your ends, if that's okay. And if you'd like, I could add some long angles through your hair to give you a little bit more shape."

"Angles? Oh, okay. If you think that would be nice. I've always had just a straight cut, but I guess I could try something new. Why not? It's New Year's."

"Are you sure you want me to do this in here? I'm going to get hair all over the floor. I don't have anything to put under you," Adrianna apologized.

Sarka shook her head. "Don't worry about it."

While Ade got to work on Sarka's hair, I decided to get going on my own task. "I imagine it must be very difficult for all of you to lose Oliver. I heard he and Barry grew up together."

Sarka nodded. "Yes. I've known Oliver since Barry and I have been together, which is almost fifteen years. I met Barry when I first moved to Boston. I had a little apartment by myself in Somerville, and we met at a café where I was waitressing at the time. I had almost no money, and he and Oliver were just starting the Full Moon Group, so we were all young and broke, but all very happy. The four of us spent all our time together. Oliver was practically family to us. As difficult as he could be, it's just unimaginable that he's gone."

"Fifteen years," I echoed. "A long time."

Sarka smiled. "Barry and I got married six months after we met. We just had a small ceremony with our families and a couple of friends. I wanted to keep it simple, and I couldn't see paying thousands of dollars for one day, even though my parents wanted us to do some big, elaborate ceremony. Do you know the original Filene's Basement downtown? I got my dress there. I was even on television that day. All the news stations were down there filming the annual wedding gown sale, and there was a shot of me pulling a dress up over my clothes. Barry and I thought it was hysterical—my parents would've had a fit if they'd found out I bought my dress for only two hundred dollars. I told them I went to New York and bought one at Kleinfeld. Why waste all that money when I could go to Filene's Basement? Oh, it was such fun!"

It was hard to reconcile the Sarka who'd had a great time getting a bargain wedding dress with the snooty, haughty woman she'd been at Food for Thought. I bent my head down as I sipped my tea in the hope of hiding the expression on my face.

"Sounds like you got to have just the kind of wedding you wanted," Adrianna said, tilting Sarka's head to the side while she shaped her hair with scissors.

"It was. My parents said that if I wanted a simple ceremony, we could all fly out to Greece, and they'd arrange everything. That was the last thing I wanted. I spent my entire childhood traveling from one country to another. Not that there weren't nice things about traveling, but I didn't have any kind of stability growing up. The minute I made friends at one school, my father would be transferred for work, or my mother would decide we needed to experience Africa, so we'd pack everything up and relocate. I think that's why I don't like to travel anywhere now. I just want time at home with my husband. Barry loves to travel, though, so we've just decided that he should go alone when he wants to, and we'll just make time for ourselves when he returns from his trips."

"Well, your house is just amazing," I said. "It's such a nice place for the two of you to be together. I really admire how you've decorated. Did you do this all yourself?"

Sarka nodded shyly. "Thank you. I'm still a bargain hunter. Some of the furniture I've redone myself. I got that coffee table at a Boy Scout fund-raiser for sixteen dollars. I stripped it down and then stained it, and I think it came out pretty well. Even the couches I got when a furniture store was going out of business."

"Tilt your head down for a minute," Adrianna instructed Sarka. "Is Barry going to be working more now that Oliver is gone? I imagine there's a lot that needs to be taken care of."

"Oliver had him working all the time anyway, so it won't be much different now. There were times when it felt like we never saw each other. Oliver was exceptionally good at the financial aspects of their clubs, but Barry is the one who really knows how to open a new place and get it up and running and keep it successful, so he was dealing with a lot of the daily grind of owning so many places. I'd like things to calm down a little, maybe have a baby. I'm not getting any younger, so if we want to be parents, we should do it sooner rather than later." Maybe getting pregnant would encourage her to eat enough to put some weight on?

She continued. "But we might adopt. As much as Barry wants to open a fine dining restaurant, he's very good at what he does for Full Moon, and he doesn't want to lose that. I've told him he should sell his share and open the kind of restaurant he's always wanted. Like the restaurant we're going to tonight with Dora."

"Dora told us you were going to Simmer. My boyfriend, Josh Driscoll, is the chef there, so we'll be there, too," I said proudly.

"Oh, that's right! Barry told me Josh made him a fantastic meal in the kitchen there. That was so generous of your boyfriend to do that. Barry really needed a morale boost. Opening a new restaurant must be so exciting for Josh. And for you. He was cooking at the gallery the other night, too, right? Those charity art events aren't my style, but Barry and Oliver needed to go, and Dora asked me to go with her. She loves those things. Dora is sweet in many ways, but she and I are very different from each other. She's a little older than I am, but it's not the age gap thing. We just don't have much in common other than the fact that our husbands are in business together. Or were in business."

For a second, it seemed to me that I'd misjudged Sarka the other night at the gallery by mistaking her boredom for standoffishness and arrogance. But did her boredom at Food for Thought really explain the difference between her coldness then and her friendliness now?

"Dora seems like she's holding it together, considering what she must be going through," I commented.

"For now. I don't think it's really sunk in yet, though. I asked her to come out with us tonight because I'm afraid if she sits in that house all alone she might suddenly realize how depressed she is and have a breakdown. It's bad enough that her husband died, but the fact that he was murdered makes it even worse. At least she wasn't the one who found him. Barry said he'll never forget seeing Oliver like that. So, I just think Dora should be with friends right now. She was crazy about Oliver, and, in his heart, he was crazy about her, too, even if he didn't always act that way."

"Did they fight a lot?" Ade spoke with clips held between her lips. "He was almost never around anytime I've been to their house."

Sarka shook her head slightly. "No, they didn't really fight, but I think Oliver met and fell in love with Dora before he should have. Not to badmouth him now that he's gone, but he probably needed a few more years to date other women before he settled down, if you know what I mean. He had a bit of a wandering eye," she explained.

"Really? I wouldn't have guessed that based on the way Dora speaks about him." Adrianna was very good at eliciting gossip from people.

"Don't mention this to Dora, but Oliver was quite a flirt. Over the years he made a number of suggestions to me. You know, suggestions that we be more than just friends. I was never really sure if he was kidding or not, and I didn't want to make a big deal out of it."

I perked up. "Did he ever try anything with you?"

"Not really. But he would touch me all the time, you know, put his hand around my waist, hug me a little too long, that sort of thing. I think it bothered Barry a lot, but I asked him not to say anything to Oliver. There was no point, and I didn't want to start a fight. Oliver never really crossed the line with me. It was more about the idea of crossing the line."

"Chloe, can you hand me the dryer?" Ade asked me. "Okay, Sarka. I'm done cutting, and now I'm just going to blow it out smooth and rounded under at the bottom. But you think Oliver was coming on to other women besides you?"

"I don't know for sure. Dora might have had her suspicions, for all I know, but it's not the kind of thing we talk about. Dora is too proud to discuss anything like that with me. We spend a lot of time together, but we're not really very close friends. She did seem jealous of that new girl that they hired to do publicity. Hannah something?"

"Hannah Hicks." I snarled and handed Ade the blow dryer.

Adrianna rubbed a smoothing serum through Sarka's hair and began pulling long sections through the brush as she aimed the dryer at them.

"Yes, that's her," Sarka yelled above the din of the blow dryer. "They were spending a lot of time together working on new ways to promote the clubs. And I know Dora didn't approve that the Full Moon Group was paying for that girl's apartment downtown. As opposite as we are, I do have a certain loyalty to Dora, and I'd hate to find out that Oliver was cheating on her. But maybe Dora just resented the money it was costing. The fact is that she can be quite a cheapskate."

"Dora?" I blurted out. "I thought she . . . uh, I had the impression that she . . ." I just couldn't finish the sentence, or I couldn't have finished it without calling Dora an outright liar.

"Not that she's stingy, really," Sarka said. "Not with her friends. Or with the people who work for her. But that's where her generosity ends."

No time ago, she had unambiguously stated her intention of donating tons of her newly acquired money to charity. Someone was lying. I thought it was Dora.

Adrianna finished styling Sarka's hair and pulled the hand mirror from her bag. "Tell me what you think." She positioned the mirror in front of Sarka.

"Oh, my God," Sarka turned her head back and forth. "I really like it. I do! I never would have thought to put in these layers like you did, but it does soften it out. What did you put in it before you dried it?"

Adrianna showed her the product she'd put in, and while they discussed a new hair-care regime for Sarka, I started packing up. Sarka paid Adrianna well and continued to gush over the subtle change in her hair.

"It was so, so nice to meet you both. Thanks for listening to me talk on and on about myself. Things have been so weird with Oliver's death, it was nice to just talk about things."

"Call me anytime. It was wonderful to meet you, too." Adrianna handed her one of the business cards that I'd done for her on my computer. Adrianna had the typing and computer skills of a turkey, so she'd enlisted my help to create more professional cards than the ones she'd attempted on her own.

We stepped back outside, which felt even chillier than before after the warmth of Sarka and Barry's cozy house. We drove back toward Brighton and talked about Sarka.

"God, she is so much better than Dora!" Adrianna said with relief. "I was afraid we were heading into another house of the dull."

"She was friendly. But there are a few . . . problems."

"What kinds of problems? That she didn't pay you, too?"

"No! Now, please keep your eyes on the road when I say this, but she could have killed Oliver."

Adrianna nearly choked laughing. "Sarka killed Oliver? Why?"

"I don't like the idea very much either, but she did have a reason to want him gone. First, she did say he'd been after her, and it might have been more than she let on. What if Oliver was really pressuring her to have an affair? She might've been protecting herself. Or protecting Dora from a philandering husband. Second, she obviously doesn't care how much money Barry is making, and she's sick to death of him working so much for the clubs. She even said she wanted him to sell out now and open a restaurant with higher-quality food. With Oliver gone, it'd be easy for Barry to get out of the Full Moon Group. He'd have enough money to hire people to oversee a new restaurant, and he'd have more time with her. Like she said, with the way she grew up, she wants stability, and Oliver's work demands were making a normal life with her husband pretty difficult."

Adrianna shook her head. "She is too nice to have killed somebody."

"Nice has nothing to do with it. She is nice, but there's something off about her, too. Something creepy. Not just that she's borderline anorexic, either. It's that, plus talking about having a baby. How could she deal with being pregnant? If she could even get pregnant. And then there's how thin she is and how fat all her furniture is."

"I liked her furniture."

"I did, too. I loved it. It's just that the contrast is rather noticeable. Also, there's how warm and open she was just now and what she was like at the gallery. She was two different people. And that's creepy."

Ade dropped me off at my place. "You're taking social work too seriously," she said.

"Probably. I'll see you and Owen tonight at Simmer, right?"

"Sure. If he's not too busy pulling strings on those damn puppets." She looked down at her watch. "I've got to go. I've got another two appointments."

"Hey, are you two okay?" I asked. "I know you're not a big fan of Owen's new job, but it'll be all right. Think of how creative it is."

"No," she shook her head. "Cooking is creative. Being a chef is creative. This is bullshit, and we both know it. I'll talk to you later."

"Bye." I shut her car door. Adrianna was right about Owen. As much as I loved him, his constant job switching was beginning to look aimless. I mean, was he really going to become a professional puppeteer and handle marionettes until he retired? I highly doubted it. Every job Owen had was as an *assistant* fill-in-the-captivating-blank; whenever the chance of promotion presented itself, he quit and moved on. Granted, we were all still in our twenties and had some leeway before we settled our lives, but Owen was pushing it, and I couldn't fault Ade for getting frustrated with her boyfriend. They'd been together long enough for her to have a right to worry about stability.

At least Josh had an actual career and a regular job. His work meant horrible hours, but it was a good step above Owen's slew of odd vocations. What's more, Josh was clear and realistic about the downside of his vocation. A chef was lucky to have Christmas off. At hotels, chefs worked on all or almost all holidays. On Mother's Day and Valentine's Day, restaurants were swamped. Chefs not only worked on weekends but were fortunate ever to have two days off in a row. When I thought about the long term—not that Josh and I were there yet—if we got married and had a bunch of kids, I'd be alone on all those holidays and alone on most nights. Anniversary dinners? Josh would probably be working. I'd grown up watching *Friends* and, as far as I could remember, Monica the chef had never missed any important coffeehouse chitchat and had definitely never had to work on holidays. Some weeks, Josh had practically no time to sleep. A lot of doctors, of course, worked nights and weekends and holidays, too, but they made five times what Josh did, and the high incomes probably eased the scheduling difficulties. As to the vision of Josh off feeding and tending to other people while our kids and I were home alone, well, it rubbed me the wrong way. The nerve! There he was, out creating romantic experiences for loving couples, and here I was, stuck in the house dealing with domestic chaos.

Realizing that I was seriously jumping the gun and, even worse, starting to sound like Heather, I shook our imaginary bratty children out of my head and, avoiding the back stairs, where I felt doomed to run into stupid Noah, headed up the front steps. As I struggled with my keys and fought with the ancient lock on my condo door, the phone inside began to ring. I won the battle with the lock in time to answer it.

"Um, Chloe? This is Isabelle." The clatter in the background announced that she was calling from the restaurant.

"Hi. Sounds like you're at work. How's it going?" I asked excitedly.

"Oh, um, well . . . it's good. Really. I wanted to thank you for getting me this job. It only took me twenty-five minutes to get here, which is so much better than that other job I was going to interview for. And everybody has been really nice to me here."

I sensed a "but" coming.

"Isabelle, is anything wrong? Did something happen?"

"Oh, no," she tried to assure me over the din of shouting. "It's just . . . is it always this crazy at a restaurant?"

My stomach dropped. I glanced at the clock and saw it was just after one o'clock. If things were bad now, Isabelle was in for a long day ahead. "What do you mean by crazy?"

"Josh and Gavin are fighting, and Gavin keeps talking about God and stuff. Is this a religious restaurant of some sort? Because I haven't been to church in years. And Josh got mad because someone burned the bottom of a skillet, and so Josh slammed it into the trash can, and then Gavin said that if he was just going to throw new equipment away, why not get rid of everything, and so Josh threw out a blender and a serving tray and then—"

"Isabelle, take a breath, okay? I'm sorry it's so wild there right now, but you have to remember that this is their opening day, and Josh and Gavin are both really nervous about tonight. It won't always be like this. You guys will find a routine and a rhythm after a couple of weeks, I'm sure. Just hang in there and lie low for now. I'm sorry they're freaking you out," I apologized. "No matter what Josh or Gavin, or anyone else for that matter, does today, don't take it personally. If they're being idiots, it has nothing to do with you. Why don't you see if you can trail Snacker today," I suggested. "He might be less worked up than Josh."

"Who's Snacker?" she asked.

What the hell was his real name again? Josh always called him Snacker. Oh, yeah. "His name is Jason. He's Josh's sous chef."

"Oh," she giggled. "The really cute guy? Tall with dark hair?"

"Yes." I laughed. "That's him. Tell him I asked him to take care of you today, okay?"

"All right," she promised. "Thanks again, Chloe."

It was midafternoon, and I was tired and hungry again. I started a pot of coffee and put the kielbasa on the stove to simmer for a bit so that the kale would cook through. As I waited, I checked on Ken and decided to give him a bath, as the Web site had advised. I found an old plastic bowl that would have to become Ken's, since I wasn't about to use the same container as a food-storage bowl *and* as a hermit crab's spa. I filled it a third of the way full with water and carried the bowl over to his cage.

I hadn't counted on my inability to reach inside the cage, touch Ken, and—terrifying prospect—actually pick him up in my bare hands. I was overcome by visions of an irate crab sticking his claws out of his shell and gouging my hands. So what if his pincers were only a few millimeters long? I still put on winter gloves. After that, by squealing and stomping my feet in disgust, I worked up the courage to lift the little monster and plop him into the bowl. Just as the Web had promised, Ken emerged from his shell and made grotesque scratching noises in his effort to find traction on the smooth curves of the bowl. Thirty seconds of that revolting nonsense was all I could endure. I went to pluck Ken out of his bath only to face the challenge of grabbing him without touching his actual body, which was now halfway out of his shell. Stupid pet. With one eye shut, I mustered enough bravado to return Ken to his cage. There wouldn't be another bath any time soon for that crustacean.

The phone rang. I yanked off my Ken-handling gloves and picked up.

"Happy New Year, Chloe!" Naomi greeted me.

"You, too. What's up?"

"I called to talk about the list you've been working on."

Uh-oh.

FOURTEEN

THE list, which I had e-mailed to Naomi, had evidently left her speechless. I waited out her long pause until the fear overcame me that she'd get me kicked out of social work school for my lack of aptitude for self-exploration.

"Why don't I pull up my copy on the computer?" I sat down in front of the monitor, opened the document I'd entitled crp.doc, and cleared my throat. "Okay. I'm ready to be analyzed!" I said cheerily. Last night I'd added a few last-minute items in an attempt to beef up my list. I scanned the computer screen to make sure I'd deleted the phrase *psychotic supervisor.*

"First of all," Naomi began, "why is the file called 'crp'?"

What had possessed me? Why hadn't I changed the file name before e-mailing it to her? "Well . . ." I cleared my throat. "That stands for Chloe's Real Problems."

"Hm. Okay." Another long pause.

I said nothing.

"As I'm reviewing your list, I'm finding a general theme of irritation with daily life, and, um, I wonder if you could speak about why things like putting duvet covers on comforters cause you anger. And your intense hatred of shower-curtain hooks?"

"I've been giving this a lot of thought," I lied. "I've discovered that I tend to become angry with daily challenges that are *preventable*. There is enough needless red tape in the world, and with all the incredible technology and resources available in this country, I cannot accept the idea that no one has invented shower hooks that stay on the rod, or easier ways to make the bed, or some sort of little tool that would remove leaves from oregano stems. I mean, it's the overwhelming number of seemingly small challenges that we face each day that add up to create hour after hour of frustrating experiences. So, at the end of a twenty-four-hour period, we have each come across a multitude of annoying hindrances that roll themselves up into a giant ball of anger. So, at first glance, my list may *look* like it's made up of trivial things, but, really, it's the effect of such a large number of preventable frustrations that lead me to a state of anger."

"Chloe, I'm sure that all the people waiting in long lines at food banks would sympathize with your being forced to endure Jessica Simpson's rendition of 'Let It Snow' throughout the entire month of December." Perhaps I should have left that one off the list? "Why don't I forward you a copy of my list of things that cause me anger? And then we can compare."

I heard the clicking of her keyboard, and, thanks to high-speed Internet access, I got her e-mail almost immediately. "Great," I said. "Here it is."

I skimmed Naomi's lengthy list: *"Lack of resources allotted to social services agencies. Continued tolerance of chauvinistic/abusive behavior in the workplace. Inequality in . . ."* Okay, I got the message. I was a terrible human being.

I said, "This is quite an extensive list. Perhaps you could share your insights into yourself with me, and I could use you as a role model for future self-exploration."

Thirty minutes later, which is to say, after thirty minutes of listening to Naomi express her passionate intolerance for social injustice, I hung up the phone feeling like a heartless moron. While I was infuriated by things like the reappearance of Josh's ex-girlfriend and the ubiquity of sidewalks that hadn't been shoveled, Naomi was driven to action by the unfairness of the world.

Driven to action. More than ever, I was shaken by the fear that it was Naomi who had murdered Oliver. If I believed that Naomi was guilty, didn't I have an obligation to turn her over to the police? I still had Detective Hurley's business card. But if I called him, what could I report? I had no proof that Naomi had done anything wrong. Furthermore, I highly doubted that Naomi was in the midst of some crazed killing spree, so it wasn't as if my silence were putting other lives in danger. At least I hoped not. For all I knew, though, she was so incensed at my frivolously subpar performance as an intern that she was loading a gun right now. And if I told Detective Hurley about my suspicions of Naomi, I'd have to share my suspicions about Hannah, Dora, and Sarka, too, wouldn't I? And I had no evidence to implicate any of them, either. For the first time, however, as I mulled over the possibility of talking to Detective Hurley, it occurred to me that my suspicions fell mainly on women and that the murder weapon had been a Robocoupe. According to pop culture, poison was one kind of woman's weapon. What about a food processor, even a gigantic one? Was it a woman's weapon, too?

FIFTEEN

HAVING resolved not to call the police, I went on to formulate my New Year's resolution, which was to become a social superhero: an individual selflessly dedicated to fighting atrocities on the planet Earth. Today, however, was December 31, so I could enjoy doing my hair and makeup and dressing up for dinner without feeling ashamed that I was already breaking the resolution, not to mention neglecting the world. I filled a bowl with the steaming kielbasa and sat down in front of the television. After all, Naomi's high level of social awareness might have driven her to commit murder. To save myself from homicidal fanaticism, I had to counteract Naomi's influence with some truly socially unaware *Laguna Beach* reruns.

Doug showed up at five wearing a red T-shirt announcing: Gays Do It Better. Between that and the black leather pants and jacket, he wasn't planning a don't-ask-don't-tell kind of night. He'd let the hair on his formerly shaved head grow back an inch, and I wondered whether his New Year's resolution was to stop looking like Mr. Clean. Doug's appearance made me hesitate to ask his advice about what I should wear tonight, but I took a chance and stood him in front of my closet.

"No black," I instructed. "I'm sick of always wearing black to dress up."

Posed there, Doug was staring at hangers full of black clothing. "Sexy but not rude, since Josh will be busy all night, and we don't want him distracted by a plunging neckline, do we?"

I disagreed. "Plunging and distraction are fine. Go nuts. And don't *Mommie Dearest* me about all the wire hangers." I flopped onto my bed and flipped through *Us Weekly* while Doug plowed through my wardrobe options.

"What about this top?" Doug suggested, waving around a sleeveless red top that tied at the back of the neck.

"Have you lost all of your gay aesthetic?" I shrieked. "Doug, redheads have no business wearing red. Heather gave that to me after she had Walker and her breasts tripled in size and she got rid of all her clothes. Are you feeling ill?"

"No, I'm not feeling ill. Redheads can totally pull off red if it's the right shade, like this is. It's not like it's stop sign red or anything. This is a gorgeous deep red, and the material is just right for a holiday—sort of linen with a shimmer thing. Try it on. But you'll have to wear black pants. Oh, leather ones! We'll match!" Doug grinned and tossed me my pair of leather pants that I'd worn only once before, to my five-year high school reunion, where I'd hoped to run into Andy Peyton, who'd stood me up for a spring dance and left me single while all my friends were making out with their dates to Savage Garden and Chris Isaak. And he didn't even bother to show up at the reunion. I was still pissed about that.

I made Doug turn around while I squeezed into the pants, which after about forty-five knee bends, I decided would stretch out enough to fit. I put on the red top and said, "Okay, turn around. What do you think?"

"I told you. You look hot. High-heel boots and some earrings, and you'll be good to go."

Good thing we'd be sitting down most of the night, since the odds of my successfully walking too far in the tight pants and heels were slim to none.

"Is Owen coming with Adrianna?" Doug called to me as I was in the bathroom fiddling with my hair.

"Yup. And, no, he's still straight."

"Damn." Doug and Owen had met a few months earlier, and Doug was still harboring a secret crush on Ade's boyfriend. "Anyway, how did your semester end up?"

"Fine, I guess. But I need some advice. Come in here and keep me company." I filled Doug in on my list, on the conversation I'd had today with Naomi, and on my general inability to take to the streets to riot for justice. I didn't want to involve him in my obsession with Naomi as a psycho killer. For one thing, he might decide that I was crazy. For another, the more I talked about my obsession, the worse it would become, which is to say, the more possible and even likely.

"Chloe, you've got to relax. This Naomi character has got her own style, her own niche in the world of social work. You've just got to find yours. And your professional style will probably be very different from hers, but you can be equally effective in working with people. Naomi is totally dedicated to fighting sexual harassment, but I don't think that is *your* calling. I know you care about the women you've been working with, but don't feel bad that you aren't Naomi. The field placements are designed to give you insight and experience into social service agencies in general. It's part of a process of learning about yourself and what you want to do. Look, when you graduate, you might want to work for a nonprofit, but you might want to try to get into private practice, or work for a large corporation doing organizational psychology work. Whatever you want. There are a million different opportunities."

"So I won't flunk out of school? Go look at my list. It's on my laptop in the kitchen."

"No, you won't flunk out," he said from the other room. "But I agree that your list was pathetic." Doug returned to the bathroom and looked at me with well-deserved irritation. "I know you're a more caring person than that list suggests. I mean, come on, 'People who stand too close to me in line,' is not what Naomi was looking for."

"It's an infringement on my personal space, and I find it highly upsetting!" I snapped back.

"And, 'Mail that comes from Delaware because it will be a credit card offer with ridiculous interest rates'? You don't like the way Naomi pushes you, right? Instead of letting your interests and concerns come out naturally, she expects you to voice your outrage at the world the same way she does. Why don't you try giving her a little more on a daily basis, and maybe she'll lay off these stupid exercises."

"Yeah, you're probably right. She just expects me to walk around constantly proclaiming my opposition to sexual harassment. Like I should be carrying banners and protest signs with me everywhere I go!"

"Why *did* you go to social work school?" Doug asked.

"You know why! I had no choice!"

"Yeah, I know your uncle's will required you to get a master's degree in something. You could have picked anything. Business school, broadcasting, art history? But you didn't. You chose social work. Why?"

"I don't know. It seemed like it would be, uh, okay," I stammered.

"That's not a reason, and that's what you need to think about. You'll work it out. But for now"—Doug pushed me aside to get a glimpse of himself in the mirror—"remember that even negative experiences are part of learning. It's important to know what you *don't* want to do so that you can figure out what you *do* want to do. Hurry up so we can go. It's already six, and it's going to take forever to get downtown tonight. I'm a gay man, and *I* get ready faster than you."

"Yes, but you practically don't have any hair," I pointed out. "Anyhow, I'm ready."

I realized that I was fussing over my hair and makeup more than usual tonight, probably because that stupid Hannah had reappeared in Josh's life and I was feeling threatened and insecure—dumb of me, because until she showed up, everything between Josh and me had been going great, and there was no reason to imagine that Hannah could come between us. Right? Even so, I double-checked my lip gloss and added another spritz of eucalyptus spearmint body spray to my wrists.

Boston's chronically nightmarish traffic always became unbearable on New Year's Eve, so Doug and I had ruled out driving ourselves or taking a cab. We left my condo and walked the short distance down the hill to reach a T stop in the middle of Beacon Street. This section of the Green Line ran above ground and descended to become an actual subway as it approached Kenmore Square. Public transportation ran for free tonight, and, even at this relatively early hour, the cars were jammed. We pushed our way to the middle, grabbed onto a pole, and clung to it as the car lurched forward. As I'd neglected to mention in my list of anger-inducing items, the unflattering lighting in the subway cars irritated me. Under the fluorescents, Doug looked positively jaundiced. When we dove underground and reached the Kenmore stop, a mass of people attempted to board the already crowded car, and I found myself smashed up against Doug in a position that under other circumstances might have been considered pornographic.

"I'm not enjoying this any more than you are," Doug assured me.

The two of us practically gasped for fresh air when we emerged from subterranean Boston. "Thank God I used extra deodorant." Doug sniffed his underarms. "What a revolting form of transportation!"

"Funds were running low for my private limo service," I said, winking at Doug. "Sorry."

I pulled my date along the sidewalk toward Simmer. Lights were strung up on lampposts, wreaths hung suspended over the streets, and everywhere were large signs wishing everyone a happy New Year. The sidewalks were full of families and students eagerly admiring ice sculptures and applauding street performers, and the whole city had a wonderfully magical feel to it. Tonight was going to be so exciting! Josh was going to astound everyone with his superb culinary skills. By midnight, he'd be on his way to fame and glory as Boston's hottest new chef!

"There's Simmer," I said excitedly, pointing out the restaurant to Doug.

"Good. I'm dying for a drink. Do you think they'll comp our drinks for us?"

"They better." I laughed. "Because after enjoying an incredible dinner, I plan on getting happily wasted on expensive cocktails. And then dragging Josh home to make drunken love all night long!"

We crossed the street and opened Simmer's front door. Just inside the entrance, Gavin was welcoming a couple and directing them to the hostess. He was dressed in a formal suit and practically oozed pride at the opening of his restaurant. Tonight was the result of months, if not years, of dreaming and planning. Furthermore, Gavin had sunk a tremendous amount of cash into Simmer. He deserved the pleasure he was radiating.

"Welcome, welcome, Chloe! Can you believe it's happening?" Gavin enthusiastically shook my hand and introduced himself to Doug.

I said, "Congratulations, again. This is wonderful. I can't believe all of that work got done on time. You've really pulled it off." Looking around, I saw that the installation of the ceiling light fixtures was complete. Now, everything basked in exactly the kind of flattering glow that would have boosted the morale of T riders throughout the city. The lighting brought out the earth tones of the textured walls and the tiled floors. Behind the bar, the bottles shone. The glasses in the racks and in people's hands twinkled. The tables were covered with linens in a shades of cream and pale rust. Best of all, people were everywhere. Customers! Diners here to enjoy my Josh's genius!

"You know," said Gavin, "I really think this place was meant to be—that Simmer was meant to be mine. Somehow we got the lease and everything just came together. I thank God for that! So let's get you two to your table."

"We're meeting a couple of my friends here. Are they here yet?" I looked around the room, trying to spot Adrianna's blonde hair in the almost full dining room.

"You have a whole table of people waiting for you." Gavin gestured to a large table in the front of the room, right by the window.

I couldn't believe it. "What the hell are they doing here?" I muttered to Doug. Why did my family have to turn every event into a great big fat family reunion? Seated at the table, with bemused expressions on their faces, were Owen and Adrianna, with both of my parents and Heather and Ben and Walker and, incredibly, baby Lucy. What twenty-five-year-old wants to spend New Year's Eve with her family? Her *entire* family! And what had possessed Heather and Ben to bring the kids here? Of all the nights not to get a babysitter! Walker was seated in a booster chair and hanging sideways off the arm clutching a blue train. A giant bowl of Cheerios sat in front of him, which led me to believe that at least my sister wasn't going to ask to see a children's menu.

"Surprise!" My mother beamed at the family's success in having snuck in here without my knowledge.

"Yeah. Surprise!" I smiled weakly. "I had no idea."

No idea that I'd be doomed to celebrate the New Year's Eve opening of Simmer by laboring to make conversation with my relatives. So much for a night of ogling my boyfriend in an alcohol-induced haze. Now I really needed a drink.

SIXTEEN

ADE had done her best to rescue me by saving two seats between hers and Owen's for Doug and me. At least I wasn't pinned between my parents. Doug immediately grabbed the seat next to Adrianna's boyfriend.

I scooted in next to Ade and whispered, "Did you know they were coming?"

She stifled a laugh. "No. I swear I didn't. Holidays with the Carters. Who knew?"

"We just had dinner together the other night! I wanted tonight to be about Josh. Well, Josh and me. Anything but a night with my entire family staring at me and analyzing my relationship. Can I have a sip of that?" Without waiting for an answer, I picked up Adrianna's glass of wine.

It looked untouched, but I didn't care whether it was or not; I needed a quick gulp.

"So you must be Doug?" Heather introduced herself and the rest of the nut jobs at the table. I wasn't sure if I was dreading an evening with my family because they irritated me on an individual basis or if it was the collective group of them that had the capacity to drive me insane. Well, I reasoned, dinner would last only so long, and I would still find some alone time with Josh late tonight.

For reasons beyond me, Heather had tied a gigantic red silk scarf into a headband and sat across from me with a mammoth bow on top of her head.

"What are you? Cindy Lou Who?" I couldn't help myself. "You look like you hopped right out of a Dr. Seuss book."

"Lovely to see you, too, my dear sister." She lifted a glass of what looked suspiciously like a martini to her mouth.

"Heather! You're still nursing! You shouldn't be drinking," I scolded, looking at Lucy to see whether the baby was intoxicated—although how anyone could tell, I had no idea, since babies had no muscle control to begin with.

"Your sister stopped nursing this morning," Ben informed me. "And now she's drunk."

"That is correct. I am." Heather reached into her glass and removed an olive, which she peered at intently for a moment before throwing it up in the air and catching it in her mouth. "And it's wonderful." She smiled happily.

Oh, goody! With one sister loaded, no one would notice if I had a few too many drinks myself. Better yet, with any luck, Heather would make a spectacle of herself for the rest of the night and leave me alone. On second thought, if she did anything to ruin the night for Josh, I'd kill her.

"Look, there's Dora." Adrianna pointed to the entrance.

"With Barry and Sarka," I said as the couple entered behind Dora.

Gavin was politely shaking Barry's hand while at the same time gloating over his acquisition of the prime Newbury Street spot that Barry had coveted, or so I suspected. Dora was monstrously overdressed in a long ivory gown with sequined patches—tacky, if you asked me, but it was probably some Badgley Mishka million-dollar design. Gavin showed the trio to a small table in the center of the restaurant.

"So, Doug, tell us," my father began, "as one of the few male students at social work school, you must be quite busy dating, I would guess. Anyone special?" Dad smiled innocently.

"No, not at the moment. Although"—Doug stood up and took his jacket off to display his T-shirt—"I'm keeping my options open."

My family leaned in and slowly read his shirt. I watched their faces as the realization sank in.

"So, probably no girlfriends, then?" Heather removed herself from her martini long enough to ask.

Our waitress came to the table, took drink orders from Doug and me, and left all of us with the menu.

APPETIZERS

Seared Shrimp with Corn Polenta and Sweet Corn Sauce

or

Grilled Lobster Tail
with Black Beluga Lentils and Truffle Oil

or

Seared Scallops with Chanterelles
and Pineau des Charentes, Served in Puff Pastry

SALAD

Baby Greens Wrapped in English Cucumber
with Sesame-Honey Dressing

ENTRÉES

Grilled Steak with a Stilton Potato Cake,
Roasted Baby Vegetables, and Peppercorn Sauce

or

Pan-Seared Salmon Roulades
with Saffron-Tomato Coulis, Served over Jasmine Rice

or

Roasted Vegetable Wellington
with a Red Pepper Vinaigrette and Balsamic Reduction

DESSERT

Layered Chocolate Torte with Fresh Raspberries

or

Banana Three Way

One look at the mouthwatering menu made me mind my family's presence less. Josh's food made even Heather's comments less grating!

"This looks like heaven," my father crooned. "What a way for Josh to open the restaurant!"

"Sure," Heather said, ignoring Walker, who was busy folding a menu into a paper airplane, "but everyone seems to be forgetting the fact that this isn't Josh's restaurant. He just works here."

I was about ready to grab her son's paper airplane and fly it into her eye when our drinks came. I swallowed some wine and focused on deciding which mouthwatering entrée to have. Doug and I consulted with each other and agreed to order different things so we could share. When our waitress returned, I ordered the shrimp appetizer, followed by the steak and the banana dessert.

Heather giggled. "A banana three way!"

"Somebody cut her off," I begged.

Adrianna excused herself to go to the ladies' room. The rest of us struggled to achieve relatively normal conversation.

My father cleared his throat and whispered conspiratorially, "Did everyone see who's here? The restaurant reviewer, Mishti Patil. I recognize her from her picture."

Josh was going to be more than unhappy about her presence. As this woman should know, it's unfair to subject any restaurant to a review on its first night. It was obvious even to me, an outsider in this industry, that you cut a new place a lot of slack early on; you wait until it works out its kinks before you tear it apart. So far, nothing had gone wrong, but the evening had just started, and we hadn't tasted any food yet. As confident as I was in Josh's skill as a chef, I was worried that his food wouldn't come out of the kitchen the way it was supposed to. It's one thing for a chef to come up with fantastic dishes, but the quality of the food that actually gets plated and served depends on many other people besides the chef. Even with Josh and Snacker cooking on the line tonight, I was still afraid that some incompetent person had left bones in the salmon or had oversalted the salad dressing. I glanced around to see whether anyone was puckering or making faces. So far, everyone looked happy and festive. I tried to comfort myself by remembering that since Mishti had evidently been bribed to write a review, she'd presumably do a good one, no matter what. Furthermore, Josh had been so insulted about the bribe that I knew he'd outdo himself by proving that there was no need to *buy* good reviews of his food. Mishti and her dining companion were five or six tables away. Although I couldn't get a good look at them, they seemed to be doing all right for now.

Our appetizers began to arrive, and I lit up as I saw Josh coming to the table carrying mine.

"Hi, honey. Oh, this looks beautiful," I said, gazing with admiration at my plate. Four huge shrimp, delectably butterflied, rested on a fluffy polenta circle dressed with a creamy yellow corn sauce. Josh shook hands all around and accepted praise and congratulations from everyone—well, everyone except Heather, of course, who busied herself with her napkin.

Josh leaned in to me and said quietly, "So, you decided not to come to *my* restaurant with Sean, huh?"

My stomach dropped. "What?" I whispered back.

"Check your cell phone messages once in a while," Josh snarled angrily. "Like I really needed this shit right now, Chloe."

He left the table. I immediately pulled my phone out

of my purse and punched in my codes. The only message was the extremely pissed-off one from Josh: "Chloe. Glad you had a good time last night with Sean at Eclipse. Seems like a great guy." *Click.*

That damn Hannah! She obviously *had* seen me at the bar with Sean. So much for my covert getaway. That bitch had probably waited all of thirty seconds before scampering back to Josh with news of my supposed infidelity and luring him back to her lair to cook her a romantic dinner. Although Josh had no reason to be jealous, I hadn't planned to tell him about my harmless date-that-wasn't with Sean. I mean, the conversation had centered around Hannah and the murder. Still, I'd been spotted out with an ex-boyfriend. And what had Josh himself been up to with Hannah? I still didn't have an explanation about the shopping list in his handwriting. Not that I'd asked him yet.

"What was that about?" Doug asked me.

"Long story," I answered.

I sampled my shrimp and, as cranky as I now was, knew that it was one of Josh's best dishes ever. The sweetness of the polenta and corn were a delectable match for the spiciness and saltiness of the shrimp. Josh had taught me that to make flavors balance out in a dish, you needed to combine opposites.

Our salads arrived. Long lengthwise slices of cucumber were wrapped about brightly colored greens to form low cylinders. Enoki mushrooms sprouted out of the tops of the salads, which were covered in a glistening sesame-honey dressing. I took a taste. My salad was as delicious as it was beautiful.

But until I'd straightened things out with Josh, I was going to be crabby and upset for the rest of the night. And where was Adrianna? She still hadn't come back from the ladies' room, and I needed her. In situations like this, I had a tendency to blow things out of proportion and act rashly, whereas Adrianna had a contrasting tendency to retain her sanity.

I excused myself from the table, but everyone was too occupied in savoring the food to notice. It's amazing how quickly complete confidence in the solidity of a relationship can change to incredible fear that everything is about to collapse. I just hoped that Josh would believe me when I assured him that nothing nefarious had transpired between Sean and me. I also hoped, of course, that Hannah hadn't taken advantage of Josh once she'd made him doubt my devotion.

As I hurried through the restaurant, I was so focused on finding Josh that I barely noticed any of the other diners. Reaching the doors to the kitchen, I suddenly realized that I couldn't just barge in. This was opening night, the tension was high, meals were now being prepared and served, and, for all my sense of involvement with Simmer, I didn't work here. For a moment, I stood there helplessly. Then one of the doors flew open, and I nearly collided with a server carrying an overloaded tray of food.

"Sorry," I muttered apologetically and ran off to the bathroom to figure out what to do. I was such an idiot! Why hadn't I just told Josh about meeting up with Sean? Now it just looked like I was hiding something.

I pushed open the bathroom door to find Adrianna in front of the mirror shaking her hair out and applying lipstick.

"Where have you been? I need your help," I whined. "It's Josh."

"Sorry. Just preening, you know. What's going on?" Ade leaned toward the mirror to get a close-up view of her perfectly applied makeup.

"Cheater."

Ade stood bolt upright. "How do you know?" She stared at me in the mirror, disbelief running across her face.

"That's what Josh thinks." I explained Hannah's dirty deed and went on to say that not only did I look like a cheater but that Hannah had probably tricked Josh into cheating on me.

"Oh." Her face relaxed a little. "That's ridiculous. You did nothing wrong, and we both know Josh wouldn't touch that little rat girl again. You're being silly. Go find him and straighten this mess out. Is our food there yet? I'm starved."

"The appetizers came. And the salads. I'll be back at the table in a minute."

"See you then." Adrianna left me alone.

Everything was going wrong! The last thing I wanted was to fight with Josh at Simmer's opening. As I'd gathered from Isabelle when she'd called me, Josh had been in a foul mood all day. Poor Josh! Instead of being free to devote himself exclusively to the preparations for opening night, he'd been plagued by thoughts of my hooking up with Sean! Was it narcissistic to imagine that Josh would be so overwhelmed with misery over me that he wouldn't be able to function? So what if it was narcissistic! I didn't care. I had to fix everything right now.

Determined to clear up the misunderstanding, I pushed open the restroom door. As a server returned to the kitchen, I followed him into the madness. Josh and Snacker were moving at warp speed, finishing plates that were lined up across one of the counters. The two chefs garnished dishes with herbs, wiped drops of sauce off the edges of plates, and adjusted the positions of food to give the most artful effect. Snacker had a dish towel in one hand and was cleaning sauce off the edges of the dishes, and Josh was glaring at the plates as if daring them to be more outstanding than they already were.

"Okay, Chef. These are ready to go." Snacker stood back proudly.

"And they would've been ready to go sooner if you hadn't kept disappearing on me." Josh didn't even look at Snacker. "I don't know what the hell is going on with you tonight, but get it together."

Snacker had the decency to look ashamed. "Gotcha. Orders are up!" he called out.

"Thank God. What took so long?" growled a waitress.

I slipped out the door. This was not, after all, the time to explain myself to Josh. I returned to our table at the front and sat down.

Our appetizer and salad plates had been cleared. Doug was raving about his lobster tail. "That was ridiculously good. You better watch yourself, Chloe, because if I get the chance, I'm going after Josh myself."

I willed Heather not to applaud, but she was too busy chugging down a glass of water to celebrate the possibility that my gay friend would swoop in and steal my boyfriend. By the time my steak arrived, I felt significantly more positive about resolving this misunderstanding with Josh. He was under monumental stress today; his snapping at me probably had less to do with me than with the pressure to pull off opening night.

Obligatory or not, my steak was phenomenal. The tangy taste of the Stilton potato cake worked beautifully with the peppery seared beef. The baby vegetables were still slightly crunchy and full of flavor. When Doug fed me a bite of the roasted vegetable Wellington, I nearly groaned with delight: the pastry was light and crisp, the vegetable filling was delectable, and the red pepper and balsamic sauces were heaven. Now I was really feeling better about Josh; this food was like make-up sex.

Another glass of wine later, and we had all cleaned our plates. I was totally stuffed, but had I been in the privacy of my own home, I'd have picked up my plate and licked it. I wasn't sure how I was going to cram a dessert into my stomach, but there was no way I was going to miss out on the banana creation, which I knew from Josh consisted of caramelized banana slices served with banana ice cream and topped with a rum sauce and banana chantilly.

Josh and a server brought out our desserts.

"I'm sorry," my chef whispered in my ear. "I've been an asshole. I'm just really edgy tonight with the opening. Snacker talked me out of my mood, but I don't like the thought of you with another guy."

I looked up at him and smiled. Yay! He was over it!

"But," he added, "what were you doing out with Sean last night?"

Okay, he wasn't quite over it.

"Sean called me and asked me to meet him, so I did. And what about you? Were you at Hannah's place last night cooking for her?"

"What are you talking about?" Josh looked at me, stunned. "I didn't cook anything for Hannah. I was busting my ass here all night."

My family was even more interested in this interchange

than in the food being served. To the best of my recollection, this collective distraction from food was completely unprecedented. A family first! And an unwelcome one, of course. Josh and I needed to continue our discussion away from the table and, especially, away from my parents.

"Josh," I said, "can you come talk to me for a few minutes? Somewhere else. Not here."

He nodded. "Yeah, things are calming down in the kitchen. Snacker's taking another break, but it's mostly dessert orders that are in, and the rest of the guys can handle that. We can go to my office." Heather's face sank with disappointment that she wasn't going to witness a fight between Josh and me.

Adrianna stood up with us to use the ladies' room again. "That wine is just running through me," she explained, although I was pretty sure I'd consumed most of her glass.

I followed Josh through the maze of full tables. At least he was holding my hand.

"Josh, it's no use pretending nothing is up with Hannah, because I saw the shopping list you gave her. It wasn't just that it was your kind of food—it was in *your* handwriting. She made me pick her up from the police station the other day and then forced me to chauffeur her around town to shop for the ingredients for the dinner *you* were making her."

Josh stopped so abruptly that I nearly smashed into

him. He turned around to face me. "Yes, I did write out a shopping list for her. The other night at the gallery, Hannah told me that she'd changed, that she was interested in food and cooking, and that she wanted to make a wonderful dinner for some guy. She asked me for suggestions, and then she had me write out everything she needed. So I did. If she told you I was cooking for her, she was just screwing with you. One of the many reasons she and I are no longer together. Okay?" He resumed walking, pulling me along and shaking his head in obvious disbelief at how gullible I was.

As we neared Barry, Sarka, and Dora's table, Josh stopped to speak to a waitress. Standing there waiting for him, I couldn't help eavesdropping. Dora was speaking rather loudly to Barry and Sarka. To my dismay, I overhead her describing how she'd gotten rid of Oliver's pets. "If you can even call hermit crabs pets!" she exclaimed. "I don't know why he fussed over them so much. He had an enormous fish tank filled with sand for four of those disgusting, slimy crabs! Can you imagine? I just flushed them down the toilet last night. Good riddance!"

I held Josh's hand tightly. As unlovable as Ken had at first seemed, he was growing on me, and I was appalled that anyone would simply send a living animal off to the city sewer system. The same idea had admittedly occurred to me when I'd first seen Ken, but I wouldn't actually have done it! How could Dora so easily have flushed away Oliver's beloved pets? She must be totally heartless. Did her violence against small creatures mean that she was capable of violence on a larger, say Oliver-sized, scale?

I looked away from Dora, whom I now saw as a ruthless crab-killer . . . and maybe more. At another nearby table were Naomi and Eliot. The trendy owner of a trendy gallery, Eliot had obviously taken pity on Naomi. I felt touched by his kindness in giving my wallflower supervisor a night on the town, and not just any night, either, but New Year's Eve. Because of Naomi's granola-based social skills, it seemed particularly generous of him to put up with her on a holiday.

I hurried past them before they noticed me.

I looked away from the ill-matched couple only to catch a glimpse of Sean and Hannah, who were cozily seated at a table for two. Aha! *That's* who Hannah was cooking for! Those two had met at the Food for Thought and must have hit it off. In other words, Hannah had somehow gotten her claws into poor, trusting Sean. Knowing Sean as I did, I suddenly realized that after telling me about the incident he'd witnessed at the gallery between Oliver and Hannah, he must have gone to Hannah and believed whatever self-serving explanation she'd given him. I couldn't imagine, however, why Hannah had picked Simmer as the place the two of them would celebrate New Year's Eve. It had been Hannah, I felt certain, who'd made the selection. What could she possibly have said? *Hey, Sean, let's go to my ex-boyfriend's new restaurant, where we can also see your ex-girlfriend and, with a little luck, her entire family!*

There was something highly disturbing about our two exes hooking up, but as far as I was concerned, the two of them were welcome to each other, especially if my ex would keep Josh's ex away from Josh from now on. As tempted as I was to stop at their table with Josh and spit out a witty, biting comment, I realized that it would be a mistake to give Hannah any kind of attention. Besides, although the general concept of spitting out a witty, biting remark felt wonderful, I wasn't able to translate the idea into particular words.

We got to Josh's office, which was no bigger than a closet but had two doors, one that opened inward from the kitchen, the other that opened inward from the dining room, both propped open to allow Josh to keep an eye on things. The combination of the two doors sticking into the tiny room, two chairs, and Josh's desk left almost no room for the two of us. I crammed myself into one of the chairs and looked at Josh, who stood in the one square foot of floor space left.

I said, "Look, the only reason I went to Eclipse last night with Sean was because he called and said he really needed my advice on something, and I didn't see any reason to say no to him. But more than that, I wanted the chance to poke around in one of the Full Moon Group's restaurants."

"Why? What do you care about that for?" Josh looked totally irritated with me.

"I found out that Oliver had been harassing female employees, and I wanted to see if I could find out if anyone else was doing the same thing. There's such a thing as an atmosphere of harassment. I wanted to see whether there was any sign of that. But when I met Sean, he told me that he'd seen Oliver forcing himself on Hannah at the art gallery the other night."

"What? That's horrible."

"The thing is, when Hannah was trying to fend off this creep, Oliver, she must have spilled her disgusting snap peas on him. That's why the police questioned her all night. They must have found the green powder on his body and suspected her of killing him. Sean wanted to know if I thought he should tell the police about what he'd seen."

"What did you tell him?" Josh asked.

"I told him no. And the reason I told him that is because Hannah didn't kill Oliver. Naomi did."

SEVENTEEN

"NO, you're wrong. Naomi wouldn't kill anyone." Josh let out a deep sigh and looked away from me. "Gavin did it."

"Gavin? Josh, listen to me. Hannah had been calling the Boston Organization. She wanted help because Oliver had been harassing her on a regular basis, and Hannah was getting desperate. You know how overinvested Naomi gets in her work, so Naomi took it upon herself to solve the problem. She whacked him over the head with your poor Robocoupe. Then, like most criminals supposedly do, she even returned to the scene of the crime on the pretext of taking Eliot a thank-you present. And now she's going to rot in prison!"

Josh stared at me confused. "I guess I could see why

she'd give Eliot something, but it's not as if a Full Moon partner needs anything. They're all loaded," he scoffed.

"Barry and Oliver are the partners. Were the partners."

Josh sighed. "Chloe, a *group* is not just two people. Didn't you just finish a class on group therapy? Wasn't Doug out there the teaching assistant in that class?"

Like I needed yet someone else pointing out my terrible performance in school! "Hey, I tried very hard in that class, but the professor had the personality of a rock, and the textbook was about as scintillating as the fine print that came with my credit card."

"Well, anyhow, the Full Moon Group is a *group*. Eliot stays out of the actual running of the business, but he's a silent partner, meaning he contributes and makes money. It's no secret. You just didn't happen to know it. Probably a lot of people don't know about it, actually, because he's pretty low key about being a partner, but he and I were talking about it the other night at his gallery. I don't think Gavin realizes it either, now that I think about it. Eliot was too polite to say anything when Gavin was bragging about beating them out for this location." He paused. "Speak of the devil . . ." Josh waved at someone.

I looked out into the dining room to see Eliot and Naomi, who were passing by the office door, hand in hand.

"Oh, Josh. Nice to see you again." Eliot stopped and

stuck his head in the office. "Wonderful, wonderful meal. Everything was exceptional," he said. "Gavin invited us in to take a peek at the kitchen. Hope you don't mind? Naomi said she's never seen a professional kitchen."

"Sure, go ahead. Don't mind the craziness going on," Josh said, waving them into the office. "You can cut through here."

Naomi beamed at me. "Hi, Chloe. Happy New Year's!" She winked at me before sliding past us and through the open door to the kitchen.

"Josh, do you know what you just did?' I whispered. "If it's no secret that Eliot is a Full Moon partner, then Naomi must know about that from Hannah. Josh, she talked to Hannah all the time! And now Naomi is cozying up to Eliot with the intention of murdering him, too!"

Suddenly panicked, I stood up and spoke softly. "She's going to kill Eliot. She killed Oliver at the back of the gallery with a heavy kitchen appliance, and now she's going to kill Eliot at the back of this restaurant with a similar weapon. Josh, your kitchen is full of murder weapons! She's got some sort of crazy repetition compulsion, and you've sent her into a room full of lethal appliances! Come on!" I grabbed a stunned Josh by the hand and pulled him into the kitchen.

"No, you're acting crazy," Josh informed me. "You need to listen to me!"

I scanned the kitchen, but Eliot and Naomi were nowhere to be seen. I did see Isabelle, though, in a corner of the room. The shy girl I'd met the other day looked positively radiant. She was sweaty and exhausted, but she had clearly found her calling in the kitchen.

I dragged Josh behind me. "Isabelle."

"Oh, Chloe," she gushed. "I love it here. You can't believe how much work this is and how nuts it got in here, but I love it. And Chef has been taking care of me." I was pretty sure I saw a slight blush creep up her cheeks. I couldn't blame her for having a crush on Josh.

"Good, I'm so happy for you. Listen, have you seen a woman with crazy braids and a man with big eyes come through here?"

"Yeah, I did. They just went in there." Isabelle pointed to one of the walk-ins, as Josh called them, meaning walk-in refrigerators and freezers the size of small rooms.

"Quick! Grab something!" I instructed Josh.

"Like what?"

"Anything! Here." I handed him an oversized metal soup ladle. "I'll open the door, and then you go in and hit her on the head with that."

Josh started to laugh. "You want me to hit your supervisor on the head with a ladle?"

"She's probably killing him right now. Go!" I reached for the handle of the walk-in, pulled open the heavy door, and pushed my brave chef in ahead of me.

The scene was just what I'd feared: she was killing

again! Specifically, Naomi had Eliot pinned against a wall, and, vampire fashion, appeared to be biting him.

"Stop it!" I screamed.

Naomi spun around, saw the two of us, and screamed right back at us. Since Josh had failed to raise the ladle in a protective manner, I steadied myself on my feet in preparation for Naomi's attack.

Eliot stumbled forward, his head hanging low. I looked him over for wounds, blood, or other signs of assault but saw none.

"This is so embarrassing," he said. "We shouldn't be using your storage area like it's the backseat of a car. I really apologize." Eliot adjusted his shirt, which had slipped out of his waistband.

Oh, my God. We'd walked in on Naomi mauling Eliot, all right! Just not mauling him in the manner I'd expected. Gross. It took me a few seconds to process the information that Naomi was not attempting to murder Eliot and was not a lesbian. I'm not sure which realization was more shocking.

"Eliot and I met in a yoga class a few months ago," Naomi explained, brushing her braids back from her face. "I've been wanting to tell you, Chloe, but the relationship is sort of new and, well, anyhow . . . Chloe, I have something to share. Eliot is now the man in my life." She put her arm around his waist and leaned into him.

Eliot cleared his throat. "When Food for Thought came around, obviously I suggested that Naomi and I pair up, but we were trying to keep up professional appearances."

"Eliot's gallery was a very desirable spot," Naomi said. "We felt that the larger, more powerful agencies might be so resentful that there'd be accusations of favoritism."

"So," Eliot continued, "we didn't mention our being together to anyone. Now that that's behind us, I guess there's no reason to keep this a secret anymore." He and Naomi smiled at each other, clearly smitten. "Naomi was telling me over dinner that she'd never been behind the scenes at a restaurant, so Gavin said it wouldn't be a problem if I showed her around. Sorry. I guess we got a little distracted."

"No problem," Josh tried to reassure them. "I'm very happy for you two. Since you're here, why don't I give you a personal tour?"

The horny couple followed Josh out of the walk-in and, still in a state of shock, I plodded after them. Huh. So either Naomi had committed a one-time murder and was going to give her new love, Eliot, a reprieve from death by small kitchen appliance, or she hadn't killed Oliver at all.

Josh was showing off a still-new-looking gas stove, complete with eight burners and a flattop grill. When Eliot jumped in to explain the differences between professional and home stoves, Josh took the opportunity to step back and continue our previous conversation.

"See, I told you it wasn't Naomi. She's a lust-driven

social worker, just like you!" He nudged me and gave an exaggerated wink. "I'm kidding! But seriously, I'm pretty sure Gavin was the one who killed Oliver."

"Why do you think that? He got the location from the Full Moon Group. He had no reason."

"As I've learned over the past couple of weeks, Gavin thinks God meant him to have this location. Chloe, you've probably heard him. He keeps saying that getting this place was *meant to be.* Like it's fated or some bullshit like that."

"Now that you mention it, Gavin said that tonight, when Doug and I got here. And something about thanking God."

"And I don't think he was talking about God in a true religious sense, since as far as I can tell, he's not particularly devout in any other sense of the word. He's more caught up in the idea of some vague higher power," Josh explained, gesturing wildly into the air. "As nice a guy as Gavin seems, he's a nut job, if you ask me. I bet he killed off Oliver because Oliver was the Full Moon partner with the most clout, and that group had tried to interfere with Gavin's so-called destiny."

To me, Gavin had seemed so normal. Perhaps I wasn't paying enough attention at school; clearly, my diagnostic skills were weak. "When I talked to Isabelle today," I said, "she tried to tell me that Gavin was talking about God, but I guess I wasn't really listening. I'm going to be a crappy social worker," I moaned.

"You're going to be great. I didn't say anything to you about Gavin having this weird side to him because I didn't want you to worry. And selfishly, I thought Simmer could be a great restaurant, and good executive chef jobs are hard to come by. I really don't want to get involved in this, and I don't exactly have any proof that Gavin is a killer, so I'm just trying to stay out of this whole mess. I don't want this to be happening," Josh confessed.

I couldn't fault him for feeling that way. Half of all restaurants close within the first six months. If Josh had found a professional home for himself, a place that could not only survive but become highly successful, he wouldn't want to lose it.

"The thing I don't understand," I said, "is, why kill Oliver? Yeah, he seemed to be the leader of the Full Moon Group, but Barry is the one who's been making jokes about buying Simmer from Gavin. Barry is the one who really appreciates great food and is nuts about the whole culinary industry. Oh, whatever." I shrugged my shoulders. "We can't figure this out. And as long as it's not Naomi and as long as Hannah leaves you alone, I don't want to be in this mess. So for now, since we know Eliot is no longer in any danger of losing his life at the hands of my supervisor, and since Hannah is otherwise engaged with Sean, do you want to come sit down with us for dessert?" If there was no reason to miss out on my Bananas Three Way, my stomach still had room.

Josh laughed. "Food always comes first with you.

One of the many things I love about you." He put both hands on my cheeks and turned my face up to his for a soft, slow kiss.

Was that Josh saying he loved me? We hadn't actually said "I love you" to each other, although it was clear that's how we felt. For some reason, we were both being cautious about saying it out loud, and it wasn't something I needed to hear to be happy with Josh. Still, I couldn't help thinking that it would be nice when it happened.

Eliot and Naomi had wandered off and were exploring the other side of the kitchen, where the vegetables and sauces sat lined up in stainless steel containers at the back of a long counter.

"Come on." Josh took my hand. We were turning to leave the kitchen when Snacker hurried through the door from the dining room.

"Happy New Year everyone!" he shouted to no one in particular.

"Where have you been?" Josh looked exasperated. "Dude, stick around once in a while, will ya?"

"Sorry, sorry, sorry. I'm all yours again. What do you need?"

"Just make sure all the desserts go out, okay? Things are going fine, and I don't want that to change. Then head up the cleanup. Good thing Gavin only wanted one seating since you've been MIA most of the night."

Snacker placed his hands on his chest. "I will handle everything from here on out. You have my word. That way, you and your lovely lady will have the rest of the evening to yourselves."

"You got yourself a deal," Josh happily agreed.

We ran into Adrianna in the middle of the dining room. Yet again, she was returning from the ladies' room.

"Are you feeling all right?" I asked her, as we reached our table. "You've been to the bathroom, like, a hundred times tonight."

"Yeah. I'm okay," she said vaguely. "Nothing serious."

Josh pulled over a stray chair for himself and scooted in next to me. Everyone else at the table had finished dessert, and Doug glowered at me for having left him stranded with my family for so long.

"I'm sorry," I apologized. "Are you okay?"

"Yes. But you owe me one. Your nephew spent ten minutes telling me more than I wanted to know about Thomas the Tank Engine and all of Thomas's little train friends. Did you know that Thomas is a boy and has a penis?"

I glanced over at Walker, who was busy examining the underside of his train.

"I thought I might die of boredom. You better have worked things out with Josh." Doug looked hopefully at me. "Don't leave me again!"

"We have. I'll go hang out with your right-wing parents as payback. Deal?"

Doug nodded, happy in the knowledge that my spending an evening with his less-than-liberal mother and father would more than compensate for having abandoned him at Simmer.

My banana ice cream had melted, and the caramelized bananas were now cold, but even so, my dessert was wonderful. Doug had saved me a bite of the rich chocolate torte and had even left me a couple of raspberries. One taste and I had yet more reasons to be head over heels for my chef!

"Is something going on with Owen?" Doug wondered aloud.

"What do you mean? He looks fine to me," I said, licking my fork in a display of uncouth table manners. "Adrianna's the one I'm a little worried about. She's spent half the night in the ladies' room. It's not the food, obviously. Everyone else is fine, and Josh is a fiend about fresh ingredients and a sanitary kitchen. What do mean about Owen?"

"I don't know. He's all fidgety tonight, like he's anxious or something."

"I have no idea."

As if on cue, Owen stood up from his chair. Unfortunately, he had tucked the tablecloth into his pants, so we all spent a few moments picking up spilled glasses and rearranging dinner plates.

"My apologies," Owen said formally. "I'm a little nervous. But I have something to say." He buttoned his jacket and ran a hand through his hair. "Adrianna—" he began with a loving look at my best friend.

Oh, my God! He was going to propose! This was so exciting! It's not often that you get to witness a proposal. Usually you just get a giddy phone call from a friend, or one day your girlfriend holds up her hand to show off a new ring. But to be right here while my best friend got engaged was too exciting for words!

No wonder Adrianna hadn't been feeling well! She must have suspected that Owen was going to ask her tonight. She wasn't sick; she was nervous. I looked wistfully at Ade and prepared myself for what was bound be a totally romantic proposal from Owen.

Adrianna was ashen. Seriously. No color in her face whatsoever. Wow, maybe she hadn't suspected after all. Maybe she really was surprised, and now the monumental significance of what was about to happen was sending her into shock. I wished that Owen would hurry up. What if Adrianna collapsed and had to be rushed off in an ambulance? Well, I'd miss witnessing my first marriage proposal, that's what.

Josh grabbed my hand tightly. "Uh-oh," he said softly.

Uh-oh? What does he mean by uh-oh? She was going to say yes. Why wouldn't she? I turned to Josh with irritation. What was he talking about?

". . . I am completely in love with you," Owen was saying.

We all made appropriate oohing noises in support of Owen's declaration.

Josh squeezed my hand tighter. "Oh, no."

"What?" I whispered confused. " 'Oh, no' what?" I was really annoyed at him for interrupting my enjoyment of Adrianna and Owen's engagement.

"Snacker," Josh whispered back.

Snacker? What did Snacker have to do with anything? Everything was under control in the kitchen. Only a few minutes earlier, he'd taken a solemn oath to handle everything. I knew that Snacker had been slacking off tonight and taking too many breaks, but . . .

Oh. Shit.

I spun around to face Adrianna, who looked as though she might go into cardiac arrest at any moment.

Snacker hadn't been taking those breaks alone.

Ade caught my eye and silently begged me to get her out of this mess. No matter how seedy and slimy it had been of Adrianna to do whatever she'd been doing with Snacker tonight, she was still my best friend. But I felt more sympathy for Owen than I did for Adrianna. No matter how unpromising poor Owen was as a potential husband and no matter how vocationally lost he was, I couldn't let him get shot down in front of everybody. I had to rescue Owen before he had his heart broken in public.

I had to brainstorm quickly. I'd cause some kind of a scene, any kind, and ruin the moment so tremendously that Owen would be unable to finish his proposal. My two friends could talk about their six thousand conflicts and differences and dissatisfactions later. If Heather had only kept drinking, she could have been provoked to jump atop the table and perform a scene from *Moulin Rouge.*

Owen was closing in on the big question. ". . . so what I want to ask you, Adrianna, is . . ."

I was on the verge of faking a dramatic mental episode when noises from the back of the restaurant preempted me. Loud crashes sounded from what I thought was Josh's office. A second later, someone or something slammed into what was definitely the door to the office, a door that was now closed.

"What the hell is going on?" Josh took off across the dining room, dodging alarmed customers. Not to miss out on the action, I was right behind him. As we approached the source of the noise, I recognized Gavin's voice, but he was shouting so frantically that I couldn't make out his words. Still, there was no question that he was bellowing madly. Josh must be right about Gavin's being the killer! He was in Josh's office trying to finish off his second victim!

Josh tried the handle on the door. "Dammit, it's locked. Where are my keys?" He fumbled around in the pockets of his baggy chef pants until he produced a huge key ring and eventually found the right one and opened the lock. He was able to push the door open only a few inches when it snapped shut.

"Snacker!" Josh called out. "Help me open this door." I was mildly offended that Josh solicited help from Snacker. Typical for men to ask other men for help when it came to physical demands! I could have been just as useful as Snacker. I'd have to flex my biceps for Josh later.

"Is that Gavin in there?" Snacker asked as he appeared. He threw a dish towel over his shoulder, and he and Josh leaned on the door together.

"Yeah," Josh grunted against the weight of the door. "We have to get in there. Push!"

Like a silly cheerleader rooting for her team, I stood behind them.

After two tries, the chefs forced the door open to reveal Gavin and Barry locked tightly together in a struggle. Just visible between them was a large handgun.

Josh and Snacker took major steps back.

So certain had I been that Josh was right about Gavin that it took a moment to absorb what I was seeing. The man clutching the weapon was not Gavin, but Barry. Barry was the one who held the gun, and Gavin was furiously trying to wrest it out of Barry's hands.

While in the process of trying to save his own life, Gavin was shouting, "You are not getting my restaurant from me, you maniac! It is meant to be mine, and you will not take it away!" This didn't seem the time to be arguing with Barry, but it didn't stop Gavin from screaming that he wouldn't make Barry a partner if he were the last fruitcake on earth.

I looked behind me in search of some large object to

hurl at the two men. Where was that lethal ladle when we needed it? The couple at the table nearest me had a full bottle of red wine, so I reached between the horrified-looking pair of diners and grabbed the glass bottle. Raising my arm up, I aimed for Barry's head and hurled the bottle as hard as I could.

The bottle completely missed Barry and hit the ceiling light, shattering glass and knocking out the bulb. I momentarily remembered why I had always been the last kid chosen for teams in gym class. Apparently age hadn't improved my pitching skills whatsoever, but the noise startled the two men long enough for an enraged Gavin to secure the gun from Barry's hand.

Gavin held the gun on Barry, who seemed to accept his defeat and was kneeling on the floor, the fight drained out of him.

"See this creep?" Gavin hollered. "He thinks he's some kind of godfather. Trying to make me an offer I couldn't refuse. When I told him no amount of money could get him my restaurant, he pulled this gun on me. As if I would ever let you get your hands on my place. You're disgusting, Barry."

I heard sirens wailing outside, and I was hoping that those were for Simmer and not for some other New Year's crisis. With all the traffic and people crowding the streets outside, I hoped the police could get here before Gavin hauled off and shot Barry.

"Barry!" Dora said angrily. "You fool!"

She and Sarka appeared now and stood next to me, Dora looking furious and Sarka looking near tears.

"I knew you must have been the one who killed my husband. You and your idiotic ideas about opening an expensive restaurant. As if wasting all that money on grand tours of Europe wasn't bad enough, then you wanted to sink all of Full Moon's profits into some money-eating restaurant?" Gone was the meek, sorrowful Dora from this morning. This woman was on fire.

"You ungrateful little shit!" she continued, shaking and pointing her finger at Barry. "After everything that Oliver did for you! You would have been nothing if Oliver hadn't taken pity on you and let you become part of his company. He was the one with the brains and the business savvy, and you just kept trying to muck that all up. But he wouldn't let you. Oliver blocked you at every step, at every stupid, costly step you tried to take."

Dora turned to me, tears streaming down her face. "Barry couldn't take it anymore." Then she paused and eyed me suspiciously. "Weren't you at my house today?"

I nodded.

"Huh." Even in her crazed state, she seemed confused that someone of my low status could be present during this high drama. She turned back to Barry. "So, the night you killed Oliver, you'd had it with him ridiculing you for your pompous, contrived love of art and fine food! And you thought killing him would give you what you wanted?"

Dora lunged toward her husband's killer, and Josh and Snacker grabbed her before she could get more than a few feet.

The police entered the restaurant, pushed their way to Josh's office, relieved Gavin of the gun, and took Barry into custody.

Sarka whimpered next to me. "Oh, God, Barry. What have you done?"

Eighteen

"NEW Year's Eve was not what I expected." I lay snugly in bed with Josh spooning me.

"You're not kidding." He let out a roaring yawn. "Barry seemed completely harmless. I cannot believe he's the one who killed Oliver."

In spite of what he'd just said, Josh seemed more insulted than surprised by the revelation that Barry was the murderer. It was, I thought, a deep and personal offense to Josh that a fellow food devotee, someone who shared Josh's own passion for fine cuisine, had twisted and even perverted that zealous love as Barry had done. As I mulled over the murder, I could see that years of Oliver's dismissive attitude toward Barry and toward his dreams had finally provoked Barry beyond endurance.

Had Barry also been enraged by Oliver's interest in Sarka? I didn't know. But Barry's principal motivation had certainly been his ardent desire to make his fantasy restaurant become a reality. He must have realized that with Oliver alive, the Full Moon Group would never take the financial risk of opening a fine-dining establishment but would continue to limit itself to glorified and lucrative bars. On the night of Food for Thought, Oliver had poked fun at what he'd viewed as Barry's pretensions about art and food—or so it must have seemed to Oliver. Barry, however, must have felt that his most profound dreams and passions, together with his most cherished images of himself, were being ridiculed and dismissed. In my view, Oliver's taunting had been only one trigger for the murder. What had inflamed Barry, I suspected, and what had incited him to kill Oliver at the earliest moment, had been hearing Oliver's mockery at Simmer's booth. At the booth, Barry had been confronted with the reality of a man, Gavin, who was realizing the dream stolen by Oliver. Furthermore, Barry had tasted and loved Josh's delectable medallions of beef. I hoped that Josh would never realize that his culinary genius had helped to provoke a murder. Indeed, when Barry killed Oliver, the taste of Josh's food must still have been lingering on his palate. Last night, on New Year's Eve, when Barry had tried to make Gavin an offer he couldn't refuse, the scene had almost replayed itself: savoring Josh's food at Simmer itself, not merely at the booth, Barry had lashed out at the man who was denying him access to his unrealized fantasy of owning a fine restaurant with Josh's marvelous food.

I was admittedly disappointed that Hannah had nothing to do with Oliver's murder, but it was comforting to realize that having sunk her claws into Sean, she'd probably leave Josh alone. Furthermore, with Eliot the only partner in the Full Moon Group left alive or out of jail, the future of the group's establishments was uncertain, and Hannah's PR work in Boston was over. I prayed that she'd move back to New York and disappear permanently from our lives. Sean was a decent person who deserved a healthy relationship with someone who adored him. That relationship wouldn't be with me, and I hoped it wouldn't be with Hannah, who, besides everything else, is a manipulative liar.

When the police arrived at Simmer last night, Detective Hurley was among them. When he questioned me, I happened to mention that I'd picked up Hannah after he'd held her all night at the station. And he'd done no such thing! Detective Hurley got defensive: Hannah was nothing more than a witness, and the police certainly did not subject her to any kind of all-night interrogation. With typical self-dramatization, Hannah had set up a phony crisis from which she intended to have Josh rescue her. On the night of Oliver's murder, she'd slept in her own bed, or maybe in someone else's; and in the morning, she'd gone to the police station, stood outside, and pretended to have been inside all night. I probably won't tell Sean. He wouldn't believe me. He'll have to figure out Hannah for himself.

The great news was Naomi's innocence. After the police took Barry into custody and removed him from Simmer, I spent some time with Naomi. As I'd guessed, she had recognized Hannah's voice at Food for Thought and had realized that Hannah was the hotline caller in need of help. Even though Naomi had known that Hannah was being harassed, she hadn't taken violent action. In quintessential Naomi style, she'd been trying to convince Hannah to file a complaint against Oliver and had been in the process of locating a good lawyer to represent Hannah in her lawsuit. Naomi told me last night that the toughest part of helping Hannah had been keeping the secret from Eliot, who *she* knew was a silent partner in Oliver's business and who was oblivious to the way Oliver treated women. Eliot's relationship with Barry and Oliver had been strictly business. Nonetheless, it had been a struggle for Naomi to find herself plotting a nasty lawsuit against one of her new love's partners.

With Oliver dead and Barry in jail, Dora and Sarka were now both without husbands. I had no sympathy for Dora, but I felt sorry for Sarka. I couldn't help wondering whether her longing for what seemed to me a stereotyped version of a normal, stable home life, together with what I guessed was a mild eating disorder, hinted at some perception of her husband's disturbance and his potential for violence. No matter what, I could only begin to imagine how hurt and betrayed she felt by Barry's actions.

Even though it was eleven thirty in the morning, I'd had only a few hours of sleep and was totally bleary eyed. The sleep I did get was restless and filled with bad dreams. I sat up in bed and rubbed my eyes, thinking a good hit of caffeine might help. Josh looked as exhausted and drained as I was.

"Why don't I start a pot of coffee and then go downstairs and take someone's paper, okay?" I hoped Noah hadn't picked up his, since it gave me a sick sense of satisfaction to steal his newspaper whenever I could.

When I'd successfully returned with Noah's paper, and we both had steaming cups of coffee, we curled up on the couch together. I flipped through the pages to see if Mishti Patil had reviewed Simmer.

"Here it is!" I cried excitedly.

"Stop, Chloe. I don't want to see it if she did. It'll be a fake review that she was paid off to do." Josh tried fervently to grab the newspaper out of my hands, but I stood up, spilling coffee all over myself, ran across the room, and locked myself in the bathroom.

I skimmed the review while Josh rattled the door, saying, "It doesn't count! I don't want to hear it!"

"Listen, listen! 'Although there are issues to be addressed at Simmer, I am happy to report that Simmer is a welcome addition to Newbury Street.' Blah, blah, 'beautiful decor . . . the wait staff struggled to keep up at times . . . ' "

Josh was now pounding on the door. "Stop reading!" he begged.

I paid no attention. " 'The food was worth the wait . . . outstanding lobster tail . . . lentils still had a bite to them . . . best salad dressing in Boston . . . salmon was overcooked but had potential . . . average chocolate torte . . . ' "

Josh stopped banging. " '*Average* chocolate torte'? *Average?* Who does she think she is?"

"Do you know what this means?" I said excitedly.

"It means she doesn't know the first thing about chocolate," Josh said angrily.

"Yes, but it also means that she wrote a real review. Gavin didn't pay her off! Or, if he tried, she didn't accept his offer. No one bribes someone to write a mediocre review. And for Mishti, this review is pretty good. She doesn't give out compliments easily. And, God, she said you have the best salad dressing in all of Boston!"

After a long pause, Josh said, "I guess that's pretty good."

"It's more than pretty good. Can I come out now?"

He laughed. "Yeah, let me read the whole thing."

I unlocked the bathroom door and handed him the paper. When he was done, I was going to clip out the review and make copies of it. I took the crossword out of the paper and left Josh alone for a few minutes to read Simmer's first review in its entirety.

"I'm going to call Adrianna and see how she's doing."

"Do you think she got any sleep?" Josh asked with concern.

"I hope so," I said doubtfully and went and sat down in the kitchen.

Learning that Barry was the murderer would have been enough shock for one night without the preceding revelation about Adrianna's messing around with Snacker. When I reached her on the phone, practically the first thing she said was that she was pregnant.

"I suspected I might be," she said, "but I didn't use the test kit until after I got back from doing hair yesterday." The positive result had thrown her into a total tizzy. She'd freaked out, she said, because as much as she loved Owen, she hadn't planned on getting pregnant and settling down with a puppeteer's assistant any time soon.

"So what were you doing running around having clandestine meetings with Snacker in the bathroom last night?" I did my best not to yell at her since she'd been talking to me through sobs.

"God, Chloe, I don't know! I just was freaking out and trying to pretend I didn't know I was pregnant and trying not to feel like my life was set in stone and that I would be with Owen who can't figure out what the hell to do in life, and . . . I don't know. I just wanted to feel free one last time. I don't have a good reason. Owen was being all weird with his marionette bullshit that night at your parents' house, and Snacker seemed so cute and funny, and I was feeling frustrated with Owen. I went to Simmer the other night to see Snacker," she confessed. "Nothing happened then, but I was flirting and he was hot and . . . and then when Owen started to propose, I thought I would die." She blew her nose loudly into the phone.

I could not believe this. "How is Owen taking everything?"

"It could be worse. He's not mad I'm pregnant, but he is pretty furious about the whole Snacker thing. I mean, of course he is. I'm pissed at myself. But I think he understands that I was having some sort of panic attack last night and wasn't really myself. Not that that excuses me making out with someone else while he's gearing up to ask me to marry him!" She started wailing and choking on her tears. "And why was I attracted to Snacker in the first place? What is wrong with me?"

My heart just broke for her. I hated to hear my best friend so miserable. "Honey, look. You and Owen will get through this. Maybe you weren't planning on this happening, but you guys love each other very much. Owen is crazy about you, and he'll understand that he's going to have to stop jumping from job to job if you two are going to be parents." I had to ask: "Ade, you are going to keep the baby, aren't you?"

"Yes, it's not a question. Maybe under other circumstances, if it wasn't with Owen. You know, if we hadn't been together so long. Of course I love him. But, Chloe, I don't even *like* kids! I never thought I'd have kids, and now I am! What if I don't like my own baby? Then what? This just all feels so hard right now. I don't know what to do. This wasn't the plan, and I'm scared." I thought the poor girl might hyperventilate from crying so much. Her distress made me worry about her and the baby. She pulled herself together enough to tell me that after she and Owen had a huge blow-up fight, they'd spent two hours talking and crying before Owen had gone home. Owen was supposed to go to her apartment this afternoon. I hoped that by then she'd have had some rest. She was going to need it.

After I'd told Josh everything, I asked, "Are you going to talk to Snacker?"

Josh ran a hand through his hair. "Yeah. What an ass. He knew Adrianna had a boyfriend. For Christ's sake, he had dinner with Owen. He's not usually such a pig, I promise. It sounds to me like she was throwing herself at him, so it's not entirely his fault. Who wouldn't want Adrianna all over him?" I raised my eyebrows, and Josh quickly defended himself. "Well, not *me*, but you know what I mean."

"I know. This whole thing is crazy. As much as I love Adrianna, I can't see her as a mother. She can barely stand to be in the same room with Walker and Lucy. I don't know how she's going to parent her own child."

Josh kissed the top of my head. "She'll have Owen and

you to help her. And me. I'll make her homemade baby food. She and Owen will be all right. I really think so."

"Okay," I said, although I was doubtful that homemade baby food would do much to ease Ade and Owen's stress. "I guess there's nothing I can do right this minute. So, tell me what you thought of the review."

"It's okay," Josh said with unusual modesty.

"Give it to me." I held out my hand and took the review from him. "I'm going to cut it out and frame it, and one day you'll acknowledge that having Mishti Patil write anything positive about you is an amazing feat."

We spent the next couple of hours snuggled on the couch, reading the paper and watching football, until my stomach started rumbling.

"Josh, I'm hungry," I complained. "And there's nothing to eat here. Do you want to order something in?"

He rubbed my feet and smiled. "On my new budget? Not really. I'm sure we can find something."

"Seriously, there's nothing. We finished off the kielbasa at three last night, so there's like, potatoes and spices and weird frozen meat samples. I'm not in the mood for venison steaks right now."

Josh pulled me up from the couch. "Come on, we'll find something good."

I followed him into the kitchen.

After discovering four frozen pork chops and rooting through my cabinets, Josh announced that he'd come up with something. "Curry. It's freezing cold and snowing outside, so we're hunkering down for the day with a steaming pork curry on rice."

"I have curry powder?" I asked. So far as I could remember, I'd never made curry in this kitchen.

"No, but that's okay. I'm going to make my own version."

Despite my confidence in Josh's culinary abilities, I was a little uncertain about the idea. Josh heated a deep skillet and began sautéeing chopped onions and garlic in a little olive oil. After a few minutes he started shaking cumin, coriander, nutmeg, ground ginger, cayenne, and red pepper flakes into the dish, and, within moments, my kitchen magically started smelling like curry. Soon, he added carrots, potatoes, coconut milk, butter, and chicken broth and brought the whole thing to a lovely simmer.

"There you go, baby. Let's let that develop some more flavor." He put a lid on top and turned the heat down. "In a few minutes, I'll start the rice and then sear off the pork chops."

"You *are* a genius!" I hugged him. Nothing made me happier than spending the day with both Josh and delicious food.

"And you doubted me!" Josh teased.

Forty-five minutes later, we were back on the couch with steaming bowls of pork curry over yellow rice balanced on our laps. One of the good things about living alone was that no one made you sit down and eat every meal at a table.

The dish had just the right amount of saltiness, sweetness, and spicy heat but, as comforting as the curry was, I was worried about not hearing from Adrianna. I tried her phone, but she wasn't picking up.

"She'll call when she's ready, Chloe," Josh tried to reassure me.

"All right," I agreed, scooping up a mound of rice.

An unpleasant scratching noise made me look up from my food. "What was that?"

Josh looked around the room. "Is it Gato?"

"No, he's asleep on the chair." The sound continued, and I prayed that I didn't have strange animals crawling behind the walls.

Josh pointed to the cage across the room. "I think it's Ken."

He was right. Ken, who had finally chosen to emerge on his own from his shell, had one crabby claw stuck out and was scratching the side of his glass house.

Josh said, "Hey! He's alive! And sort of cute!"

I put down my bowl and went to peer at Ken. He wasn't nearly as disgusting looking as I'd previously thought. He had a red body and claws, two big black eyes, and funny antennae that projected from his head in a manner that I tried to see as whimsical. I'd learned from my online research that he must be a strawberry hermit crab and thus much more interesting than the typical brown crabs. "I like him! He's not so gross!" I felt sorry for the little guy, just left to crawl around on boring sand with nothing to do. I would go to Petco tomorrow and buy him special snacks, tunnels, climbing branches, and decorated shells.

Ken had made it through New Year's. Now I could look back and say, "*Last* year, Ken slept most of the time, but *this* year, Ken has become comfortable enough in his environment to explore new activities." So, Ken had come out of his shell, but I would stay nestled in mine with Josh.

Josh interrupted my Ken daydreams. "I almost forgot. I have something for you." He disappeared into the bedroom and emerged with a blue candy box in his hands. "I hid these under your bed, so once you wipe off the dust bunnies, I think you'll be happy."

Josh held out a ten-piece box of Baci chocolates. "Open one."

I didn't need another invitation before tearing into the treats. The rest of my curry could wait. I unwrapped a chocolate, but before I could pop it into my mouth, Josh stopped me. "Wait, Chloe. Look, each one is wrapped in a little note. Read it."

Why speak? The entirety of love can be said in a kiss.

And so Josh kissed me.

Recipes

Trying to get a chef to write out a recipe for fewer than sixty people is trickier than you might think. When we asked Jessica's husband, Bill, for the recipe for the Sesame-Honey Vinaigrette, it began with two pints of salad oil and one pint of rice vinegar. The entire recipe would have made enough to last the average household a year. After much nagging and complaining, we finally convinced him to write out all the recipes in traditional serving sizes. The vinaigrette still makes more than you'll need for four salads, but Bill swears that when you start breaking down a recipe too much, you risk losing the integrity of the dressing. The extra will keep nicely in the refrigerator.

Each of these recipes makes enough for roughly four

servings, and all were created by chef Bill Park, with the exception of the kielbasa dish, which is Jessica's own recipe and her favorite winter dish.

If you plan to make all four courses from the New Year's Eve menu, be sure to give yourself enough time. The vinaigrette can be made ahead of time, and you can plate and cover the cucumber salads until dinner. Although making the entire meal is fairly labor intensive, a little help from your dinner guests will go a long way. Besides, everyone always hangs out in the kitchen at dinner parties, so you might as well put your friends to work! Each dish is also wonderful on its own and could be served on separate occasions with different side dishes.

That Kielbasa Thing

Olive oil
1 package kielbasa, sliced into 1½-inch-thick pieces
1 large onion, sliced thickly
2–3 cloves garlic, minced
½ tsp. dried basil
1 tsp. dried parsley
½ tsp. dried savory
½ tsp. dried marjoram
½ tsp. crushed bay leaves, or 1 whole bay leaf

¼ tsp. dried oregano
¼ tsp. black pepper
¼ tsp. salt
1 can whole tomatoes
1 can cannellini beans, drained
¼ cup chicken broth
1 large bunch of kale, thoroughly washed, excess water shaken off, and roughly chopped
1 tbsp. sugar (optional)
Additional salt and pepper to taste

Heat a bit of olive oil over medium-high heat in the bottom of a stockpot or large pan. Add the kielbasa pieces and sauté until lightly browned. Add the onions and cook for a few minutes until they begin to soften. Add the garlic and all the herbs and spices, and cook for 2 to 3 minutes, making sure not to burn the garlic. Add the salt and pepper. Add the entire can of tomatoes with the juice, leaving the tomatoes whole, and the beans and chicken stock. When this comes to a hearty simmer, begin adding the kale, one handful at a time, covering the pot after each addition so that the kale will wilt down and give you room to add more. When the kale has softened enough, you may gently stir the pot, incorporating the kale into the broth. Cover the pot and turn the heat down to a light simmer. Let the dish cook for at least an hour. The kale will lose its bright green color, but will soften beautifully. Taste the broth and add up to 1 tablespoon of sugar if needed. Depending on the brand of canned tomatoes you use, there may be a higher level of acidity than you'd like, and the sugar will sweeten any sourness. Reseason with salt and pepper.

Although good on the first day, this dish is best made a day ahead. Reheat the entire dish over medium-high heat and then turn the stove down to low. You can leave the dish on low for a bit, but be careful not to overcook the kale, since it can break down entirely and ruin the dish. Chloe likes this served over rice or with a big piece of crusty French bread.

Note: If you have fresh herbs available, you may certainly substitute those for the dried herbs, but make sure to triple the amounts.

Josh's Curry

Olive oil
1½ medium onions, sliced thickly
3 garlic cloves, peeled and smashed with the flat of a knife
½ tsp. cumin
1 tsp. coriander
½ tsp. cardamom
1 tsp. nutmeg
2 tsp. ground ginger
1 pinch cayenne

½ tsp. crushed red pepper
3 carrots, peeled and chopped into 1-inch-thick pieces
1 large potato, cut into 1-inch cubes
1 tbsp. butter
1 red pepper, chopped into 1-inch pieces
1 can unsweetened coconut milk
¾ cup chicken broth
4 pork chops, bone-in or boneless, about ¾ inch thick
Salt, pepper, and sugar to taste
½ tsp. sesame oil

Heat a skillet deep enough to hold all of your ingredients over medium-high heat. Coat the bottom of the skillet with a little olive oil, and sauté the onions and garlic for a couple of minutes. Add all of the herbs and spices, and continue sautéing for another few minutes to toast them and bring out their flavor. Add the carrots and potatoes, and cook for 5 minutes. Add the butter, red pepper, coconut milk, and chicken broth. Bring the dish to a simmer, and then turn the heat down to low. Cover and let this cook for 45 minutes.

About 10 minutes before the vegetables and sauce are done, heat a separate skillet on medium-high heat. Dust the pork chops liberally with salt, pepper, and sugar, and lay flat in the skillet. Check after 4 minutes, and when they are nicely browned, flip them over and cook on the other side. Sprinkle each pork chop with 3–4 drops of sesame oil. Make sure they are thoroughly cooked through before serving.

Serve the pork chops with a hearty amount of the vegetables and curry sauce over them. This is a great dish with any kind of rice and a simple side salad.

JOSH'S NEW YEAR'S EVE DINNER

Baby Greens Wrapped in English Cucumber

2 large English cucumbers
4 handfuls mesclun mix
6–8 oz. fresh enoki mushrooms

Tools: at least one cylinder, about 4 inches in diameter and 2 inches deep

Cut the cucumber into 4 paper-thin slices. You may use a mandoline to cut the slices. If not, you can certainly use a knife, but make sure that the slices are thin enough to bend easily. Place a cylinder in the center of an individual serving plate. Line the inside of each cylinder with one or two cucumber slices, depending on the length of the cucumber. Fill with a good handful of your mesclun mix, making sure the cylinder is full, but that the greens are not packed tightly. Cut off the bottom of each enoki mushroom, leaving the stem long. Using two fingers, gently make openings in the greens and insert the mushroom stems. Separate the mushroom tops to give each one the appearance of a crown. Slowly and delicately remove the cylinder from the salad, keeping the nice round shape. Drizzle a bit of the sesame-honey dressing over the salad, and pour more decoratively on the plate around the salad.

Sesame-Honey Vinaigrette

¼ cup rice vinegar
¾ cup sesame oil
¾ cup salad oil
2 tbsp. soy sauce
2 tbsp. orange juice
2 tbsp. honey
½ tbsp. minced ginger
¼ tbsp. minced garlic
2 tsp. black sesame seeds
2 tsp. white sesame seeds

Combine all ingredients and let rest for at least half an hour before serving. This makes about two cups of vinaigrette, but if you are going to the trouble of making your own dressing, you might as well make a little extra to store in the fridge!

Seared Shrimp with Corn Polenta and Sweet Corn Sauce

It takes a few steps to make this dish, but it is really very simple to put together!

Corn Polenta

3 ears corn
1 tbsp. olive oil
2 tbsp. butter
Salt
4 cups chicken stock
½ cup heavy cream
Pepper
½ tsp. nutmeg
1 cup instant polenta
½ cup Parmesan cheese

Remove husks from all the ears of corn. Hold one ear vertically on a cutting board and, using a sharp paring knife, slice off the kernels from top to bottom. Repeat with the other two ears of corn so that you have about two cups of corn kernels. Heat a sauté pan on high heat with the olive oil and 1 tbsp. of the butter. Toss the corn kernels in and season with ½ tsp. of salt. Cook for a minute and a half, stirring occasionally, and then set aside.

In a medium pot, bring the chicken stock, 1 tablespoon of the butter, cream, salt, pepper, and nutmeg just to a boil. Whisk in the polenta and stir well until thoroughly incorporated. Keeping the heat on medium-high, add the sautéed kernels of corn and the Parmesan cheese. Check the seasoning, and add more salt and pepper if needed. Turn the heat down to low and set aside until serving.

Sweet Corn Sauce

6 ears corn
½ cup heavy cream
½ cup chicken stock
Salt and pepper
¼ tsp. dried thyme, or 1 tbsp. fresh thyme
3 tbsp. parmesan cheese

Remove the husks and stems from the ears of corn. Grate each ear lengthwise against a grater to produce a chunky but milky corn puree. Set aside.

In a medium saucepan or pot, combine all ingredients except for the cheese, and bring to a nice simmer. Stir in the Parmesan cheese and mix until well incorporated. Set aside while you cook the shrimp.

Shrimp

1 tbsp. butter
1 tbsp. olive oil
20 large shrimp, or 16 jumbo (U12) shrimp, peeled and deveined
½ tsp. salt
½ tsp. black pepper

Season the shrimp with the salt and pepper.

Heat the butter and olive oil in a sauté pan over medium-high heat. When the butter has begun to foam, toss the shrimp in. Stir as needed until the shrimp have turned pink and are thoroughly cooked through, about five minutes.

To serve: In the center of each plate, ladle out a generous serving of the corn polenta. Place 4 or 5 shrimp on top of the polenta and then spoon the sweet corn sauce over the shrimp. If you are using fresh thyme, you can garnish the dish with a small sprig of the herb.

Stilton Potato Cake

5 large potatoes, washed and peeled, sliced into ¼-inch-thick pieces
4–6 oz. Stilton cheese, crumbled
3 tbsp. chopped parsley

Salt and white pepper
3 cups heavy cream
2 eggs, beaten

Preheat oven to 350°. Grease a 9×9-inch baking pan and layer the bottom of the pan with potato slices. Sprinkle on some of the Stilton and the parsley, and then add a light sprinkle of salt and pepper. Repeat the layering process, beginning with the potatoes, until you have filled the baking dish. Bring the cream to a simmer in a small pan and remove from heat. Temper the beaten eggs by adding a small amount of the hot cream and whisking until incorporated. Slowly add the rest of the cream, whisking as you go. Pour this mixture evenly over the potatoes and bake uncovered at 350° for 45 minutes or until the cream sauce is bubbling and the potatoes are tender.

Roasted Baby Vegetables

Depending on where you shop, you may or may not be able to find true "baby" vegetables, but you can simply buy larger sizes of your favorites and cut them down into roughly one-inch chunks. For this dish, you can use whatever vegetables you choose and select from the best of the season, but you'll want to select hard, dense vegetables (butternut squash, carrots) as opposed to softer ones (summer squash, tomatoes). If you are making the Stilton Potato Cake, you can pop your tray of vegetables in to cook with it.

Recommended Vegetables

All of your vegetables need to be well washed, peeled, and destemmed. Use any or all of the following to total about four cups:

Baby carrots (not the prepackaged, bagged ones)
Cauliflower florets
Butternut or acorn squash
Baby onions or any larger onions
Baby or regular-sized beets
Brussels sprouts, sliced in half
Celery root
Parsnips
Beets

Other ingredients:

⅓ cup olive oil
1 tsp. each salt and pepper
Optional: 3 sprigs fresh rosemary or thyme or both, or 2 tsp. of dried herbs

Preheat the oven to 350°.

Once you have your vegetable selection prepared and cut into uniform sizes, simply toss them in a bowl and mix with generous amounts olive oil, salt, pepper, and herbs if you are using them. If using fresh herbs, you can simply add the whole stems without removing the leaves. Spread your vegetables out on a baking sheet and cook them in the oven for about 12 to 15 minutes until just tender but not mushy.

Grilled Steak with Peppercorn Sauce

4 steaks, any good cut, for example, tenderloin, sirloin, or rib eye
Salt, pepper, and sugar to season

Whenever Josh is cooking a simple meat dish, he begins by generously coating each meat portion with a good dusting of salt, pepper, and sugar. This dusting gives a delicious crust. About twenty minutes before serving dinner, grill the steaks. If it is not grilling season where you are, or if you do not have a stove-top grill, you may certainly sear the steaks in a skillet set over medium-high heat. After cooking, set the steaks aside while you make the sauce.

Peppercorn Sauce

1 cup Madeira wine
2 tbsp. ground tricolored peppercorns
1 beef bouillon cube
2 cups water
1 bay leaf
1 tbsp. cornstarch

Pour the Madeira and the peppercorns into a skillet and set the pan over medium heat. If you've cooked your steaks in a skillet, you can use that pan for the sauce. Bring to a simmer and reduce the wine down to a syrup. Add your beef base or bouillon cube, water, and the bay leaf and bring this back up to a simmer. In a separate bowl, mix the cornstarch with a little bit of water, so that you have a thick liquid, and then add this to the sauce. Remove from heat and pour over steaks. Serve with the Stilton Potato Cake and Roasted Baby Vegetables.

Banana Three Way

Eggroll Cups

1 tbsp. sugar
3 tbsp. Chinese five-spice powder
Canola oil
4 eggroll skins

Mix the sugar and the five-spice powder together. In a deep skillet or pan, heat around four inches of canola oil over medium-high heat. Measure the temperature of the oil with a cooking thermometer. When the oil reaches 350°, lay an eggroll skin in the oil and press down with the bottom of a ladle, forming a cup shape. Hold in the oil for 2 to 3 minutes until nicely browned. Gently remove and dust with the sugar and five-spice powder mixture. Set aside. Repeat with the other three egg roll skins.

Chocolate Rum Sauce

¼ cup dark rum
½ cup heavy cream
¼ cup brown sugar
2 tbsp. butter
1 cup bittersweet chocolate

Add the rum to a saucepan and reduce to about half, over medium-high heat. Add the rest of the ingredients, stirring constantly with a wooden spoon, until well combined. Set aside.

Banana Chantilly

1 pint heavy cream
1 tsp. banana extract
2 tbsp. powdered sugar

Put all ingredients in a large bowl and, using a hand blender, mix at high speed until you have a fluffy, whipped cream. Set aside while you cook the bananas.

Sautéed Bananas

1 tbsp. butter
2 bananas, sliced
1 tbsp. sugar

Heat the butter in a sauté pan over medium-high heat. Add the banana slices and toss in approximately 1 tablespoon of sugar or enough to coat the bananas well. Sauté for 2 to 3 minutes and remove from heat.

Plating the Banana Three Way: Banana or vanilla ice cream. For each serving, put 1 tablespoon of the Banana Chantilly in the center of a plate and place an eggroll cup on top. Fill with ice cream and pour one-fourth of the sautéed bananas on top and then a good dollop of the chantilly. Drizzle with the rum sauce, pouring a bit around the plate as well.

Turn the page for a preview of the next Gourmet Girl Mystery by Jessica Conant-Park & Susan Conant

TURN UP THE HEAT

EARLY May in Boston. There's nothing else like it. After almost six straight weeks of apocalyptic rain, the sky had suddenly turned an all-but-forgotten blue, the temperature had risen to the miraculously high sixties, and, best of all, the outdoor dining area at my boyfriend's restaurant was finally open. Josh Driscoll, love of my life, was the executive chef at the five-month-old Newbury Street restaurant, Simmer, and tonight, for the first time ever, Simmer's fortunate patrons would be able to savor the fruits of Josh's culinary genius while dining on the sidewalk patio. When Josh had called me earlier today, he'd practically been singing into the phone. "Chloe Carter, my lovely lady, you better get your ass down here to the patio tonight! It's going to be nice!"

Josh's slight case of spring fever was highly contagious: I was as excited as he was.

As Josh's girlfriend, I obviously had a major in at Simmer. Even so, my friends and I had had to wait forty-five minutes for an outdoor table that could accommodate all five of us, the five of us being me; my best friend, Adrianna; her fiancé, Owen; my social work school buddy and teaching assistant, Doug; and his new boyfriend, Terry.

Newbury Street restaurants were jammed tonight. The good weather seemed to have awakened everyone from hibernation, and all the outdoor eateries in this high-end area were packed with diners. Simmer was no exception. As we waited inside for a patio table, I looked around and, as I'd done before, felt amazed at how beautifully the place had turned out. I'd been around while Gavin Seymour, the owner, had been renovating the location, and I'd seen Simmer at its worst, with electrical wires dangling from the ceiling, holes in the walls, and floors made of crumbling concrete. Now, beautiful dark brown tiles covered the floor, modern light fixtures hung from the high ceilings, and wood moldings framed the textured walls. Gavin had wanted to create what he'd called a "worldly" feel to the restaurant; he'd been eager to have the decor and the ambiance announce that Simmer's menu wasn't limited to one style of cooking but was inspired from cuisines around the globe. The room was filled with square tables and high-backed chairs.

Because Josh had helped Gavin to pick out the china, the glassware, and the silver, I knew that all of it had been as expensive as it looked. Votive candles placed at each table gave the room a wonderful glow and flattered everyone's complexion. I loathe eating at restaurants where the lighting casts a yellow tone or a weird shadow on my face; no matter how good the food is, it's hard to enjoy myself if I'm worried about resembling a ghoul.

And God forbid one not look sensational on Newbury Street, right? The problem with coming here to see Josh all the time was that I felt obliged to dress up. I mean, everyone in this sophisticated section of Boston was either independently loaded or living off of someone else's money and, in either case, was a regular customer at Barney's. There was hardly an uncoiffed head of hair, a manicured hand not weighed down with Cartier jewelry, or a wallet not busting with platinum credit cards. I was torn between feeling totally nauseated by the disgusting display of wealth and pathetically eager to look as if I belonged. My deceased uncle Alan's monthly stipend kept me easily afloat, but I didn't have the money to go flinging bills around at Agnes B. and BCBG. I'd long ago run out of appropriate outfits to wear to Simmer and did my best to make my T.J. Maxx pants look like Chanel. Granted, there was a Gap on Newbury Street, but there were hardly streams of diners here in oversized hooded sweatshirts. It always took me at least an hour to get out of my apartment when I was going to Simmer. It never occurred to me to leave without pressing my wavy red hair between the burning blades of my flatiron; people on Newbury Street did not have frizz! And then I had to spend twenty minutes pretending that my L'Oreal makeup actually was from Paris, all the while slathering my blue eyes with brown liner and trying to color my pale cheeks a fresh-from-Barbados bronze. By the time I'd finished, I always felt passable on Newbury Street, but I remained basically disconnected from the obscene wealth that hit you at every snobby shop and from the stick-thin bodies that you passed on every corner. Not that there was anything horribly wrong with my body. But the average twenty-five-year-old around here weighed a hundred and ten pounds, and I was about fifteen over that.

We'd just sat down at one of the ten tables that had been squeezed into a gated area on the sidewalk in front of Simmer when Josh appeared at our table. "Chloe, I just heard you guys were here. I'm sorry you had to wait so long." Josh leaned down and kissed me before brushing his arm across his sweaty forehead. He was dressed in his once-white chef's coat, now covered in permanent food stains from previous months plus fresh stains from today. His dirty-blond hair was damp at the hairline, and his eyes were heavy with exhaustion, but even the dark circles and puffy bags couldn't take away the sparkle of excitement in his blue eyes. Business had been steady, and if tonight was any indication of how the spring and summer were going to go, Simmer was about to really take off.

Josh tossed a filthy dish towel over his shoulder and reached out to shake hands with Owen, Doug, and Terry, and then circled around the table to give Adrianna a kiss on the cheek. "How's it going, Mama?" he asked affectionately. Adrianna was almost five months pregnant but already looked about to go into labor before tonight's dessert.

She rolled her eyes. "Going great if you don't mind constant heartburn, fatigue, swollen hands, and having your ribs kicked from three to five in the morning."

"Owen kneeing you in his sleep again?" Josh grinned, and then rubbed her shoulder. "I'm sorry. I know you're having a hard time."

"Yeah, it's okay. I'm just grouchy. And starving." She looked up at him hopefully.

"*That* I can help with." Josh nodded assuredly. "I gotta run. I think Leandra is your waitress. Order whatever you want, and I'll comp it for you." One of the perks of being the executive chef at Simmer was that the owner, Gavin, let Josh sign off on orders so we didn't have to pay for anything except a tip. "I'll try to come out again later if I can." Josh made his way between tables to the front entrance. One couple seated near the door stopped him. Josh smiled as he accepted what I knew were compliments about his food.

Leandra appeared moments later. I'd met her a number

of times before, because Josh's overwhelming work schedule meant that I was spending lots of time hanging around Simmer trying to catch glimpses of my boyfriend. In fact, I was beginning to look and feel like a barfly. Leandra was petite with very short white-blonde hair that somehow upped her femininity. (If I chopped off all my hair I'd look brutish!) She needed no makeup on her annoyingly symmetrical face, and Simmer's unisex staff T-shirt and pants left no doubt that Leandra was voluptuously female. I saw Adrianna, her usual super model body now rounded, scowl and toss her long blond-hair back over her shoulder. I involuntarily ran my hand down my own hair, checking for any dreaded frizz.

Leandra handed out menus. "Sorry. Hope you haven't been here too long. I can't believe how busy we are tonight, and they didn't schedule enough servers. Can I get you some drinks to start?"

"I'll take a Kirin," Doug said. "You want one, too?" he asked Terry.

Terry nodded and put his hand on Doug's knee. I still had a hard time grasping that Doug and Terry were a couple. Their homosexual relationship didn't bother me in the least; what alarmed me was Terry's style. He looked like a woman-obsessed rock star or maybe the host of a VH1 show on hair bands of the eighties. Every time he opened his mouth, part of me expected him to burst out singing, "Once Bitten, Twice Shy," "Unskinny

Bop," or "Eighteen and Life." With thick, wavy, highlighted brown hair and rocker clothes, Terry was a total contrast to my social work school mentor, Doug. Doug was anything but conservative—on occasion, he wore neon—but it took most people, my parents excluded, about four seconds to figure out that he was gay.

Social work school was one thing, but I wasn't sure how Terry's image went over with his presumably more uptight professors and fellow students at MIT, where he was getting a PhD in physics. Studying at the Massachusetts Institute of Technology clearly put Terry in the category of überintellectual. More importantly, he seemed genuinely to adore Doug.

Avoiding alcohol out of sympathy for Adrianna, Owen ordered lemonades for the two of them. I, on the other hand, felt the need to celebrate the arrival of spring with a crisp glass of Pinot Grigio.

Leandra reappeared a few minutes later with our drinks. As she set our glasses down, I wondered how she was going to get through the brutally hot and humid Boston summer in Simmer's required attire. Her heavy cotton short-sleeved black shirt looked like it didn't allow for much airflow, and the long black dress pants were stylishly tight with a slightly flared boot cut at the bottom. As if to assure a minimum of heat loss, all the servers and bartenders wore long black aprons with *Simmer* written across the top in white lettering.

"Okay, we need to toast," I said, raising my glass. "To

the appearance of the sun, the end of school, and dinner with good friends," I proposed cheerily.

"Not so fast," Doug stopped me before I could take a sip of wine. "You still have finals to get through."

I sighed. "I haven't forgotten." Actually, I *had* forgotten about exams, at least momentarily, until Doug mentioned them. Doug was a teaching assistant at the Boston City Graduate School of Social Work, where I was finishing up the first year of a master's program. He took great pleasure in humorously reminding me that as a doctoral student, he was superior to me. Finals were going to be a nightmare. I had two long papers to finish writing and three two-hour in-class exams. It was at times like this that I regretted enrolling in social work school. Although I was finding more and more things to like about the experience, I still hid my ambivalence about school from my peers. Most of the other students were avidly devoted to their studies and their field placements (social work speak for internships), and I had enrolled only because of a clause in my uncle Alan's will that required me to accept an all-expenses-paid trip to the land of graduate school. In my late uncle's opinion, I evidently needed a master's degree in *something*. Anything. Only then would I receive my inheritance. I'd been pretty resentful of this obviously manipulative and controlling plan that came from the other side. When I'd originally chosen social work school, the choice had felt as if I'd drawn it out of a hat, but as the end of my first year approached, I was beginning to think that my choice hadn't been so random after all. The fit between me and the profession was better than I'd expected, and I was finding that social work skills actually applied to daily life. For instance, instead of just seeing Terry as a complete oddball, I was interested in the personality characteristics that pushed him to deviate from the norm. How did he manage to remain independent and unique? Why didn't he cave in to societal standards?

"Well, we're going to toast anyway, finals approaching or not." I raised my glass and clinked drinks with everyone.

I smiled across the table at Adrianna, who, despite feeling ghastly during her pregnancy, was as beautiful as ever. Maybe because she was feeling so terrible, she was making an extra effort to look as stunning as possible. Her hair and makeup were done to perfection, and she was wearing an adorable navy blue wrap-around maternity top that hugged her round belly and her full chest. When my sister, Heather, had been pregnant with each of her children, she'd always worn voluminous tops that covered her body and hid her weight gain. Ade was doing the opposite: embracing her body's changes and accentuating her growing curves. But as much as she was displaying the pregnancy with her usual confidence, she was pretty tight-lipped about the entire concept of motherhood and had yet to express any feelings about being on the verge of becoming a parent. Children had never topped her favorites list—I'm not sure that she'd ever intended to become a parent, and I suspected she was more afraid than she was letting on. At least her fiancé, Owen, was enthusiastic, in fact, sometimes irritatingly so. But unlike Adrianna, he was practical. He had already started shopping for clothes, diapers, and baby equipment. Remarkably, Owen still had the sense to give Ade the emotional space she needed. As to physical space, I had no clue about how they expected to fit all that baby gear into their new apartment.

I did, however, feel sure that Adrianna and Owen would have a beautiful baby. In terms of looks, Owen was as attractive as Adrianna. His black hair, fair skin, and bright blue eyes, coupled with his charming personality, made him a dream. The hitch was his garish taste in clothing. The T-shirt he wore tonight had an arrow pointing to the left and the words, That's My Kid in There! To make sure that the ridiculous T-shirt would deliver its message with full impact, Owen had been careful to keep Adrianna on the correct side.

Although Adrianna and Owen had not planned on having a baby, the two of them were managing this enormous surprise fairly well. They were moving in together next week and had found a decent two-bedroom apartment around the corner from me in Brighton. To describe their new apartment as having two bedrooms was pushing it, since the second bedroom was actually a walk-in closet, but the tiny room did have a radiator and a small window, so it would work as a nursery, at least for a while. What's more, although Adrianna and Owen hadn't set a wedding date—they couldn't even decide whether to get married before or after the baby was born—they were nonetheless officially engaged. I was just happy that they were together at all, especially since Adrianna had freaked out when she'd found out she was pregnant and had foolishly made out with Josh's sous chef, Snacker, a number of times in some sort of rebellious denial. On the night the unsuspecting Owen was going to propose, in fact, just as he was about to propose, right here at Simmer, Adrianna had suddenly announced both her pregnancy and her recent history with Snacker. Owen had understandably flipped out, but fortunately, the two of them had quickly worked things out. Owen and Snacker, on the other hand, loathed each other but remained coldly polite, mostly for my sake.

"So what are we ordering?" asked the ever-hungry Adrianna. Despite complaining about heartburn all the time, the girl couldn't get enough to eat. "The cod with vegetables looks really good. This is a new menu, right?"

"Right. They've only been running it for a few days. It's got all the new spring items on it. Josh had to teach the kitchen staff all the recipes and how to plate the food. I think it looks awesome." I was bursting with pride at Josh's food.

I'd watched him sit at my kitchen table, pen in hand, while he brainstormed to come up with the perfect dishes for the menu. I'd also learned how he went about pricing them out. It was fairly appalling to learn how little it costs to make some plates and what restaurants charge for them. The basic rule was that you figured out what the protein portion of the dish would cost, like the steak or the tuna, then you'd estimate the cost of the other ingredients, add those together, multiply by three, and then add three dollars. So, a twenty-four-dollar entrée might only cost the restaurant seven dollars in actual food costs. Josh had explained to me that after following the basic rule, he would then adjust the price depending on how a dish sold. Pasta dishes were great because they sold really well, and the pasta was cheap to buy, so chefs could up the price on those menu items. It was also easy to up the prices for lobster and tuna dishes, which were obvious luxury foods and sold a ton. Chicken, on the other hand, often had to be on a menu to please the occasional customer who wanted it, but it generally didn't sell well, so a chicken entrée price would stay close to the formulated pricing cost.

Terry put his menu down on his plate. "I'm definitely getting the seared scallops with grilled pancetta, honey parsnip puree, and warm pear chutney. No question. Thank you for inviting us, Chloe. Doug has had such nice things to say about Simmer, and I've really been looking forward to coming here."

"I'm with you on the scallops," Owen agreed. "And the roasted pork quesadilla with apple salsa." It was very Josh to do something traditional like quesadillas but then serve it with a unique topping.

Leandra came to take our orders. "Everybody set?"

Despite having eaten at Simmer many times, I was still impressed that the servers didn't write anything down. Order pads were apparently beneath the upper-crust atmosphere of Newbury Street. If I'd been Leandra, I'd have had to run to the register, scramble to remember every order, and immediately enter it into the computer. She showed no signs of strain.

Just as Doug finished telling Leandra the entrée he wanted, Gavin Seymour appeared and welcomed us with the charm that's so useful to restaurant owners. Gavin was in his late thirties, very handsome, and dressed in his typically and somewhat misleadingly casual style. Tonight he had on soft khaki pants and a simple cotton shirt, but I knew from Josh that Gavin did most of his clothes shopping through his personal dresser and that his clothing all came from high-end shops. The plain shirt was probably from Brooks Brothers. If I ever have the luxury of having a personal dresser, I'm going to instruct my assistant not to waste my money on overpriced clothes that might as well come from Old Navy.

"Have you all ordered?" Gavin asked. We nodded. He took our menus then turned to Leandra. "Why don't you ask Josh to send out a few extra appetizers for this crowd? They all look especially hungry tonight."

"Of course, Gavin. I'll go put these orders right in." Leandra smiled directly at her boss and smoothly took the menus from his hand. I'd heard that she and Gavin were seeing each other. Gavin was another Simmer male known for his many romantic flings, but according to the wildly active restaurant rumor mill, Gavin and Leandra were having a full-blown relationship and not just making out in the backseat of Gavin's Jaguar after service. Although Josh said the two did their best to avoid public displays of affection, it was hard to ignore the glint in Gavin's eye as he watched her walk away from the table.

With all the love in the air, it really felt like spring. Doug and Terry, Adrianna and Owen, Gavin and Leandra, Snacker and whatever girl of the week, Josh and me. Things with Josh were great, but looking around the table at the happy couples, I found it hard not to miss him. Visiting him at the restaurant was the best chance I had of catching a glimpse of my chef—that or the late-night visits at my place. Not that I was complaining about that department. But I wanted him with me for dinners like this, too. Josh had repeatedly assured me that his crappy schedule would ease up over time. But Simmer had opened on New Year's Eve, and I was still waiting.

Best friends are good at reading thoughts. "I'm sure

Josh will come out again when he can," said Adrianna in an effort to comfort me.

"I know, I know," I said. "I'm happy it's so busy tonight, but it also means Josh might have to stay late." *Again*, I thought.

Josh was working at least ten, if not twelve to fourteen, hours a day and had perpetual dark bags under his eyes. He caught me one morning covertly trying to apply cold cucumber slices to his exhausted eyes while he slept. I hated Josh's schedule, but he wasn't the least bit surprised by the hours he was putting in. Josh felt strongly that Simmer's success rested on him. Gavin might be the owner, but it was Josh who seemed to feel the most pressure to have the restaurant succeed. The majority of restaurants fail within the first six months, and Josh was determined that Simmer wouldn't be one of them. Now that he'd finally found the perfect place to showcase his culinary, artistic, and managerial talent, he was giving Simmer everything he had. The menu was all his, which didn't happen at every restaurant, and Josh had complete control over every dish that was served. Gavin had been really great to Josh, too, and promised him that when things settled in, Josh's hours would become more regular. The better the restaurant did, the better Josh would do in terms of both hours and pay. Right now Josh's salary was almost laughable, but Gavin just didn't have the money to pay him what he deserved. The initial start-up costs involved in opening any restaurant are astronomical. Josh's salary would increase in proportion to Simmer's success, or so Gavin promised. I wanted to believe him, even though it seemed odd that an executive chef working on Newbury Street didn't get a decent salary, never mind a fat paycheck. In spite of everything, though, I was thrilled for Josh and convinced that Simmer would be the place he'd really make a name for himself in the competitive world of Boston restaurants.